BAD THINGS WILL ALWAYS CATCH UP WITH YOU....

After a while, Coach called us out for the second half, and we started to run a layup line to get warm. I was looking around at the crowd and the gym like they belonged to me. That's when I noticed that Marcus wasn't out on the court. I thought maybe he hit the bathroom or needed to get taped up, and after another run through the line, I went to check.

I looked back inside the locker room and two guys in suits were handcuffing Marcus. Casey and Ms. Randolph saw me at the door and pushed me back outside. Then Casey wiped a tear from his eye and huddled everybody up around our bench.

"Marcus was just arrested," Casey said, steadying himself. "I can't say why. There's nothing we can do for him right now, except play the rest of the game like it means something to us."

After we broke the huddle, kids were looking at me for answers. But I didn't have anything to say. My legs got weak, and I thought I was going to pass out. I tried not to look anyone in the eye, and walked onto the court. Then the ref blew the whistle to start play.

OTHER BOOKS YOU MAY ENJOY

BLACK AND WHITE

PAUL VOLPONI

speak

An Imprint of Penguin Group (USA) Inc.

SPEAK

Published by the Penguin Group

Penguin Group (USA) Inc., 345 Hudson Street, New York, New York 10014, U.S.A.

Penguin Group (Canada), 90 Eglinton Avenue East, Suite 700,
Toronto, Ontario, Canada M4P 2Y3 (a division of Pearson Penguin Canada Inc.)

Penguin Books Ltd, 80 Strand, London WC2R 0RL, England

Penguin Ireland, 25 St Stephen's Green, Dublin 2, Ireland
(a division of Penguin Books Ltd)

Penguin Group (Australia), 250 Camberwell Road, Camberwell, Victoria 3124, Australia
(a division of Pearson Australia Group Pty Ltd)

Penguin Books India Pvt Ltd, 11 Community Centre,
Panchsheel Park, New Delhi - 110 017, India

Penguin Group (NZ), Cnr Airborne and Rosedale Roads,
Albany, Auckland 1310, New Zealand (a division of Pearson New Zealand Ltd)

Penguin Books (South Africa) (Pty) Ltd, 24 Sturdee Avenue,
Rosebank, Johannesburg 2196, South Africa

Registered Offices: Penguin Books Ltd, 80 Strand, London WC2R 0RL, England

First published in the United States of America by Viking,
a member of Penguin Group (USA) Inc., 2005
Published by Speak, an imprint of Penguin Group (USA) Inc., 2006

5 7 9 10 8 6 4

THE LIBRARY OF CONGRESS HAS CATALOGED THE VIKING EDITION AS FOLLOWS:
Volponi, Paul.
Black and white / by Paul Volponi.
p. cm.
Summary: Two star high school basketball players, one black and one white,
experience the justice system differently after committing
a crime together and getting caught.
ISBN: 0-670-06006-2 (hc)
1. African Americans—Juvenile fiction. [1. African Americans—Fiction.
2. Race relations—Fiction. 3. Basketball—Fiction. 4. Juvenile delinquency—Fiction.
5. High schools—Fiction. 6. Schools—Fiction.] I. Title.
PZ7.V8877Bl 2005
[Fic]—dc22 2004024543

Speak ISBN 0-14-240692-9

Printed in the United States of America

THIS NOVEL IS DEDICATED
to the loving memory of my father.

*He showed me the angles on a basketball court
and how to look inside them.*

*Special thanks to my mother, wife, and daughter,
who kept a place in their hearts warm for me
while I was busy with this work.*

Thanks to the people who helped me along the way to write:
Anthony Cipollone
April Volponi
Bob Fierro
Jim Cocoros
Lenny Shulman
Rosemary Stimola
Jill Davis

 BLACK

I admit it. I've been scared shitless lots of times. But I was never as shook as when the gun in Eddie's hand went off. It thundered inside that car like the whole world was coming to an end. I never expected Eddie to pull the trigger, by accident or any other way. I guess that was a big part of it, too. In all the time Eddie had that gun, we never shot it off once. It was just for show, so we could get our hands on some quick money. That's all. We never flashed it around in front of our friends or anything. It was just for us to know about.

I was more scared for that man we shot than anything else. I didn't even know he got clipped in the head until Eddie told me later. The gun went off and I closed my eyes. I shut them so tight, I thought my eyelids would squeeze them right out of their sockets. I only opened them again to find the handle on the door, so I could get out of that car and take off running.

That damn sound was ringing in my ears. There was no way to outrun that. I couldn't hear the air pumping in and out of my lungs, or the sound of my feet hitting against the concrete. And I didn't know that Eddie wasn't right behind me until I was halfway home, and peeked back over my shoulder. Then I looked back for him again, even though I knew he wasn't there.

I ran to my crib on instinct, and I guessed Eddie did the same. But I wished he was right there with me to explain what happened. I had to know right then. My brain was going twice as fast as my feet. I didn't know how to slow it down or what to think about first. I just needed to tell Eddie I had seen that man someplace before. I could still see his round, black face in front of me, like he was somebody I passed on the streets a hundred times. And I was praying to God with every breath I took that the man wasn't dead.

My name is Marcus Brown, but almost everybody outside my family calls me "Black." That's because they're used to seeing me all the time with my boy, Eddie Russo. Eddie is white. Kids who are different colors don't get to be that tight in my neighborhood. But we got past all that racial crap, until we were almost like real blood brothers. So somebody came up with the tag "Black and White" for us, and it stuck. It got more hype because we played basketball and football for Long Island City High School. We were two of the best players they ever had. Everybody who goes there knows about us. We even made the newspapers for winning big games a couple of times. Scouts from lots of colleges came to see us play. Some of them wanted to sign up the both of us, and keep what we had going. But that's all finished with now.

I don't remember if the idea of robbing people came up before Eddie snuck out his dead grandfather's gun or not. But once the two of those things were square in front of us, they fit together right. We weren't trying to get rich off it. We were just looking for enough money to keep up.

Lots of kids we knew either hustled drugs for their loot or pulled little stickups on the street. But drug dealers and ballplayers usually hold down opposite ends of the park, shooting looks at each other over who runs the place. That's how it was for Eddie and me with them.

The football team always had two or three posses that ripped people off. They would wave their dough around at parties and latch on to the best girls. Some of them even bought rides with their money, while Eddie and me wore out the bottoms of our good kicks walking. And whenever those dudes went out to celebrate after a big win, we were like two charity cases. Then word started getting out among the right females that Black and White were strictly welfare.

Eddie's family has more money than mine. They live two blocks down and across the street from the Ravenswood Houses, in a private house with a front porch. Eddie has a mother and a father, and they both work. Eddie gets an allowance that's only a little bigger than what I get to go to school with every week. But if Eddie ever needed twenty bucks for something, he could put his hand out and probably get it. My mother has always been tight like that. The only money coming in is from her sewing jobs, and what the state sends her every month to take care of me and my little sister.

Senior dues were $150, and the end of February was the deadline. You either paid it or missed out on everything good that went along with graduating, like the class trips to Bear Mountain and Six Flags. It took me almost three months to save that kind of money. Eddie put a lock on his wallet, too, and we were just about there.

Then around the middle of January, Nike came out

with the new Marauders. Everybody on the basketball team was buying a pair because they came in maroon and powder blue, the same as our school colors. We were the main attraction on that squad. There was no way we were getting caught behind the times like that. So we spent most of our dough on new basketball kicks. That left us with just over a month to get the money we needed for dues. We didn't know how we'd do it. But we made a pact that either both of us would come up with the cash, or we'd miss out on everything together.

Teenagers can get a job easy in some place like McDonald's or Burger King. It's honest, but it's low-rent, too. Kids at school and around our way already treated us like stars. And we were going to be even bigger one day. First in college, and then the pros. So we decided Black and White shouldn't be serving up fries in those stupid hats for everybody to see. Besides, there was almost no way to juggle going to practice every day and having a job.

That's when Eddie first snuck out the gun, thinking we could sell it. We knew a kid who paid almost $300 for a .38 caliber just like it. But Eddie's father knew where the gun was supposed to be and might go looking for it one day. Eddie couldn't blame something like that on his sister. His father would have known it was him, straight off. So we figured that we could borrow the gun anytime, then put it back. That's how we came to do stickups.

We kicked it around a lot first and knew everything we could lose. But it was only going to be a problem if we got caught. Eddie and me weren't going to be that dumb. We were just going to pull enough stickups to get the money for dues. Then we'd call it quits.

Eddie was sold on the idea before I was. "It'll be too easy," he said. "And whatever we can take, we deserve." That hit something inside, and pushed me over the line.

We knew enough not to rob other kids. They could get stupid right in the middle of it, or might have a posse of their own and come back after us. We were looking for a payday, not a war. Adults are just easier. Most of them don't want any trouble. They're scared of kids they don't know. And unless you get unlucky and try to heist an off-duty cop or corrections officer, you're usually home free. We even thought about taking the bullets out of the gun, just to play it safe. But we stressed, thinking we might have to shoot it off in the air, if there was ever any real drama.

Growing up, kids all around my way would boost

little things from stores, like candy and soda. If you got caught, the owners would beat your ass good before they'd even think about calling the cops. But I was more worried about what my mother would do to me, and how it would make her feel to know her only son was a thief. It wasn't worth it to me back then. I would rather watch everyone else getting over than turn my own mother against me.

But things were different now. I was already seventeen. I had to start pulling my own weight, until playing ball paid off in cash. It was the same for Eddie. He was my best friend, and the only one I would ever trust on something like this.

We practiced coming up on people, over and over. Eddie said we should watch how they did it on TV, because they copied things like that from the way it really goes down. So we worked on it, like any play we ever ran in a game. Then we scouted out a good-sized parking lot just off the end of Steinway Street, where people shopping might have some real cheese on them.

The lot was laid out in front of a P.C. Richards electronics store, and always deep with rows of cars. There was a big hardware store on one side of it, a movie theater on the other, and a pizza restaurant across the street. There was a sign that read, PARKING

FOR P.C. RICHARDS CUSTOMERS ONLY! But we watched, and everyone going into those other places used that lot, too. In between everything, there was a little park without a basketball hoop. It just had kiddie things in it, like a seesaw and a jungle-gym set. It was empty during the day because of the cold, and we knew it would be the same at night. So we used it as a sort of base to look things over.

Our first time out, it took almost an hour before we moved. We sat on the swings going back and forth, figuring out if we had the nerve to pull it off or not. Lots of people walked by alone, but we just watched them all. Then we started dissing each other about who was going to chicken out first. When all that ran dry, we got quiet and moved closer to the gate. We picked out a white lady carrying a shopping bag. She walked real slow. That was good for us because we wanted to keep our timing right. Eddie and me were walking even with each other, maybe twenty feet apart. And if that lady had turned around, she never would have thought we were together.

We waited until she got all the way to her car. Then Eddie came up from behind and showed her the gun. She got hysterical right away and started to cry. I took the package out of her hand so she could open her pocketbook. Her wallet was sitting right on top.

She was so scared, she couldn't pull it out. Finally, Eddie reached in and grabbed it. Then we got our asses out of there quick.

I didn't want to throw the lady's package down in the street and have somebody take a second look at us. So I just held on to it tight, and dropped my face down behind it. We weren't even a block away when she started screaming for help.

I hated the way she sounded. It was like we did something really terrible to her. After that, Eddie and me decided we'd never rob another woman.

"It's like if somebody did that to your mother," Eddie said. "How would you feel?"

I was just happy we got away with it. We were so nervous that almost a half hour went by before we looked in her wallet. There was $92 inside. So we did a little victory dance, and gave each other high fives out behind my building. We looked at the picture on her driver's license for a second, but neither one of us wanted to know her name. Then we walked a couple of blocks and threw her wallet into a big trash bin behind a supermarket, credit cards and all.

There was a brand-new Walkman in the package. Eddie said he wanted me to keep it for acting so smart and holding on to it. I scratched up the cover so it wouldn't look like it was right out of the box. Then

I gave it to my little sister, Sabrina, and told my mother I found it outside of school. Sabrina had the earphones plugged into her head for a week straight. And every time I saw her with it, I thought about what Eddie and me had done.

Two weeks after that, we robbed an old white man just before the stores closed that night. We were about to step to him when somebody passed by out of nowhere. Eddie and me just froze for five or six seconds. When I looked up again the man was already halfway into his car. I was surprised when Eddie went ahead and pulled the gun on him anyway.

Eddie's face turned mean-looking. He made the man slide over, and got into the driver's seat next to him. Then Eddie unlocked the back door, and I got in, too. He screamed at the man to empty all his pockets. I didn't see much because my eyes were glued to the side window, watching for trouble. But after the man took out his money, he had his eyes shut tight. When we bounced, Eddie grabbed the man's car keys and left them on his back bumper.

"The cops probably won't even find them back there," Eddie said.

And we walked away fast with confidence, like we were professionals now.

That job got us $129 in folding money, almost $3 in

loose change and a token to drive across the Triboro Bridge.

I remember, we stopped at the McDonald's underneath the train tracks on Broadway and each had two Quarter-Pounders with Cheese. Then we left the token on the table like a tip for anybody who wanted it.

Between our loot and what we had saved, there was enough for dues. We held on to the money over the weekend just to look at it some more. But when we went to pay that Monday, the school secretary got bent out of shape because it was March first already.

Eddie knows how to fast-talk most people good, and he didn't waste a second after the last word left her mouth. He told her I was busy celebrating Black History Month. That he thought it was a leap year, and February had the one extra day to it. She smiled at all of that nonsense and made us each out a receipt.

We were happy the way everything turned out, but were flat broke again. It all went down too easy to just walk away. And neither one of us mentioned quitting the stickup business.

Our last stickup was on the next Friday night, after basketball practice. Before we left, Coach Casey called everyone over to the bleachers and gave his usual speech for the weekend.

"Gentlemen, I know the city never sleeps, but try not to get into anything stupid over the next couple of days," Casey told the team. "Don't get into fights and don't get locked up. Do your families a favor—stay home at night and study. I want to see everybody back here on Monday the way we left."

Eddie and me would always smile at each other while Casey talked like that. Not because we didn't appreciate it, but because we knew his rap inside out. We heard him make that same speech every Friday for almost four years. But Casey was solid with us. And we knew he meant it.

On our way up to Steinway Street, Eddie asked me if I wanted to be the one to hold the gun this time. It felt good in my hand the couple of times I played around with it. But I didn't have any real practice pulling it out on somebody. Eddie had been perfect twice already. I didn't want to screw things up, so I took a pass.

It was freezing out that night. We started to shiver, waiting in the back of the parking lot, across from the park. We had our eyes locked onto everything around us, looking for somebody easy. We even passed on a man with a cane because it didn't feel right, and the wind came up strong against us.

Eddie said that holding the gun was like squeezing a piece of ice, and his fingers were going numb. So I let him have my gloves. After a while, I started blowing into my hands to keep them warm. I could see my breath coming out between my fingers, and anybody who saw us there probably thought we were smoking weed.

The man was just a shadow to me when he first came out of that hardware store. It was really dark, and he had his coat buttoned all the way up around his neck. Eddie gave me a nod, and I nodded right back. I didn't even know the man was black until we walked up to him, and Eddie told him it was a stickup.

WHITE

By the time I made it home, the sweat was pouring off of me. I was breathing harder than ever. Every part of my body was on fire. I couldn't go inside, or everyone would know something was wrong.

My right hand was in my coat pocket, still wrapped around the gun. I could smell that it had just been fired. But I wouldn't pull it out again.

I bit down hard on the tip of a finger, and pulled Marcus's glove off of my other hand with my teeth. I wiped the sweat from my face with it, and stuffed the glove into the empty coat pocket. I turned the knob on the front door and opened it.

Gotti jumped up and hit me in the stomach with both paws. But I pushed him down with one hand and scratched him behind the ear. My sister was lying on the floor watching TV.

"Isn't Marcus with you?" she asked.

I wasn't sure what would come out of my mouth. So I just shook my head.

My folks were in the kitchen. I heard my mom call out something to me about dinner, but I went right upstairs, and locked the bathroom door behind me. When I turned back around, I was staring straight into the mirror.

The sweat was starting down my forehead again. The skin was stretched tight across my face, and my eyes were bulging out. I could have been looking at a murderer. I took the gun out of my pocket and put it in the sink.

I heard my sister coming up the stairs, talking on the phone. That's when I felt a *bang!* Like I had shot that man all over again. Only I could feel the trigger slip between my finger and Marcus's glove this time. I could feel myself jerk backwards, and could see the blood.

I listened until I heard my sister's bedroom door shut. Then I peeled off the other glove and grabbed the gun. I opened the door just wide enough to check the hall, and when I saw that it was clear, I bolted for the attic.

My mom hadn't changed a thing up there since my grandpa died in his sleep last year. Sometimes, it almost felt like he still lived with us. The pictures of him with my grandma were on the table next to his bed. My mom dusted them almost every day. In all the times I took his gun, it never bothered me. But now I felt sick to my stomach.

I reached up to the top shelf of his closet and took down the brown shoe box. There were a dozen rubber bands wrapped around it. They were old and stiff. But I undid them all without any of them snapping. I had left a brick in its place. So I put the gun back inside, and hid the brick on the closet floor under some old magazines. Then I slipped the rubber bands back around the box, and put it away.

I got out of there and grabbed a basketball from my room. Halfway down the stairs, I held the ball out in front of me to stop any questions about where I was headed. My mom saw me at the bottom step and called out my name. Then my dad turned around to look at me. I lifted the ball up in front of my face and said, "I'm going out to find Marcus."

The wind ran through my wet clothes. I tried to dribble the ball to keep warm. But it would hardly come back up off the ground. It was just too cold. I knew that Marcus would be either in his house or at the courts in the Circle. I turned in between the first two buildings of the projects and could hear a game going on.

I turned the next corner and the wind dropped off behind the big buildings. Moses and X were playing one-on-one at the basket under the light. Marcus was sitting by himself on a bench next to the court. His hands were in his pockets, and his face was down into his coat.

X yelled, "Now we can play some two-man."

When I heard that, I knew that he hadn't told them what happened.

It was the first time I could remember that me and Marcus didn't give each other a pound or a slap on the back. We just looked at each other.

"It just went off," I said to him in a low voice.

I flipped Marcus the ball and he cradled it in his fingertips. He made an excuse to Moses and X about not playing, and we headed out of the other end of the park together.

"Look at them go! They're so scared!" Moses echoed through the Circle.

"They're feeling the pressure, big time," hooted X. "They know it could have been the end of Black and White tonight."

And they both laughed.

When we got out of earshot, Marcus asked me, "Do you think he's dead?"

I told him that I didn't think so. That the bullet just grazed him, and there was blood on the back of his head and neck. I knew the window next to him got shattered. But, I wasn't really sure about anything.

"Oh God, not in the head!" Marcus cried out loud. Then he jumped up and smacked a street sign with the basketball. The sound rattled down the block and I turned around to see if anybody was watching.

We talked about going back there to see what was going on. Maybe there was police tape around the car already and a bunch of cops asking people about what they had seen. We thought we could find out if the man was still alive that way. But in the end, we decided against it.

"What if he's still in the car, and nobody's found him yet?" Marcus asked. "Do we call an ambulance? Do we leave him there?"

"I don't know," I said. "I can't think straight."

So we just kept walking in circles around the projects.

Then Marcus said, "I thought I recognized that man from somewhere."

I told him that he was just imagining things. But he said how that could have been the father of some kid he knew, and his eyes started to tear.

"I know I fucked this up for us, and got that man shot. I shoulda took the gun when you asked. I punked out!" Marcus said.

I didn't want to hear any more, so I started to walk off. Marcus grabbed my shoulder to turn me back around. That's when he saw the blood on my coat. I rubbed the spots hard with spit and some napkins I found up against the curb. But it wouldn't come off.

And I wasn't about to take it home for my mom to wash.

We ditched the coat into an open trash bag out behind White Castle. I tied the bag up tight with two strong knots. The gloves looked clean, but we didn't want to hold on to them, or leave them in the same place as my coat. So we stuffed them down a sewer on the next street corner.

I was freezing. But I couldn't go home without a coat, or somebody might put two and two together. Marcus took me back to his place. We were always trading jackets anyway, so I'd be able to get away with that. But as soon as I walked in the door his mother asked me, "Where's your coat, child?"

I told her that I took it off to play ball and somebody walked away with it.

"What some kids won't do to get what they want," she said, shaking her head.

It was almost like lying to my own mother. But before it got any worse, Marcus came out with another jacket and told her that he was going to walk me home.

"Don't you boys go looking for who took that coat now," she said. "Just let it go. Maybe some poor child needs it to keep warm. It's cold as the devil out there."

I promised her that we wouldn't, and Marcus said

he'd come straight home. After we left, we didn't say a word to each other for a while. I knew how terrible I felt. But I knew that Marcus was feeling even worse than I did. Maybe because that man was black, too.

We passed back through the Circle, and it was empty.

Everybody calls that park the Circle because it's right in the middle of the Ravenswood Houses, surrounded by the buildings on every side. I'd been playing there since I was thirteen. Marcus brought me down after we met at the courts on 21st Street, over by the Department of Sanitation. I'm the only white kid that hangs out there. Nobody took to me right away. I had to fight plenty of times before I got any respect. But the Circle is where "Black and White" was born. And now we ran that court because nobody else could deal with the two of us.

I stopped us on the corner of my block. I didn't need to take Marcus inside with me and risk having to answer any more questions. So we clamped our hands together, and gave each other a pound. But it didn't feel like usual.

I got into the house and up to my room without having to say a word to anybody.

BLACK

Every time I shut my eyes that night, I saw the man's face. The shadows moved around under my eyelids until he came out clear. I'd look over every line and bump. And sometimes, he'd stare straight back at me. I couldn't figure out where I knew him from. But seeing his face that way made me feel like he was still alive.

I wouldn't go out of the house for anything the next day. I watched the news on TV and listened to the radio, waiting for a story about a man who got killed in a Queens stickup. But there was nothing.

Eddie didn't call me at all that day. I didn't dial his digits, either. I helped my sister with her homework and folded some clothes in my room. When my mother saw that I wasn't going out that night, she asked, "What's got you pinned down inside this apartment on a Saturday night?"

I looked at her like I didn't know what she was talking about.

"Let me hear it!" she demanded.

I told her I was saving my strength for the game against Grover Cleveland on Tuesday night. That at least three or four college scouts would be there, and maybe I'd finally pick a school. But she didn't buy that.

"I just hope it's a girl you're hiding out from, and not some street gang," she said, straight out.

Eddie's sister, Rose, called me on Sunday. They had cousins visiting from Long Island and were taking them to the movies. Her mother was making Eddie go, too, because it was family. So Rose invited me, too. She even talked her mother into buying my ticket.

I had it bad for Rose, and thought she felt the same. She would kiss me on the cheek almost every time I saw her. And when Eddie wasn't around, she'd catch the corner of my lips, and give me a sexy smile. Rose went to school at LIC with Eddie and me, but was a year behind us.

Eddie caught me staring at her from behind one time. I didn't know how to pretend that I wasn't, so I didn't even try to come up with an excuse. He just shook his head and said, "Don't even think about it, Black! Don't even think about it!"

I never thought about going out with a white girl before. Every girl I ever went out with was black. But my best friend was white. So I didn't see the difference.

Eddie rang me a half hour after Rose, worried to death. He said Rose and the cousins wanted to see something that was playing at Kaufman Studios. That was just across the street and down the block from where we shot that man. He tried to talk them into seeing another flick or going to a different theater. But they wouldn't budge.

I was nervous about going back there, too. But I cupped my hands around the phone and told him it would be all right. That maybe we could find out what happened.

We met at the bus stop across the street from my house, just after four o'clock. Their cousins had never seen the projects before, and were looking around like they had just landed on another planet. Rose showed them the police station built right into one of the buildings. There were a couple of squad cars and some scooters parked outside. I gave Rose a wink and said, "Without those cops on scooters, it would be a jungle out here."

Rose was laughing under her breath. But Eddie wouldn't smile. I tried to keep him loose, but something was pulling hard at me, too. I had to know where I saw that man before. I kept thinking I had it.

But it would slip out of my head with the sound of every car that zipped past.

The buses run slower than snails on Sunday. And it was brick outside, wind and all. For a second, I thought about putting on my gloves. Then it sunk in all over again.

The Number 66 bus finally showed. I lifted my leg for the first step, and something settled in my brain. I could feel my insides go numb. But I kept on climbing. By the time I reached the top and heard Eddie's change going into the box, I knew the man we shot was a driver on the 19-A that ran past my house. I looked up and could see his black face pasted on the man who was driving.

Rose wanted to sit up front, but I pushed everyone as far back as I could. Then the bus started to roll again, and we all had to grab fast for something to hold on to. There were plenty of seats, but I wouldn't sit down for anything. I stood up with both hands wrapped around the silver rail over my head. The sweat was starting down my face, and I felt sick to my stomach. I thought I was going to throw up.

I almost never rode the bus. So I didn't know how I remembered that driver. I could walk to school in the time it took to wait on the 19-A in the morning. I'd get on with my mother to go shopping, and took it with the team to the subway station when we had road games. There was no way he could have remembered me. He probably saw a thousand people get on and off his bus every day. But I remembered him.

The bus turned off 21st Street, and started down 35th Avenue to Kaufman Studios. Eddie was staring out the window. I wanted to tell him about it, but everyone was between us. When Eddie finally looked up, I pushed my jaw out at him like it was going to explode. He leaned over to me. But Rose said my name out loud, and we both backed off.

We got to our stop and I went straight for the back door. The cold wind dried my sweat. And I felt better with every step on the solid concrete. I grabbed Eddie around the shoulder and pulled him off to the side.

"He's a bus driver from right around here," I whispered to him. "I know it now. I've been on his bus."

Eddie slipped out from under my arm. Then he turned back to me and said, "He had to be somebody."

It was less than a block before we had to turn on the next street and see that parking lot. I raised my eyes and saw the sign for the movie. The lights were turned up bright, and there was a flashing neon arrow pointing around the corner.

I couldn't look. So I watched Eddie's face as we turned. His eyes zeroed in on the lot. Then he looked back at me with a face that was almost normal. That's when I checked it out for myself. The car wasn't there. There was no police tape or crime scene marked off. There weren't any flowers or crosses that get put up when somebody dies out on the street. It was all calm, like nothing jumped off there two nights ago.

Next thing I knew Rose was buying the movie tickets. I recognized the kid working the door from school. He ripped our tickets in half and gave us back the stubs. He looked up at us and said, "Black and White, enjoy the show!"

Eddie nodded his head to me, and put a big smile across his face. We found the theater where the movie was playing. The lights went out just before we got to our seats. The two cousins went into the row first. Then I followed behind Rose, with Eddie sitting on the end.

We saw *The Count of Monte Cristo*. Rose and the cousins were the ones who picked it out. They said that sooner or later, everybody had to read that book for school, so why not see the movie first. I really got into the story and almost forgot about everything else. Eddie started to ease up, too. I heard him pulling hard for the hero during the sword fight scenes. I took turns with Rose sharing the armrest between seats, and sometimes our elbows fit in together.

When we left, Eddie took us around the far corner, away from the parking lot. The last time Eddie and me were on those streets in the dark, we were running in different directions. But everything was all right now. We were side by side, breathing easy. Everybody was talking about the movie, and how much they liked it. None of us could believe how one friend turned on the other that way, especially Eddie. But we all thought it was right on the money how that bastard got what was coming to him.

We swung back around to 35th Avenue, but there was no bus in sight. So we started walking. We were two or three stops down, when one finally came up behind us. Eddie and me looked at each other for a second. Then we dropped our heads, until we saw that the bus driver was white.

That night, I dreamed about my father. He left right after my sister was born; I hadn't seen him since I was a little kid. My mother was so pissed that she didn't keep a single picture of him. So I didn't have a handle on what he looked like anymore. In my dreams, I was always looking straight ahead. And he was standing next to me, with a hand on my shoulder.

My dreams about him were always the same. We'd be in the park or someplace thick with trees. Then we'd laugh about something and start to race. I'd run as fast as I could, and I could feel him right behind me. No matter how tired I got, I'd keep pushing myself. I'd wake up from those dreams the same way every time—breathing hard with my heart pounding.

The next morning, I walked the side streets to school, off the bus route. Eddie and me never left for school together. We tried it for a while, two years back. But one of us always wound up waiting on the other and getting steamed.

I didn't see Eddie until third period, in English class. Ms. Sussman was our teacher, and assigned us seats on opposite sides of the room. Eddie and me had her once before as freshmen, so she was wise to our act and wouldn't let us sit together.

I was already copying the work on the board when Eddie got there just after the bell. Ms. Sussman gave him a late mark, and he didn't argue. Eddie would always try to change her mind with some story. But he just took the hit.

We caught each other's eye a couple of times during class. Then Eddie cracked a joke off some kid's stupid answer. He turned straight towards me to laugh. I howled right along with him, until Ms. Sussman gave us both a zero.

Eddie's mother was checking program cards on the way into the cafeteria. She worked at LIC as a school aide. She used to be in our old junior high school, too. Then she transferred over when Rose got here.

"This is my second son," she told the teacher working the door with her. "He's my illegitimate second son," she said, hugging me around the neck.

Eddie's mother was always playing around like that. She'd tell people about me, "He watches my TV, he eats my pasta and he doesn't give me a dime for any of it. He must be my other son. My Black-Italian son from Sicily. That's just a stone's throw from Africa."

It didn't bother Eddie one bit that his mother worked in our school. I love my mother more than anything, but I wouldn't want to be running into her in the halls, or have her hanging around my teachers. Nobody would. But Eddie didn't act any different around his mother. He was always the same, either way. And I respected him for that.

We finished the day in math class together. The teacher there had assigned seats, too. Eddie sat right in front of me. Math was always the hardest subject for Eddie, but he had to pass to play ball. I knew my formulas cold and helped him study. When we had multiple-choice tests, Eddie would lay his pen down on any problem that had him stumped. Then I'd kick the back of his chair to let him know what answer I had. It was always one kick for "A," two for "B," and three for "C."

After class, we went up to the gym to basketball practice. Our lockers were right next to each other, and we took our time changing. We knew that Casey wouldn't run us hard because of the game the next night. Casey was the head basketball coach and an assistant coach on the football team. He did everything he could to make sure none of his basketball players got banged up too bad during football season, especially Eddie and me.

Casey got college scholarships for lots of kids from our neighborhood. But none of them made it to the pros yet. That's where Black and White was going to be different. We were both going to make it big. That's why schools like St. John's, Connecticut, and Michigan State were drooling over the both of us.

Coach opened practice with a fifteen-minute shoot-around. Kids were at every basket, getting loose and feeling their favorite shots. Everybody had their own rock to shoot with. And for a while, it was raining basketballs. Then Casey ran us through all our set plays, until we got each one right. He ended practice with a half hour of foul shooting. Everybody paired up at different baskets. And the freshmen had to go downstairs to the girls' gym when we ran out of hoops.

Eddie and me took the main basket in front of Casey's office. We switched on and off, taking twenty foul shots apiece and chasing the ball down for the shooter. We started off okay. But by the third time around, we both found the groove. I knocked down eighteen out of twenty shots. Then Eddie stepped to the line and made twenty straight. It felt like everything was almost back to the way it was. And the only sound in my head was the ball slipping through the net.

We walked home together after practice, and talked about how lucky we got. Eddie and me were sure the man was still alive, or else we would have heard something on the news. And since that whole mess blew up in our faces, we almost forgot about picking a college.

Eddie thought we should both stay in New York

and play at St. John's. "Black and White on the back page of every New York newspaper for the next four years," Eddie said, "unless we turn pro early."

That sounded like a sweet deal. I had never been away from home before, and didn't want my mother and sister to be alone. So I was hyped.

I put an echo into my voice, like an announcer, and said loud, "Keeping it real in the Big Apple. From the Circle in the Ravenswood Houses to Alumni Hall at St. John's University. All of N-Y-C, rec-og-nize Eddie Russo and Marc—"

But I broke down laughing before I could finish.

My mother had dinner waiting for me on a plate under some tin foil. She was helping Sabrina practice for the fifth-grade spelling bee. I sat in the kitchen, eating and listening to my sister spell out loud from the living room. I closed my eyes and took a deep breath. When I opened them again, everything was still all right.

WHITE

When I got home, my dad was waiting for me. He had a serious look on his face and wanted to talk. I was sure that he knew about the gun.

"Let me tell you something about your grandpa," he started off, as I fixed my feet to the floor. "He worked almost forty years for the Department of Sanitation, and got me the job there, too, right before I married your mother. It's an okay job. It pays the bills, and it got us this house. But things are going to be different for you. You've got a real chance in life. Sports are going to get you into college for sure. But I want you to pick a school where you're going to learn something, and not just play ball. I want you to study and get a diploma. That way you'll always be somebody, no matter what happens. Then you'll never have to lift garbage cans for a living like your old man."

He showed me the dark lines in his palms where the dirt got in so deep it wouldn't wash out. Then he

slipped a hand around the back of my neck and pulled me into a bear hug.

Before he let me go, he looked up at the attic and said, "If your grandpa ever heard me talk like that about the job that feeds us, he'd have taken a strap to me. And I still have to be careful about what I say, in case he's listening from up there."

I couldn't fall asleep that night. Little noises in the house had me jumping, and Gotti kept barking at something. Every time I opened my eyes, I thought I saw Grandpa's shadow. The next morning, I woke up with my head under the covers, soaked in sweat, and didn't feel right until I was outside and on my way to school.

The cheerleaders came looking for me during homeroom to set up a party for after the game. Rebecca Coles was there. She was the captain of their squad.

I didn't have a girlfriend. But if I did, I guess it would have been Rebecca. We had hooked up a couple of times since last year, and she was always cool about letting it lay low. She just walked up to me after a game one time and said that she couldn't stop thinking about me. It doesn't get any easier than that for a guy. But I liked her, too. Rebecca can throw a perfect spiral with a football. She said she used to play with her older brothers, until she started thinking about boys all the time.

I couldn't even think about a party until after we won that night.

"You can't talk to him now. He's got his game face on already," Rebecca said, punching me in the stomach.

I picked my hands up without thinking. Then she stepped back and smiled.

"What are you gonna to do to me, tough guy?" she laughed, dancing around like a boxer. "Are you going to knock my block off and go to jail instead of playing in the game tonight? Is that what you want?" she went on, trying to keep a straight face.

I was laughing, too, until she said the part about jail.

After last period, I went straight up to the gym, spread a towel over one of the benches in the locker room, and tried to catch some sleep. But just as I started to get comfortable, the kids on the track team showed up to change for their practice. That woke me up. So I put on my uniform and grabbed a basketball from the rack.

The game wasn't for another two hours, and the bleachers hadn't even been pulled out yet. I ran up and down the court pretending the gym was packed. I would take the pass from Marcus and could hear the crowd roaring in my head when I drove for the hoop. I could see my family in the stands. They were cheering louder than anybody. Everything was like it was supposed to be.

But when I stopped pretending, there I was, alone.

I went back to the locker room, and some of our guys were already there. Andre was our big man in the middle. He was just a junior, but he was six-foot-seven and still growing.

"Yo, White," he said with a smile. "Thanks for not picking a school yet. I love that all these scouts are still coming out to see you and Black play. That means they're all getting a peek at me for next year. Good looking out for a teammate."

That's when Marcus came in with Moses and X.

"Ravenswood Projects are in the house!" X screamed.

Marcus slapped my hand and said, "Big night for Black and White, my brother!"

Then Moses grabbed a freshman named Preston, and told him he was on the door tonight. That meant he had to wait for the Grover Cleveland team to show, and bring them up the back stairs to the visitors' locker room. Preston got really pissed off. He had the door the last time we played a home game.

"I just dig having a white doorman," snapped X.

Besides me, Preston was the only other white player on the team. He wasn't bad for a freshman. But he played guard, like me and Marcus. So he never got into the game, unless it was a blowout.

"We want them to see your skinny freshman ass first," Moses piped in. "Then when they come out and see the real players—*pow!*—they'll be in shock."

Everyone except for Preston cracked up.

If Marcus was hanging around the locker room when the other squad showed up, he'd always go to the door. He'd show them the way in and shake everybody's hand. He was totally the opposite of me. I didn't want to talk to anybody on the other team or shake their hand until the game was over.

When we were still in junior high school, me and Marcus used to sneak up those same stairs to see the games. Jason Taylor was the LIC captain back then. He lived in the projects and knew us from the Circle. We used to bang on the door while he was waiting for the other team, and he'd let us up. Then over one Christmas vacation, the team went up to Albany to play in a tournament. The newspapers said that things got tense on the court, and there was a lot of racial shit coming out of the stands. A fight broke out and the whole gym went zoo. They showed the videotape of it on TV for a week. A white kid watching the game ripped the leg off a chair and stabbed Jason through the back with it. He died right there on the court, in Casey's arms. It's something that Coach never talks about.

I don't know when a scrub started letting the other squad up instead of the captain. But that's the way it is now. Besides, we don't have a captain. This team belongs to me and Marcus. Though if it ever came down to choosing, Marcus might pull a few more votes than me.

Casey got us all together before we went out on the court.

"Stay focused out there," he told the team. "Play our normal game and forget about impressing the scouts. Depend on your teammates, and know you've got each other's backs out there."

There were just two games left in the regular season. We were in first place in our division with a record of 16–2. That was good enough to give us home court advantage all the way through the playoffs. Grover Cleveland had lost more games than they won. We beat them by twenty points when we played at their gym a couple of weeks ago.

We put our hands into a big pile. Then everybody counted to three, and shouted, "T-E-A-M!"

Right off, we jumped out to an 8–0 lead. Marcus was getting me the ball the second I broke open, and I hit my first two shots. Neither one of them even touched the rim. They were nothing but net. Then Marcus faked a pass in my direction. When his man slid over, Marcus drove to the hoop alone for an easy score.

Out of the corner of my eye I could see my sister Rose sitting behind our bench with her friends. My mom and dad liked to sit in the last row away from all the noise. So they were impossible to find.

The other team finally made a couple of baskets, but there was no way they could keep up. We were out-running them up and down the court. I could hear the kid who was guarding me gasping for air. It was 14–4 and their coach was starting to make substitutions already.

I knew at least three of the college scouts by sight. And when the ball kicked out of bounds, I was face-to-face with one of them in the first row. I tried not to notice him. I took the ball from the ref and passed it back in.

Marcus's mother missed most of our games. She always had sewing to finish. I'd listen to Marcus fill her in on how we did. But he never made it sound impor-tant enough. So I'd give her my own play-by-play.

"Come to me for the real highlights," I'd tell her. "Marcus is too modest."

The ball popped loose and Marcus grabbed it. He found me running up ahead of everyone. I dunked the ball hard with one hand. I could feel the rim shaking as I let go of it. The cheerleaders were starting up again.

On my way back up court, I flashed Rebecca a big smile.

We rolled through the rest of the first half, and went into halftime leading 43–18. Everything was on cruise control.

It's great in the locker room at halftime when you're kicking ass out on the court. Everyone is all charged up, and nobody minds that the place stinks from the smell of sweat. Not when you're winning big, and the stands outside are still rocking for you.

Andre and X were already talking up their best plays. Even kids who didn't get into the game yet sounded like they had something to do with the score. Marcus was sitting down with a towel over his shoulders. I was walking back and forth trying to keep a good sweat going, and so I wouldn't get stiff.

Casey came in and told us not to get carried away by the score.

"We made a lot of mistakes out there," Casey said. "If we were playing a better team, it might have cost us."

He went over to the chalkboard and put up the plays he wanted to run in the second half. But before he got through, the principal, Ms. Randolph, called Casey from just outside the door. He kept talking to us as he made his way over. Then he tossed the chalk to X, and went outside. That's when X started giving his own speech, and wrote "Take No Prisoners" up on the board.

After a while, Coach called us out for the second half, and we started to run a layup line to get warm. I was looking around at the crowd and the gym like they belonged to me. That's when I noticed that Marcus wasn't out on the court. I thought maybe he hit the bathroom or needed to get taped up, and after another run through the line, I went to check.

I looked back inside the locker room and two guys in suits were handcuffing Marcus. Casey and Ms. Randolph saw me at the door and pushed me back outside. Then Casey wiped a tear from his eye and huddled everybody up around our bench.

"Marcus was just arrested," Casey said, steadying himself. "I can't say why. There's nothing we can do for him right now, except play the rest of the game like it means something to us."

After we broke the huddle, kids were looking at me for answers. But I didn't have anything to say. My legs got weak, and I thought I was going to pass out. I tried not to look anyone in the eye, and walked onto the court. Then the ref blew the whistle to start play.

We beat Grover Cleveland 73–58 that night. I was the high-scorer with thirty-five points.

BLACK

The bus driver's name was Sidney Parker. He remembered me taking the bus with the team from school. The cops got him a copy of our yearbook, and he picked my picture out cold. At least I knew for sure he was alive.

The detectives read my rights to me. The tall one had it all memorized. He bent over every word, like he really enjoyed it. But I was looking at the faces of Casey and Ms. Randolph more than I was listening. I was wondering what they thought about me, especially Coach.

The cops searched my locker for the gun. The older one pulled out a shirt my mother sewed. He went in and out of every pocket. I could feel my mother standing right next to me, waiting to put her foot up my ass. This was going to be the saddest day of her life, only she didn't have a clue yet.

I changed into my street clothes, and they cuffed me. We went down the back staircase. The same one

Jason used to let Eddie and me come up to see the games when we were younger. I remember wanting to wear an LIC jersey just like him. All the way down, I was thinking how Jason was killed in that game upstate. Everybody on the tape was running in different directions. You couldn't make out a thing until the TV station put a white spot on the kid stabbing him with the chair leg. It didn't make any sense. They didn't have any beef. Jason was playing ball, and that kid was sitting in the stands, ready to blow.

People around my way said it was because of that natural hatred. That line between blacks and whites that can't get erased, no matter what. I just remember hating that kid's guts because of what he did to Jason, not because he was white. And everybody I knew—no matter what color—hated him, too.

We reached the bottom, and the detectives pushed the door open. I expected to see Jason standing on the other side, wearing his uniform with the "C" for "captain" on his chest. I knew he'd be shaking his head over everything Eddie and me got mixed up in.

The door swung open fast. It slammed hard against the red brick wall outside. I flinched. But no one was there. The street was empty, and the cops walked me over to their car.

The detectives did most of the talking on the ride to the station. I knew enough from watching police shows on TV to wait for a lawyer before I said too much. But they kept dogging me about my partner. And when I wouldn't answer, they started calling him "the shooter."

"Are you going to take the fall for this alone, while the shooter walks?" the tall one asked me.

"He must be a real good friend of yours, if you don't want to give him up," said the older one. "Who are your two or three closest friends, Marcus? Because if you don't tell us, other people will."

Eddie must have been in a real panic, stressing over getting nabbed, too. The cops already had me. And I didn't have to keep pretending it never happened. I was just worried sick about my mother. At first, she wouldn't believe it, no matter what anybody said. She'd think it was some kind of mix-up with somebody who looked like me. Then I'd have to tell her.

When we got to the precinct, Casey's wife had just come in, too. She told me not to worry. That my mother was on her way, and that Coach would be there for me as soon as he could. I should have told her to go back to the game, and to tell Casey not to come because I wasn't worth the trouble. But I just stood there with my mouth shut until the cops hustled me upstairs.

They took me to a small room with a desk, two wooden chairs, and a phone. Then they handcuffed me to one of the chairs and left. The only window in the room was cut into the wall on my left side. It was completely blacked out, and I knew the cops were probably watching me from the other side. I tried hard not to look over there. But when I did, I was looking into a black mirror. I tested the sound of my voice, and listened to it echo through the room. For a second, I thought I said Eddie's name out loud, and held my breath over that, thinking the cops must be listening in.

The detective with the gray hair came back and asked me a bunch of easy questions in a quiet voice. He wanted to go over my name and where I went to school. He asked about my family, and what I liked to do for fun. Then he took out the school yearbook and found me in the team pictures for football and basketball. The smile never left his face when he asked if a kid on one of those teams was my partner.

He asked if I knew the names Wanda Lang or William Mathes. But before I could answer, he said, "You should, Marcus. Those are the two people you and your partner robbed before Mr. Parker."

That felt like a sucker punch in the gut. He didn't smile or anything over it. His face just stayed even. He started tapping his pencil on the table, and maybe five minutes went by without either one of us saying a word. Then the phone rang. He listened for a few seconds and said, "So he's absolutely sure."

He put the phone down and pointed to the dark window next to my chair.

"Mr. Parker has just made a positive ID on you," said the detective. "He says that without a doubt you were the one in the backseat of his car that night."

I didn't have an answer for him, and sunk even lower into the chair.

I turned and looked hard into that window. I wished I could see Parker's face in it. I was scared as anything to meet him again and hear what he might say. Still, I wanted him to know how sorry I was. But there was no way to get through. No matter how hard I looked, it was just my reflection in that window. And all I could see was my own black face.

The detective started to press me more about who I was with that night. He ran down a bunch of kids' names to me, one by one. I wouldn't shake my head "no" or say anything about them. But he kept going down the list anyway. I knew sooner or later he would get to Eddie's name. I tried to get ready. I grabbed onto the thin arms of the chair until my knuckles turned white. When he finally said, "Eddie Russo," a fire shot through my body. My mouth turned bone dry, and I could feel the sweat on my temples.

They wouldn't let my mother talk to me, and I was almost happy about that. But when they were taking me out, I saw her down at the end of the hallway. She was sitting with Casey and his wife, and jumped up the second she saw me. I could see how scared she was for me. She looked straight at me for some kind of answer, or something she could do. My chest got real tight. I knew I was breathing, but I couldn't say for sure any air was getting through. Then the detective turned me in the other direction. I remember looking back over my shoulder at her, like I belonged in handcuffs.

WHITE

Rose found out from somebody in the crowd that Marcus got arrested. She was in tears, and all over me to tell her what I knew. Some of the kids were saying Marcus probably got into a fight with somebody at school, who went to the cops about it. Only I couldn't stop looking over my shoulder, waiting for the cops to show up again and just haul me away.

Casey left the second the refs blew the whistle to end the game. A few of the scouts were waiting around by his office door, trying to find out what happened to Marcus. The scout from St. John's had talked to me a couple of times before, and once with me and Marcus together. But I didn't have much time left now.

I thought about Marcus being at the police station. And everything I could lose. I had a ticket to play big-time college ball in my hand. I wasn't going to just give it away. So I walked straight up to the scout and told him I wanted to play for St. John's.

"That's great news, Eddie! We've had a scholarship

with your name on it for a while now," he said, handing me his card. "Fax us a letter of intent in the morning, and we'll make it all official."

Then he asked me where Coach was, and why Marcus didn't come out for the second half. Before I had time to open my mouth, one of the other scouts came over to tell him that Casey was gone. I sprinted for the locker room before things got any worse.

I put my street clothes on over my uniform, and went down the same back stairs where the cops took Marcus. Kids on the team saw that I didn't want to talk. They probably thought I was in a hurry to help out my best friend.

A police car passed me on the street, and I just stood frozen until it rolled out of sight. I could feel my heart pounding inside my chest. I knew that Marcus wouldn't point a finger at me. But he might say the wrong thing by mistake, or the cops might trick him into saying we were together that night.

I beat my family back home. They probably waited around for me at the gym. And that was all the head start I needed. I ran up to the attic with Gotti on my heels. I took the shoe box down from the closet, and sat on the edge of my grandpa's bed with it. He had that gun to protect his family. I used it to rob people. The pictures of him with my grandma were looking right at me. I told him how I screwed up, and that I never meant to shoot anybody. But he just stared back at me from every angle.

I opened the box with my hands shaking. I hated the idea of touching that damn gun again. So I held my breath, and grabbed it fast. The gun felt heavier in my hand than it ever had before.

It was always chilly in the attic. And the gun hadn't warmed up a bit since I put it back that night. I closed my palm around the handle with my finger way off the trigger. The cold ran up my arm, and sent a shiver through my spine. I stuffed the gun into the front of my pants and started breathing again. I put the shoe box back with the brick inside. Then I hustled my ass out of the house, taking Gotti with me this time. I wanted to look more like a kid walking his dog than somebody trying to ditch a gun.

I walked up to the projects, and past Marcus's building. Then I turned straight down 21st Street for Astoria Park. Every half block or so, I tapped on the gun to make sure it was still there. The Department of Sanitation garage was on the other side of the street. My dad picked up his truck there in the morning and dropped it off in the same spot every night. My grandpa did the same thing before him for almost forty years.

The park right next to it was where me and Marcus

first played ball together. It's not much of a park, just two full courts laid out side by side. It doesn't have a bench, a water fountain, or a single tree. And in the middle of summer, there isn't any shade at all. That park doesn't even have a name. Everybody just calls it the D.S., because it's right over the fence from the garage.

My old junior high school came up on my side, and I thought about all the fun me and Marcus had there. I waited for the light to change and crossed over at the next corner. The C-Town supermarket was right in front of me. Gotti went wild barking at the big plaster cow and chicken on the roof. And I yanked hard on his choker to get him to stop.

I checked on the gun again, and walked faster.

There's a little graveyard that pops up out of nowhere, right on the street between a tire shop and somebody's house. It takes up the space of a regular-sized building. You can see the whole thing from front to back through the fence. None of the headstones are standing up straight anymore. The graves are so old that the city can't dig them up. But the gate is always locked, and nobody can go inside to visit, either.

I crossed under the Triboro Bridge and into Astoria Park. I walked across the running track where we used to run laps for football practice. One time, we had almost fifty kids there doing laps, when a white dude called another kid a nigger. The black kid tackled him on the spot. Everybody else started pairing off, and choosing sides. Me and Marcus grabbed a hold of each other and were just dancing around in circles. There was almost a riot. But we had fun, and just laughed at everybody.

Shore Boulevard is at the bottom of a short, steep hill. There were only a handful of people hanging out along the strip there. And a few more were in cars, either getting high or making out. I looked over the railing. The East River was rolling up onto the rocks in little waves. But twenty yards out, the currents were really moving.

I walked all the way down to the Hell Gate Bridge before I found an open spot where nobody was watching. The Hell Gate is up on concrete columns as tall as Marcus's building. And it would take an earthquake to shake them. Only freight trains and Amtrak use that bridge. So it's mostly dark and quiet up on the tracks, and the same way underneath.

I wrapped Gotti's leash around the rail, and took a second look around. Then I took a deep breath, and pulled out the gun. I squeezed the handle and threw it as far as I could. I heard the splash, and felt the muscles in my arm start to burn from the strain. Gotti's head was hanging over the rail. He bird-dogged the gun all the way into the water. He didn't want to give up on it, either. But I dragged him back the way we came.

When I got home, everyone was waiting for me. They thought I was at the police station trying to find out what happened to Marcus. It didn't even hit them that Gotti wasn't in the house. I walked in the door with him, and they almost couldn't believe it.

"Where were you?" Rose said, before my mom could get out the same words.

I told them that I just had to get out and think for a while. Then I asked if they had heard anything new about Marcus.

"I called his house," said Rose. "His mother went down to the police station, and there's a neighbor staying with his sister."

"I'm just glad you're not mixed up in any of this," my dad said.

"It's where Marcus lives," my mom jumped in. "It's the projects. There's crime all around him. It was probably just too big a temptation."

Then she took a short, quick breath and said, "Listen to me. I'm talking like he's guilty of whatever it is. Maybe it was some other black boy who looks like him."

I wanted to stop all the talk about Marcus, so I told them that I took the scholarship to St. John's. My mom was so happy she started to cry. Mostly because I wouldn't be moving away.

"I told everybody he would be a success," my dad said at the top of his lungs.

Rose asked me if Marcus getting arrested would stop schools from wanting him, too. "What does that have to do with me?" I snapped.

"Nothing!" my dad said. "Not a thing!"

Rose stared back at me.

Maybe I was the worst friend in the whole world, getting myself into a school while Marcus was in handcuffs. But I threw up my arms and walked away from her.

I thought the day I picked a school would be one of the happiest times in my life. That there would be some kind of big celebration at home. I thought me and Marcus would be at a party with the rest of the team. That maybe I would celebrate in private with Rebecca, or some other girl, that night. But here it was, and it was nothing like that.

It took me almost an hour to type out a simple letter, saying that I was choosing St. John's.

I spent the whole next morning at school dodging questions about Marcus. I got to homeroom as late as I could. But the second I walked through the door, everybody wanted to know what happened. Most of them looked shocked when I told them that I didn't know anything. They were asking me about Marcus like I was his brother. Maybe they thought I was supposed to chase the cops all the way down to the station house.

Rebecca wasn't asking me to explain anything. But she talked to me like somebody in my family was sick in the hospital. I hated that kind of sympathy, especially because I didn't deserve it. I was going to tell her about the scholarship, but I couldn't find a place to start. Every time I brought it up into my throat, it didn't feel right.

Later, my mom tracked me down in the hall. I could see in her face that something was wrong. She was holding the letter I gave her to fax over to St. John's. I thought the scout had changed his mind and sent it back. But my mom gave me the letter and said, "It's all done, and I'm very proud of you."

Then she put her hand on my shoulder and said, "I went to the principal's office to fax that. Ms. Randolph told me all about Marcus. Eddie, he was arrested for a robbery with a gun, and somebody got shot. Can you believe it?"

She asked me if I was going to be all right. I told her I could handle it, and that she should worry more about Rose.

"You're right," she said. "I'm going to find her now.

I don't want her hearing about this from the kids."

She kissed me on the cheek, like that would protect me from something. Then she walked off to find my sister. I could hear the sound of her footsteps behind me when I realized that she said, "Somebody got shot," and not killed.

No matter what happened now, at least it wasn't murder. That man didn't get killed. And I wouldn't have to live with something like that forever.

All through English class, I kept looking over at Marcus's empty seat. I wondered where the cops had him, and what was happening. Marcus could be real strong. I knew he wouldn't break down, not even under those bright lights they use to make people talk.

I knew that Rose would call Marcus's house when she got home. I could get the scoop that way, and find out what was going on. I didn't know if his mother was going to think that I had something to do with it. Marcus knew tons of guys in the projects who could pull something like that. Some of them even had police records. But she knew how much time we spent together.

Marcus had the seat behind me in math. So once I sat down, I just didn't turn around. I tried to block him out of my head and concentrate on the problems on the board. But after a while, I could almost feel him breathing down my neck. I turned around all at once, and almost lost it when I saw a black face staring back at me. Some kid from a couple of rows back had moved up to see the board better. And I almost jumped down his throat.

I went up to the gym after class, but Casey wasn't around. There was just a note on his office door that read, PRACTICE CANCELED TODAY. I don't even think he came to school that day because the note wasn't in his handwriting.

The team was hanging around, talking about it.

"Do you think Coach is out looking after Marcus?" Andre asked out loud.

"No doubt," said Moses, eying me. "Coach is his *real* white brother."

X said to me, "So you don't know anything, or you just can't speak on it?"

"I told you already, I'm waiting to find out just like everybody else," I answered.

Then Preston came running up the stairs and broke the news. "Marcus got arrested for robbery," he said. "And somebody got shot."

"Shiiit," kids said all at once.

"Now don't tell me you weren't close enough to hear that gun go pop," X barked at me.

"Yo, X," Moses jumped in. "Back off, before we find

out what we don't want to know. He opens his mouth here and the DA will try to squeeze us all on the witness stand."

I went straight down the stairs with my blood boiling. And by the time I made it out of the building, the sweat was pouring off of me.

When I got home, Rose was crying. She had called Marcus's house and found out that his mother was on her way to New Jersey. She had no idea why. Neither did I. Casey had given everybody on the team his home number in case of an emergency. But I didn't want to call. And I didn't tell Rose that I had the number, or she would have made me pick up the phone.

I made it through the whole next day at school with my head down. Casey was there for practice, and everyone wanted to talk to him about Marcus. But he wouldn't open his mouth. He just pointed to the locker room for us to change. When we came back out, he was standing on the court with a whistle in his mouth for us to run drills.

We were running an easy layup line, until Casey popped his whistle twice for us to move double-time. Then he crossed both fists over his head. That was the signal for our full court press. The team ran into position on offense and defense. Without Marcus, we had ten players even. So everyone was on the court.

Casey called out the numbers for our set plays. We went through them all, one by one. We ran 5XL for big Andre, 17X for X, and 10C for Moses. I had a bunch of plays that all started with 11, because that was my number. Casey ran them all in a row for me. The last one was 11BW, and Preston took Marcus's place setting the pick on my man that got me free.

Everyone was going hard, like it was for real. We ran every play except for the ones that started with 12. Those belonged to Marcus. When we ran out of plays, Casey blew the whistle and called us over to the bleachers. He lifted the cap off his head, and his face got even more serious.

"I know it's all over school about Marcus. He should be home in the next day or two. When he comes back, give him some room to breathe. Let him concentrate on school and what's ahead of him," Casey said.

Then Casey made sure to look around at everyone and said, "Don't be surprised if the police show up asking questions. I understand they're looking for at least one other person."

I just stared straight ahead.

"Eddie," Casey said. "Do you want to announce you're college plans to the team?"

I told them that I had decided on St. John's. I thanked them all for helping me get there, and Casey, too. But when I finished, there wasn't any clapping or congratulations. There was just the sound of the air vents running through the gym.

"You worked hard for that scholarship," Casey said. "You deserve it."

Then he told us all to shower and go home.

I saw Casey sitting in his office before I left. He waved me in with one finger.

"I was hoping to hear about your plans from you, not from St. John's," he said.

"You're right. I'm sorry, Coach," I said. "I've had a lot on my mind since Marcus got locked up. I just haven't been thinking straight."

BLACK

The cops put me through the system. They took my picture from every side and fingerprinted me. I stayed awake all night in a cell with a bunch of crackheads, afraid to close my eyes on them. There was one toilet in the corner, and everybody could watch you shit and piss. The next morning they shipped me off to the courthouse on Queens Boulevard to see the judge.

I spent most of the day in the pens with a hundred other guys, trying to hold my ground. I had to put on my best ice-grill just to get a little bit of space. Some herb got ripped off for his hooded sweatshirt. And if the officers there didn't put a stop to it, he probably would have went out to see the judge in his underwear.

I was scared. But I wouldn't show it, or else I would have been shark bait, no matter how big I was.

I was wearing my new kicks from the basketball game, and lots of guys were eyeing them. "He's got

the new Nike joints, and they're just my size," some-body said.

Those damn shoes got me into this mess. But I wasn't giving anything up to a bunch of thugs. So I stood up the whole time, with all my weight planted on top of them.

My stomach was starting to make noise. I hadn't eaten since lunch at school, the day before. When they handed out bologna sandwiches with contain-ers of milk, I wolfed it down like I was eating at Red Lobster. Other guys with full bellies wouldn't touch it. And by the time I left to see the judge, the floor was covered with pink bologna.

They took me into the courtroom, and I saw my mother sitting with Casey and his wife. It meant something to me that Coach was there for my moth-er. I didn't hold it against Eddie for not showing. It would have been the same as giving himself up. But right or wrong, I couldn't stop thinking how Eddie was getting a free ride.

My mother came up and hugged me tight. I could see in her eyes how she would have liked to break me in half. I met the lawyer the city appointed to my case, Ms. Torres. She was talking to my mother before I came out. So my mother knew about every-thing I did. Ms. Torres told me what to expect, and asked if I would identify the shooter to get less time.

I told her no, flat out.

That's when my mother went off, "That's why Eddie's not here! Ain't that right, Marcus! Oh, but he's your best friend in the world. So he'll let you go to jail without him. You just think about—"

She caught herself in one quick breath, and held the rest back. Then her face turned more serious than I'd ever seen it before. She opened her eyes wide and said, "Marcus, I want to know right now if you've got a gun hidden somewhere in that house. I don't want your sister to find it and blow her head off!"

I never thought I'd hear her ask me a question like that.

"No, Mama," I said in a low voice.

Ms. Torres just shook her head.

The clerk called my name and it echoed off all four walls. I felt ashamed that my mother had to hear it. The DA came on and said his piece against me. Ms. Torres just listened and took notes on a long yellow pad. The judge said there was enough evidence to hold me, and set my bail at $20,000. I knew my mother couldn't afford anything close to that. So when it was over, an officer took me back to the pens. And I got put on the next bus to Rikers Island.

I was chained to the kid sitting next to me by the

wrist and leg. There were thick metal screens on the windows, and the driver was separated from us by a steel cage. The bus turned off the highway, and rolled down the side streets, maybe two miles from my house. Then it started over the Rikers Island Bridge.

There was nothing outside the window, except water and razor-wire fences.

Adolescents have their own houses, so the adults can't take advantage of them. I got sent to Mod #1 with all the other newjacks. That's where they keep you until you learn the system on Rikers. But the main part of what goes on there started to sink in right away. It's black people, wall to wall. There are some Spanish inmates, too. But everybody else is black.

That whole first night, I kept thinking how if Eddie got arrested with me, his family would have bailed him out. Only I'd still be there. I couldn't beef about it. It wouldn't have been Eddie's fault. That's the way it is. We could be Black and White anywhere else in the world. But not on Rikers Island.

I saw plenty of white dudes in court. I guess they were innocent, or made bail. The only white faces I saw on Rikers belonged to the corrections officers.

There weren't any cells with iron bars, like in the

movies. Instead, there were rows of cots in a big dorm. I slept in all my clothes that night, with my head under the blanket.

I spent most of the next day feeling my way around. A woman CO put a scrub brush in my hand. I was part of a crew that cleaned the bathroom until it shined. If my mother ever made me to do that, I would have blown. But there I was, cleaning the city's toilets, without making a peep about it.

To get to the mess hall, the officers took us down the main corridor. It's long and narrow, with low a ceiling. The different houses move back and forth on opposite sides, only five or six feet apart. The COs play the middle in between them.

Every time another house passed next to us, kids got tense, like something might jump off. I saw lots of dudes with fresh cuts on their faces, long buck-fifties from ear to jaw that would take more than a hundred stitches to close. And I didn't want to become one of them.

The COs put us at a table in the middle of the mess hall. The houses all around knew we were new-jacks, and kept barking at us. Especially the adults. Most of those dudes were diesel, and could have probably snapped me in half. I heard plenty of shit about taking my sneakers. But I just kept eating, like I was deaf.

On the way back, the house got stopped at the metal detector. Everybody was patted down. A CO wearing rubber gloves ran his hands down my sides and through my pockets. Some kid had snuck out a container of milk. And after the CO found it, he slapped him hard in the back of the head until the kid almost cried.

In the house, I was mostly able to hold my own. It was like summer camp for scumbags. Kids spent all day trying to prove they were gangsters. The sneak thieves stole shit. The maytags had to wash other kids' socks and drawers. The doldiers were muscle for the gangsters, and the thugs did their own fighting. But everyone was scared of being shipped upstate, and doing real time with adults.

The kids that were ready to cop out looked the most shook. They said the adults upstate didn't play bullshit games. They played for keeps. And you'd have to fight to keep from being somebody's boy.

It got to me, too, and I didn't want to think about doing years up there.

At around five o'clock, a CO called me to the front of the house. I was shocked when he told me I was going home on a bail-out. I wanted to be off Rikers Island more than anything. But I didn't know how I was going to face my mother at home.

An officer took me down to the front gate with my paperwork. My mother and sister were waiting just outside the last checkpoint. It looked like the gates at a subway station, with two COs keeping watch. I pushed the bar on the turnstile and felt it come back around and bump me from behind.

Sabrina ran up and hugged me. My mother was waiting with her arms folded across her chest.

"I brought her along because I want her to see what this place is," my mother said before she kissed me on the forehead, without ever opening her arms.

We had to take the 101-Limited over the Rikers Island Bridge, past our house to Queensboro Plaza. Then we took the 19-A back home from there. My mother walked in tight behind me, like they weren't going to let me on that bus anymore because of what I did. But the driver never said a word.

My mother begged her sisters in New Jersey to put up their house for my bail. They hadn't seen me since I was small. So I knew they did it mainly for her, and not me.

There wasn't much talk, except for Sabrina. I kept

my mouth shut and eyes down for most of the ride. I saw every crack in the sidewalk and every piece of trash on the floor of those buses.

Moses and X were hanging out right outside my building. They both gave me a pound, with my mother watching close.

"No matter what, they still got to prove their case against you," X said. "And they get it wrong a lot, brother."

Moses said how much the team missed me in the second half. Then he gave X a sideways look and said, "Your best friend took a scholarship to St. John's before he left the gym that night."

They waited for me to blink. And I won't front—it hurt like anything to hear. But I had bigger things to worry about. So I brushed it off.

My mother heard every word. She was so steamed at Eddie, you could have fried an egg on her forehead. But she didn't blow, either.

We got into the elevator, and the metal door sprung closed behind us. My sister had to jump up a little to hit the top button. We started up, and I could feel the pressure pushing down on me. It felt like my heart was sinking into my shoes.

My mother put the key in our door and opened the

locks one by one. I was never so glad to be home in all my life. But another part of me knew what I was in for that night. And I would have rather been caught stealing money out of my mother's purse than tell her everything I had done.

Sabrina turned on the TV. But my mother shut it back off inside the first minute. She told my sister to study her math and clean up for dinner. There was a knock at the door. My mother shot me a hard look. So I didn't even think about moving. She opened the door without even asking, "Who is it?"

Mrs. Johnson from downstairs was standing there with a pot of stew. She used to be my babysitter. Now she stayed with Sabrina when my mother got outside sewing jobs. They stood at the door and talked about me like I wasn't even there.

"So how is he?" she asked.

"He's still on this earth, if that's what you mean!" my mother answered.

Mrs. Johnson almost laughed and said, "Hold on to that kind of thinking, honey. It'll help you get through this."

That stew was the only real food I had in almost two days. But I didn't enjoy a bite. It was almost eight o'clock when we finished. I carried the dishes to the sink and started to wash them. Then my mother told Sabrina to go to bed early, and went to talk to her.

I heard my mother's footsteps starting back, and I scrubbed the dishes even harder. She pulled the chair out and sat down at the table behind me. I didn't want to turn around for anything. I kept at the dishes until they were whiter than they'd ever been.

"That's enough of that. Come over here and sit down," my mother said.

Her eyes were more sad than angry. We looked at each other for almost a minute without saying a word.

"Explain yourself to me, Marcus!" she finally said, her voice shaking.

Before the first word came out of my mouth, I broke down crying. I looked up and she was crying, too.

"I just wanted some extra money, Mama. I wanted to do things. I wanted to buy these shoes and pay the senior dues, too. I didn't mean for anybody to—"

"You almost killed somebody! Do you understand that? You threw away your life for some spending money and a pair of shoes. And you almost killed a man!" she said. "Now, did I raise you up, or did the streets?" she kept on through the tears.

She asked me why I wouldn't say Eddie's name. She knew he was there with me, and must have had the gun.

"Maybe you won't say his name to the police, but you'll say it here. I don't want to hear any more of this *I* business, because I know it was *we*. It's Black and White until somebody's ass is on the line. And when it's time to go to jail, it's just Black. He'll find a new boy to carry his bags in college, and you'll be an ex-con on the unemployment line!" she screamed.

Sabrina came out of the bedroom crying from all the yelling. My mother held her tight, and buried Sabrina's face in her chest. "I love my babies," she said, rocking her. "Lord knows, I love my babies."

After everything got said out loud, I went to my bed. I thought about Eddie, and what my mother said.

If Eddie had got bagged without me, I don't know how I'd have been acting. I just know I would have been keeping a low profile, too. You don't give your best friend up to the cops. No how. No way. I knew that Eddie would have played it the same way for me.

But that part about the scholarship was sticking in me.

The phone rang. It was like someone sent an electric shock through me. I was sitting up in my bed before the second ring. That's when my mother answered.

"Yes, he's home. But he's asleep now. It's been a long couple of days," she said.

Then she asked, "How's your brother taking all this?"

And I knew it was Rose calling.

"No, I can't talk to him right now, dear. But you let your brother know for me that God has a way of watching over things. Yes, you, too. Good night," she said, and I heard her put the phone down into the cradle.

The next morning, my mother was standing over me, poking my shoulder to get up. She was sending me to school. I took a shower and got dressed. There was oatmeal on the kitchen table, but no place set for me.

"You're going to start doing things for yourself more. Get a bowl and a spoon," she told me.

When I was finished, I went to scrape the last of the oatmeal into the garbage. My new sneakers were sitting right on top, covered in table scraps. The smell came up and hit me good. I just froze there for a second, sick to my stomach. I pushed what was left in my bowl right on top of them, and closed the lid down tight.

I kissed my mother before I left for school. She stood there like a stone statue. When my lips were on her cheek, I could feel everything warm inside her.

But once they came off, she was cold as anything to me again.

I turned the corner outside my building and thought about what I should do. I took two or three steps towards school. Then I stopped. I spun around quick and felt enough momentum to keep going towards Eddie's.

I waited across the street, at the end of the block, behind a thick tree. There were shadows moving inside the house. Rose walked out with her arms folded around a notebook. I called her name the second she stepped outside the gate. Her mouth opened wide. But I put a finger over my lips for her not to make a sound. She looked back towards the house. Then she ran over to me.

Rose said my name and hugged me at the same time. Then she told me what everyone was saying I got arrested for.

"You didn't do any of that, Marcus? Did you?" she asked.

I told her it was an accident that the man got shot. But I could see in her brown eyes how disappointed she was in me.

Rose wanted to know why I didn't just come to the door. I asked her what her mother and father thought about me getting locked up. She dropped her shoulders and said they were both down on me. That's when Eddie stepped outside.

He stood there looking at us while he put the other arm through his coat. I never saw Eddie walk with his arms so stiff. But he put both of them around me before I could lift mine to hug him back.

I told him I'd heard about the scholarship. He said that wasn't important. That we'd both be playing in college soon. Maybe even together.

I didn't believe that. And it didn't sound like Eddie did, either.

Then Eddie asked me about court, and I just held on to myself tight. Part of me wanted to spark off about what I was facing alone now. But I couldn't go there in front of Rose.

"How stressed is your mother?" Eddie asked.

I looked over Rose's head, and caught Eddie's eye.

"She's all over *everything* in this," I said, and watched his face drop straight off.

Then Rose asked how I could get talked into something like that. She said how it wasn't right that whoever did the shooting was off the hook, and that I had to pay for it all. I fought hard to keep my voice even.

"That's just the way the game gets played out," I

said. "The cops do the chasing. It's all about who they catch."

The school block came up fast. We took our ID cards out and passed through security. Two of the school safety officers, Jefferson and Connelly, were at the front desk. They worked security together at all our home games. Kids called them "Black and White wannabes." But they always just smiled at that, and did their jobs.

Jefferson was tall and lean. He played football and basketball when he was a high school kid in Brooklyn. Connelly was almost a head shorter, and weighed close to three hundred pounds. His nose was pushed flat, like a pig's. And if you ever ranked on him about it, he'd make sure you got suspended the same day. He could be all right, but he had a mean streak in him, too.

One day, Connelly went out and bought a brand-new basketball and football for Eddie and me to sign. We knew he wanted them just to sell one day. But that didn't matter. Those were our first autographs.

Connelly took the ID out of my hand. He looked at it like he'd never seen me before. Then he turned to Jefferson and asked, "Do you want to buy half a basketball cheap?" Jefferson didn't crack a smile at that or anything. But when I passed through, Jefferson tapped me on the shoulder, and said he wanted to talk to me about everything later.

When we got out of range, Eddie called Connelly an asshole, and Rose backed him up on it. Deep down, that made me feel better.

Eddie's class was on the first floor. Mine was on the third, the same as Rose's. Halfway up the stairs, Rose said, "I know the two of you keep that game face on all the time, and pretend it's all okay. But I can't even imagine what you're feeling, Marcus. It's been tough on Eddie, too, worrying about you. I heard him crying in his room. It must be a hundred times worse for you."

All morning, kids wanted to know what happened. I just played it cool, and told them that I couldn't talk until everything got straightened out in court. They figured I must have been innocent. Everybody knew I had it going on playing ball. They couldn't see me throwing it all away on a lousy stickup.

I was copying the English notes I'd missed when Eddie walked through the door. His face wasn't showing much of anything. He nodded his head to me. Then Ms. Sussman started her lesson, and Eddie turned back around. He didn't take his eyes off her for the rest of the period.

When the bell rang, Eddie pulled his books together one at a time. He stood up and waited for me. "Coach will probably run us like dogs today with that game on Tuesday," he said.

I would have done anything to hear what was really inside his head. Even if I had to punch him in the jaw to get it out. I pushed my toes into the floor and said, "I wasn't even thinking about that right now."

I went out the door first, with Eddie right behind me. Before I knew it, I was headed to my next class alone.

Later on, I ran into Eddie's mother in front of the cafeteria.

"Rose told me you were here this morning," she said. "I just want you to know that if you can't talk at home, you can come by our house and say anything that's on your mind. Marcus, I want you to know that we're always going to be there for you."

I looked into her eyes and knew how bad she'd feel if she ever found out about Eddie.

"Thanks, but I'll get by all right," I told her.

The noise inside the cafeteria hit me like a wave. Moses and X found me sitting by myself. They were all over me for pulling a stickup on somebody who could point me out so easy. Then they pounded me about messing up my shot at playing college ball.

"So the dude didn't remember what your partner, Al Capone, looked like?" asked Moses.

"Of course not," cracked X. "He was so shocked the black kid wasn't the one holding the gun, he couldn't take his eyes off Marcus."

No matter how bad they got on my case, at least it was real.

"You don't have a paid lawyer. You don't have a co-defendant to take half the blame. You're fucked!" X said.

"The only thing in your favor is the dude who got shot is black. Maybe the judge won't give a damn, unless the judge is black, too," said Moses.

All through math class, I only saw the back of Eddie's head. The teacher gave a pop quiz. I ran through it easy because they were questions we had from the beginning of the year. I could see Eddie was stuck on the last problem. I thought about kicking his chair twice for the letter "B." But my leg wouldn't move.

We walked upstairs to practice together, and started to change. The last time I was in that locker room the cops were handcuffing me. Now I didn't have anything to hide, except for Eddie's part.

Eddie saw me lacing up my old kicks and asked about my sneakers.

"My mother chucked the new ones in the garbage," I told him.

He stood there looking at me, until his eyes dropped down to his own shoes.

Coach was all over everybody at practice for making little mistakes or not hustling. I only screwed up one time. But when I did, Casey jumped on me, too. It felt good to take the heat for something small again, like screwing up on a basketball court.

After I caught my first wind, I fell right in step. The ball was moving back and forth between Eddie and me like nothing ever came between us. We had guys flying in every direction. No one could read our moves. And every time they tried to double-team one of us, the ball got passed quick to whoever was open.

I blocked everything else out of my mind and just played ball.

When Casey blew the last whistle, I was drenched in sweat. I didn't want to towel off. I wanted to keep playing. Eddie and everybody else went in to change, but I just kept shooting the ball by myself. It was the first time I could remember that Casey didn't give his Friday speech about keeping out of trouble over the weekend.

By the time I went inside, Eddie was already dressed. So I threw sweats and a jacket on over what I was wearing. Neither one of us said a word until we got down the stairs and the door to the school slammed shut behind us.

We were at the first corner waiting for the light to change when Eddie asked, "Is there something I'm supposed to do?"

"There's nothing to do," I came back. "That man recognized me, and now I got to deal with it."

"How rough was it?" Eddie asked.

I told Eddie the cops had me sewed up tight from the beginning. But I wouldn't tell them anything more. Then Eddie said he dumped the gun where nobody would ever find it. He didn't say where, and I didn't ask.

I told Eddie how my mother knew from the start it was him with the gun. But I didn't think I could get across how mad she was. So I didn't even try.

"You know I only took that scholarship right away in case they started to hear things later," he said.

"When shit jumps up, I guess you got to move fast," I said. "I'll be playing somewhere, too, after the judge and my mother finish kicking my ass."

We stopped a few blocks before our houses. I asked Eddie if he was worried about being seen with me in the streets. That the cops might figure it out for themselves.

He thought about it for a few seconds and said, "Who doesn't already know about Black and White?"

We both smiled at that, and went home our separate ways.

WHITE

I saw the black sedan parked outside of my house. Right away, I knew that something was wrong. There were two open spots on either side. But the car was parked in front of the hydrant anyway. I could hear my dad's voice from inside. It was loud and polite, like he was talking to company. I turned the knob and everything inside got quiet.

Two detectives were sitting on the couch, facing me. One of them stood up and stretched out his long legs. The other one stayed where he was, and said, "This must be your son, Eddie."

My mom came over and put both her hands around my shoulders. She steered me through the living room like I was blind and she had just changed all the furniture around.

The one who was standing took a giant step towards me and stuck out his hand. "I'm Detective Smoltz," he said, as my fingers disappeared inside his grip. He squeezed my hand and looked straight into my

eyes. It felt like he could pull anything he wanted right out of me. From across the room, my dad was staring me in the face. I thought he was about to scream at me. Then his eyes bounced between the two detectives, and he got himself together.

Gotti was anchored at the feet of the one sitting down. The detective got up only halfway, and leaned forward. He stayed low enough to keep petting Gotti with one hand, while he shook mine with the other. "Eddie, my name is Detective O'Grady," he said. "My partner and I want to talk to you about a string of robberies and a shooting."

O'Grady asked a lot of questions about Marcus. My mom and dad answered a couple of them before I could even open my mouth. He knew all about Black and White, and my scholarship to St. John's. He asked what me and Marcus liked to do after practice. That's when my dad got really upset, and wanted to know if they were investigating me.

"We're just trying to understand what happened that night," O'Grady said. "We know that Eddie spends a lot of time with Marcus. Maybe he can be helpful."

Rose came home right behind me, and my mom tried to take her upstairs. But she wanted to tell the detectives how nice Marcus treated everybody. She said that if Marcus had done something bad, that it was probably because somebody talked him into it. That he was still part of our family, no matter what.

Then Smoltz asked, "Do you folks keep a .38 caliber revolver in this house?"

My mom and Rose let out a gasp that sent Gotti into a barking fit. "We don't own a gun!" my dad said in a charged-up voice. Then he made a speech about how we were a taxpaying family, and that there were real criminals running around the streets. Through that whole scene, Smoltz and O'Grady never took their eyes off of me.

I didn't know where to put my hands or how to hold my arms. The detectives on TV were experts at reading body language, so I figured that they probably were, too. I went over and stood between my mom and Rose, and they both wrapped their arms around me. Now they'd have to judge me between two people who had nothing to hide.

Before they left, O'Grady gave me his card and said, "Call me if you remember something that can make it easier on Marcus. No one wants to see him get what he doesn't deserve."

The door closed behind them and I didn't know what to do next. My dad started ripping into Marcus. Rose and my mom were yelling at him to stop.

"It's where he was brought up," he said. "It's either

rob or be robbed. But everybody here goes around saying he's part of this family. Now the police are at our door."

Rose wanted to call Marcus to tell him about the detectives. But my parents wouldn't let her, and told me not to call, either. They said that we should keep some distance until the investigation was finished. My mom was so upset that she couldn't make dinner. And things didn't settle down until she sent my dad out for Chinese food.

I sat down on the couch in the spot where O'Grady had been sitting. It was still warm. I wasn't about to give the cops anything to work with. But no matter how I explained it to myself, I couldn't get away from how I was turning my back on Marcus. It wasn't Black and White anymore. It was just me looking out for my own ass.

I held O'Grady's card in front of my face. I looked at all the numbers and the police department seal up in the corner. I felt everything I ever worked for slipping away—my scholarship, the pros—everything.

I knew that the cops figured out it was me with Marcus that night. They probably just didn't have enough evidence to prove it, or they would have arrested me. I folded the card in half and buried it in my pocket.

That night I couldn't sleep. I heard the floor in the attic creak. I got out of bed. I knew I had to face what was up there. I could see a light from under the door as I got closer. When I got to the top of the steps, I pushed the door open.

My dad was staring right at me. He was sitting on grandpa's bed with the shoe box in his hands. The rubber bands were still wrapped around it. I stood in the doorway, waiting for him to say something. He weighed the box in his palm and shook it to hear the sound it made.

"I don't ever want to open this box, Eddie. Do I?" he asked.

I looked him in the eye as long as I could.

He never raised his voice. He just told me to get my ass back in bed. And I did. I don't know what he did with the box after that, but in the morning it was gone. He didn't tell my mom a thing about it, either. He acted like it never happened. Only I could see it behind his eyes, no matter how hard he tried to hide it. It was a look that said, "How could I raise you to do something like that?" And when my mom mentioned Marcus that morning, I saw the explosion inside of him.

I spent that whole Saturday trying to stay out of his sight. I didn't want to go to the Circle and run into Marcus, either. So I shot fouls for almost two hours on the courts over by the D.S. In all the time I was there, maybe twenty sanitation trucks rolled in and out of the big garage. The crews on more than half of them stopped to congratulate me on getting the scholarship. Dad had bragged to everyone he worked with. Now he was at home, pretending that he was still proud of me.

On Sunday morning at eleven o'clock, O'Grady and Smoltz showed up. They shook my dad's hand at the front door and wiped their feet on the welcome mat. Then they arrested me in my living room. My mom and Rose were at church. I was glad they weren't around to see it. Gotti growled at the detectives and showed them his teeth. So my dad had to drag him out to the backyard.

O'Grady said that the woman who had been robbed picked my picture out of the school yearbook. Smoltz went upstairs to search my room. But he came back shaking his head. They took me out onto the front porch in handcuffs. Some of the neighbors were even outside. My dad was walking right behind us. I wouldn't turn around to look at him.

"Don't say anything until I get you a lawyer," I heard him say from over my shoulder.

O'Grady pushed my head down as he put me into the backseat of the car. I could hear Gotti barking from around back until O'Grady slammed the door shut. Then they took me away, with my dad watching from the curb.

At the station house, they asked me questions for almost two hours. But I wouldn't say a word. Keeping my mouth shut and waiting for a lawyer was tough. But listening to how they had it all pieced together was even harder. Smoltz liked telling it again and again, and watching me sweat. They knew about everything, except for my grandpa's gun.

"Sooner or later, Marcus is going to fill in all the cracks for us. His lawyer will wise him up. You'll see," said O'Grady. "That will leave you holding the gun, Eddie. That's just the way it works. Time is time. There is no more Black and White. Those days are over. Nobody is going to watch your back anymore but you."

Smoltz explained how I could come clean, and maybe the DA would agree to go easier on me. Then he explained how Marcus could get that same deal for himself, and stick it to me.

"My partner and I have been together for nine years," O'Grady said. "What would you do if I shot somebody and asked you to keep it quiet, Detective Smoltz?"

"I'd turn you over in a heartbeat," answered Smoltz.

I spent the night in central booking, and everything they said started echoing in my ears. I didn't get a wink of sleep. All the thugs and drunks in the cell were acting up. But I would have fought every one of them, and kicked their asses, too, if it could erase everything I did.

The next morning, I got transferred to the court-house by bus. In the pens, I had my game face on. I heard lots of talk about me being a "white boy."

The system wasn't hard to figure out. You went into the courtroom, and unless someone knew your face from *America's Most Wanted*, the judge gave you bail. But lots of guys couldn't pay it. They came back to the pens bitching, and the guards put them on the bus for Rikers Island.

I got called out to a side room to meet my lawyer, Mr. Golub. My dad found him through his boss, whose son had fucked up once, too. He explained to me what would happen out in the courtroom, and what I should say. Then he would meet with me and my dad in a few days, after he studied the case more.

When I got back to the pens, I caught an earful.

"Tell me a white boy came back from seeing the judge and is going to the Island," one guy said.

"Get real now. Money came back from talking with his mouthpiece. That's all!" said another black dude.

I stood up in front, against the bars. That's where the officers had their desk.

"Big boy, you feel safer up here?" one of the offi-cers grinned.

I thought about how it was different when me and

Marcus had each other's backs. I knew that I was going home in a couple of hours. Then I'd only have to worry about my mom, and what the coach at St. John's would say.

There were two other white guys who got called out ahead of me. Neither one of them came back. That didn't bother me.

An officer walked me into the courtroom, and we came out from behind the flag. Mom and Rose were sitting in the first row, sharing rosary beads. Their eyes were red and swollen from crying. My dad looked me up and down, like he hardly knew me.

The DA read the evidence against me out loud, and my mom let out a sob. My lawyer said something in legal talk. Then the judge asked me if I understood everything. "Yes, sir," I answered.

I couldn't believe this was happening. But it was.

There was some more talk between the lawyers and the judge. When it was over, I had bail.

BLACK

Rose called my house on Sunday night. My mother picked up the phone, and only let me talk to her because she was so hysterical. I tried my best to talk her down. But she just kept asking, "Is it true, Marcus? Is it true?"

I kept sidestepping her, saying that Eddie would be all right. That he could handle it, and he'd probably be home by the next day. But I wasn't about to put Eddie in that car with me. Not to anyone. Especially Rose.

She said she was outside at a pay phone, so her parents wouldn't know she was calling. My mother was right next to me, listening to every word out of my mouth. When I hung up the phone, she said, "I don't wish anything on the family of those who do wrong. Lord knows, I've had to deal with that myself. But now that boy knows what it's like to be locked up, too."

My mother laid it down right. Eddie was as guilty as me. Maybe even a little more. She spent the rest of the night humming a church hymn. I remember lying in bed, staring up at the dark ceiling with the sound of it echoing through the house.

The next morning at school, Officer Jefferson pulled me aside, with Connelly smirking from behind his desk. He put a hand on my shoulder and started up the stairs with me. Jefferson worked all our home games and rooted for us hard. He knew that my father wasn't around anymore, so he cheered extra loud for me. It made me feel like somebody from my family was always at the game. I had a lot of respect for him. He put that uniform on every day, and did his best with kids. When there was drama in the halls, he'd put himself right in the middle of it. I never saw him take the easy way out once. When two black kids went at it, he'd get them both together when it was over with. He'd explain how black people had enough trouble in this world without them going at each other. So I knew what was coming. And when I didn't deny my part in the stickup, Jefferson let me have it with both barrels.

"I don't know if it was your bad idea, or somebody with even less sense talked you into it, son. But it was wrong. Just plain wrong," Jefferson started out. "If they send you upstate, you'll have real, everyday time to think about it. Time when there's nothing else between you and what you did. But I want to know what gives you the right to pull a gun on someone, especially another black man? Do you want a part in putting more fatherless black children on the street? Don't you know enough of them already?" he asked, without raising his voice for anyone else to hear.

Everything he said hit deep, and I wanted to take off running from underneath his arm. But I stayed there and took it, because I knew he was right. And I promised him I'd never be that stupid in my life again.

At practice, everybody was asking me about Eddie. It was the first time in almost four years he wasn't there. Casey raised his eyebrows, but he never said a word to me about it. Our final game of the regular season was the next day at Hillcrest High School in Jamaica, Queens. Missing practice before a game meant Eddie couldn't start. But he had more to worry about than that now.

After practice, guys were ripping Eddie for being AWOL right after getting his scholarship. I listened to it all without opening my mouth. Then Casey came in and announced that Preston would be starting the next day. Kids howled at a freshman taking Eddie's spot, and couldn't wait to see the look on his face. None of them really cared. It was a throwaway game for us before the playoffs started the next week. Only Casey was really pissed off at Eddie.

That night, I picked up a basketball and told my mother I had to blow off some steam, or else I'd bust wide open. Her face turned rock-hard. But she didn't say anything to stop me.

I dribbled right through the courts in the Circle, and headed straight for Eddie's house. The lights were on in the living room with the drapes halfway open. I walked past and tried to peek inside. Eddie's father was sitting on the sofa, talking to someone. But that was all I could see. So I walked around the block to make another pass.

The next time around, I stopped in front of the window and bent down even with the top of the gate. A car in the street honked its horn, and I almost jumped out of my skin. That's when I saw Eddie walk through the living room. I stood back up quick, and got out of there.

The next morning, I saw Rose in the hallway up ahead of me at school. She was walking in my direction, until she turned inside a classroom. It was crowded in the hall, and I couldn't tell for sure if she saw me. Rose had never ditched me before. I thought about her over the next two periods, and it just ate at me.

Eddie was standing outside the door to English, talking to Rebecca. He saw me coming and kissed her good-bye on the lips. I could see by the way his mouth was curled up that he wanted to be the first one to say something.

"Nobody else knows, and that's the way I want to keep it," he whispered to me.

I just nodded my head, and asked if he was all right.

"My lawyer says we'll both be all right if we keep our mouths shut," he came back.

Eddie said that he had to come to school, or he wouldn't be able to play at all in the game that day. Then St. John's would see his name missing from the box score, and would want to know what happened.

Ms. Sussman stuck her head into the hallway and told us to come in for class. She called us "gentlemen." So Eddie put his arm out in front of him, and bowed to her before we went inside.

All through class, Eddie had his notebook open and the point of his pen on the paper. But that was just to keep Ms. Sussman off his back. He spent most of the time glued to whatever business was rolling around in his head.

When the bell finally rang, Eddie waited for me at his desk.

"What did Coach say about me missing practice?" he asked.

I told him that Preston was starting in his place. But Eddie didn't even blink over the news.

"No way I'm getting on that bus today," he said. "We're going to make sure that everybody walks over to the train."

I hadn't even thought about it. The whole team usually hopped the bus outside of school and took it down to the subway station. The only other way was to walk the five or six blocks over to the N train, and make the next connection from there. I just knew that I didn't want to get on that bus, either.

Eddie's mother was working the cafeteria door. I didn't want to face her for anything. So I skipped lunch and headed for the library. I sat down by myself at one end of a long table.

A kid at the next table over was reading *The Count of Monte Cristo*. There was a drawing on the cover of the two ex-friends fighting each other. That was Eddie's favorite part from the movie. I tried to picture his face on one of the characters. I could see Eddie's hands and feet moving fast, and hear the swords hitting against each other. Then the flash of a red jacket went past. I looked up and it was Rose.

She stopped short when she saw me. I followed her eyes from where she was looking down at me, and swallowed hard.

Rose pulled out a chair and parked herself across from me. Her mouth opened wide like a storm of words was about to come roaring out. But she choked it all back. She took a quick breath and pushed her elbows into the table.

"How did it ever get like this?" she whispered in a strained voice.

I reached over and put my hand on top of hers. "It's mostly my fault," I said. "I let everybody down. I just—"

That's when the librarian leaned in over my shoulder. She took her glasses off and let them hang down from a string of glass beads around her neck. She cleared her throat and said, "This is not an appropriate place to hold a conversation. Can you please have some consideration for everyone else here?"

She was looking straight at me, but I couldn't tell

if she was waiting for an answer or not. So I played it safe and just kept nodding my head until she finally left.

Rose slipped her hand out from mine. She was losing it. Her fingers were pressed up against her eyes to stop the tears. Then the bell rang, and all I could hear was the sound of books being slammed shut.

WHITE

I showed my math teacher the early excuse note. Then I headed upstairs to the gym. Marcus and most of the other guys were already outside of Casey's office.

"Yo, college star, did you bring your long underwear today? I hear it can get really cold warming the bench," snapped X.

Everybody was laughing. So I put a smile on my face and sucked it up.

"Are you just too important to practice with us now, White?" asked Big Andre.

I started to answer, but Casey's door popped open and everybody turned back around.

Casey looked us over to see who was there. And I dropped my head before his eyes found mine. He reminded us what train stop to get off at, and not to get into any fights with other kids on the way.

"Eddie, what happened to you yesterday?" he asked out of nowhere.

Everybody except for Marcus had their eyes drilled into me.

"I had to be somewhere with my family," I said.

I knew that it sounded more like I had been to a funeral than to jail.

Casey sent us out, and I was the first one to the staircase. Down four flights, footsteps were building up behind me. They were right on my tail as I hit the first floor. Connelly was busy on the phone. He put up a flabby arm to stop me. I pulled up short, and the team piled up at my back. Connelly slammed the receiver down. He took a deep breath and squeezed his fat ass into a chair. Then he counted us, and scribbled the number in his book.

"I'd tell you boys to shoot the lights this afternoon, but that might make me an accessory," he laughed.

"Harr, harr, harr," X barked back at him like a seal. "That's so funny."

Everyone bolted for the front door before Connelly had a chance to jerk us around. On the front steps everybody started barking because they knew that Connelly could still hear us from inside. I joined in, too. It felt great. Then somebody oinked like a pig to really screw with Connelly's head, and everybody else started, too.

The wind had died down, and in the sun, it was

almost warm. Marcus stepped to the front of the pack, oinking louder than anybody. He walked right past the bus stop and started for the train on Broadway. The team just followed along, laughing and making different animal noises like it was feeding time at the Bronx Zoo.

We started out on a platform fifty feet above the street. The train came rolling in and we took over one end of a car. Kids were starting to jaw at me again for missing practice. But the sound of the train muffled most of it out.

At an underground station, we transferred over to the F train. The subway has a different feel to it when it's below ground. Instead of blue sky and white clouds, there's nothing but black outside the windows. The whole mood changes, and you can see that people are more uptight.

At the other end of the car, a man started screaming at a woman and her baby. At first, I thought they were together and just having a fight. Then the man really went off on her. And you could tell that he was crazy.

"Stupid niggers, you're all the same. Go back to the fuckin' jungle," he screamed at the woman, and started over in our direction.

The man had on a short black coat and brown wool

cap. He was tall, and staggering more than he was walking.

"Hitler didn't go far enough, Rabbi," he yelled at some guy with glasses and a beard, wearing a yarmulke. "He should have killed all the niggers, and your Jewish mother, too."

I thought the guy was going to get up and sock him for sure, talking about his mother that way. But he just kept on reading, and never even looked up from his book.

The lunatic was white. But the dirt was so thick on his face that it was hard to tell. He lost his balance and crashed face-first up against the doors. That's when the whole team wanted to puke, and turned their heads away. The back of his pants were brown where the shit stains had come through. Kids were holding their noses, and yelling at him to leave. He didn't want any part of us, so he started in with some white girl, who was sitting alone.

"One day, niggers are going to fuck you, too," he told her, leaning up against the doors. "They're going to fuck you good, and you'll love it!"

I looked over at Marcus, and he was looking right back at me. Other kids were howling. But not us. Maybe a month ago, we'd have been laughing, too. I kept thinking about being locked up with a nut-job like that and having to listen to his act twenty-four/seven. Besides, that could have been my sister sitting there by herself.

The two halves of the door opened at the next station, and someone pushed the man out of the train. Everybody clapped for the guy who did it. But just as the doors closed, that loony stepped back inside. He started up again with the girl, telling her that sooner or later some black guy was going to ramrod her. An old lady got up and tried to move into the next car, but the door was locked.

When the train finally stopped again, the man wandered out onto the platform. Kids had their faces pressed up against the windows, watching him. He was already hassling the people outside. After the doors closed, everyone started banging on the windows, calling him "Shit Drawers." That's when he gave us all the finger with both hands.

We got to Hillcrest before Casey, who had to teach his last class. In the locker room, Preston was trying not to smile too much about starting. But everyone was busy putting a battery in his back, telling him that he was the new "White" in Black and White.

I didn't know how hard to go in the warm-ups. I never had to get loose and sit back down before. Marcus leaned in over my shoulder at the back of the layup line and said, "Coach is just playing it straight. There are rules for everything. And everybody's got to pay some kind of price."

Casey got there about ten minutes before we started. He huddled us up at our bench and said that he wanted to go into the playoffs off of a strong last game in the regular season. Hillcrest had a decent squad, but we beat them by fifteen points at our gym almost a month back. That was right after me and Marcus pulled our first stickup. I went into that game on a real high, and scored close to thirty points. Now I was stuck on the bench with the whole world hanging over my head. The only things I could say I had going for me were the scholarship to St. John's and Marcus keeping quiet.

On the opening tip-off, two kids collided and the ball went rolling free. Marcus tracked it down and found Preston standing alone under the basket for an easy score. Like everybody else on the bench, I clapped for them.

A minute or two into the game, I saw my dad and his boss walk into the gym. They sat down in the second row of the stands, on the other side of the court. My dad kept looking at me, until he knew for sure that I saw him.

All through the first quarter, I kept an eye on the clock ticking down. I was waiting for Casey to call my name. Every time he turned in my direction to follow the play, I thought he was going to put me into the game.

We were ahead 12–10 when the Hillcrest coach called a timeout with 3:22 left in the first quarter. I stood up, while the players from the court grabbed a seat. Everyone circled around Casey. He was talking about how the other team was trapping us in the corners. I couldn't stop looking at the sweat rolling down the faces of Preston and Marcus.

The game started up again. A minute later, Casey dropped a hand on my back, and pushed me towards the scorer's table. I was down on one knee, waiting for a stop in play so I could get onto the court. For more than two minutes of game time, everything ran smooth and the refs didn't blow a single whistle. The ball finally kicked out of bounds with just eight seconds left. Preston ran right past me to the bench, slapping my hand on the way. Hillcrest in-bounded the ball, and I chased my man across the court on defense. The buzzer sounded to end the first quarter. Everything inside of me stopped again.

I missed my first couple of shots to start the second quarter. But Marcus kept working me the ball. I finally found the soft spot in the other team's zone, and got on track. My dad and his boss were clapping and calling out my name every time I scored. I had twelve points by halftime, but we were still behind by two.

In the locker room, Casey threw a fit. He said we were playing like the other team was going to just hand us the game. He challenged everyone to play harder, and come together "as a team." We all went back onto the court breathing fire, and ready to run through a brick wall to win.

All through the second half, Hillcrest had an answer for everything we did. I'd make a tough shot, and somebody on their squad would do the same. We couldn't get a lead bigger than two or three points. The score was tied with just a couple of minutes to go. Then Marcus found Moses cutting wide open to the hoop. He put the rock right on his hands. But Moses couldn't squeeze it, and lost the ball out of bounds. That's when everything went downhill.

We were down by one point with less than a minute to play. Andre had me standing alone on the baseline. I had both hands out in front of me, waiting to shoot the ball the second I got it. But the big man sailed the pass over my head. We didn't score for the rest of the game, and lost by five points.

Casey made us go over and shake hands with the other team. They had a look on their faces like they couldn't believe that they really beat us. I hated that, and just faked shaking hands down the line. Before we went in to change, Casey pulled us all together.

"We let each other down as a team today," Casey said. "It started with Eddie Russo missing practice, and carried over to some stupid mistakes we made on the court. You need trust out there. Trust to give the ball up to the open man. And trust that you'll get it back when you're open. But it was all just selfish today."

I couldn't believe that Casey mentioned me first. Not after some of the bonehead plays our guys made.

My dad was waiting at the edge of the court. When Coach finished with the team, I walked over to him. He said that his boss was going to drive us home. He didn't have to tell me not to invite Marcus.

A woman reporter who covers high school sports for the *Daily News* was talking with Casey. Me and Marcus had been interviewed by her lots of times. I couldn't believe that she was covering a nothing game like this. I knew that she had to ask Casey why I didn't start. I thought that maybe she wanted to talk about me choosing St. John's.

There was another man with her, carrying a pad and pencil, too. Coach called me and Marcus over. The other reporter introduced himself, and said that he covered the city section. All the time, Casey had his arms folded in front of him, and wouldn't budge off that guy's shoulder.

"I understand that Eddie was arrested on Sunday on the same charge as Marcus," the reporter said quietly. "I'd like to ask you both some—"

That's when Casey stopped him. My dad stepped in and pulled me away. His boss told the reporters that they should save any questions for my lawyer.

Dad waited outside the locker room door while I stuffed my street clothes into a gym bag. On my way back out, Marcus and Casey were just coming inside. I slowed up enough to see their faces. Marcus looked like he was doing all right. But Coach was staring straight ahead, and wouldn't even look at me.

 BLACK

On my way to school the next morning, I got a news-paper. There was a story about Eddie and me being charged with the stickups and shooting. The head-line over it read, *"High School Athletes Charged with Dropping the Ball."*

The story told all about how Sidney Parker, a bus driver on the route that ran past my house, had rec-ognized me. It said that he was the father of three children and hoped to be back at work in another month.

The article kept on about what Parker said. "I've never been afraid of young people. I've always been afraid for them. But I'm angry as hell, too. I'm angry these kids think it's all right to do anything to get what they want. I guess some of them deserve to be locked up like animals."

Then Parker told how he nailed me. "I just couldn't look at that gun pointing at me. So I turned my head

and was facing the other kid. Then I remembered where I saw him before."

I read his words over and over, until I knew them by heart. I tossed the paper away a block before school. But when I stepped through the front door, Jefferson and Connelly had one opened on their desk. I could see the headline upside down in front of me. Connelly buried his face in it and started reading the article out loud. Jefferson said good morning to me, talking right over his partner's voice.

Eddie didn't come to school that morning. His mother and Rose weren't there, either. In English, Ms. Sussman blew a fuse after some kid passed a newspaper around in the middle of class. When she was done screaming, her eyes started to water up. She went out in the hallway for a few seconds and pulled herself back together fast.

At lunch, Moses and X never stopped talking about my case. They said that Eddie getting charged was the best thing that could happen to me.

"Now you got somebody to take half the heat, and that somebody is white," X said.

"I'll bet Eddie's father's a Mason like most of the judges," Moses said. He'll probably throw up some secret hand signs that only other Masons know. Then the judge will go easy on him. That's got to rub off on you, too."

That sounded crazy to me, but I didn't want to argue over any of it.

X brought up the idea that Eddie might be at the DA's office working out a deal for himself. One that wouldn't cut me any slack at all. But I couldn't buy it. I couldn't believe Eddie would ever play me dirty, not even with the DA breathing down his neck—and maybe even his parents.

After school, I didn't want to go home for anything. I knew that someone would have shown my mother the paper, and she'd be steaming. There was never practice the day after a game. The playoffs were starting next Friday, and Casey would push us hard that whole week. But I wanted to feel a basketball in my hands, so I headed upstairs to the gym.

The place was empty, except for Casey and some other gym teachers working in their offices. I took the last practice ball from the rack. The one that nobody else ever wanted to use. It was probably ten years old, and the leather grips had worn down to nothing. But it always felt perfect when I spread my fingers around it.

I passed underneath the glass case on the wall

that holds Jason's white home jersey. He wore Number 15, and nobody else is ever allowed to have that number again. I bowed my head out of respect. Then I stepped out onto the court.

I raised up off both feet with the ball high over my head. At the top of my arc, I let the ball roll off my fingertips. My right wrist fell loose into a perfect gooseneck and the ball slipped through the net. I made that same shot over and over. And the deeper I got into a good groove, the more I was sure that Eddie would never stab me in the back.

I had been shooting for maybe twenty minutes when Casey came out. He started feeding me passes, and I buried a half dozen shots. Then he walked the ball out to where I was standing.

"This thing got a lot of attention today," he said. "Coaches are probably going to walk away from the idea of giving you a scholarship. You might have to play at a city college for a while, until you can prove yourself again."

He didn't even mention the idea of me sitting in a prison cell for the next few years. And I was glad not to hear it.

Casey said he had already called my mother. That she had seen the article and was spitting fire over it. He told me that he called Eddie's house, too.

But he only got the answering machine there.

My mother had calmed down by the time I got home. But she was all business that night. She had talked to my lawyer, Ms. Torres, who told her I didn't have many choices. That by the end of the week, a grand jury was going to indict me for sure. That in a trial, there was no way she could make Sidney Parker look like a liar. So unless I wanted to take a big hit, I was going to have to cop a plea. Then the state would go easier on me for saving them money by skipping a trial.

She told my mother I should work on getting letters from my teachers, saying I was a good student. I knew I could count on Coach and Ms. Sussman for that.

A *Daily News* was sitting closed on the kitchen table the whole time my mother was talking. Eddie's name didn't come up once. Then she caught me looking down at the paper.

"What kind of deal is your best friend working out for himself?" she said in a sharp voice. "Or didn't he talk to you about it yet?"

"Look, you don't know what Eddie's doing!" I answered.

"Neither do you!" she said, with a hand out in front of her to slow herself down. "Neither—do—you, Marcus."

"I know we *both* screwed up," I told her. "And you're right: he's my *best* friend!"

"And you're my son," she came back at me. "Who else is going to look after you? The Russos?"

Those words were like the last good shot in a street fight. I didn't open up my mouth again, and neither did my mother. Only she didn't have anything left to prove.

Eddie was back in school the next day. At practice, the rest of the team didn't even mention the story. Casey wouldn't touch it, either, and stuck to basketball. When practice was over, kids gave us so much space in the locker room that we wound up walking out together.

After the first block, we hit a red light and the traffic was too much to cross against. "So I guess a grand jury is going to indict us," I said.

"My lawyer says that the DA could indict a ham sandwich if he wanted to. That's why we don't even have to be there to open our mouths," he answered back, moving out into the street.

Eddie timed the cars just right and ran over to the other side. I was caught flat-footed and just watched him sail across. When I finally reached him, Eddie said, "Besides, the woman who picked out my picture isn't even a hundred percent sure."

He told me that the coach of St. John's called his house and left a message. The coach wanted to know what was going on, and for Eddie and his parents to get back to him. Eddie's father had his lawyer call back instead, saying that Eddie was innocent and would be there in September.

Eddie kept his eyes straight ahead the whole time he was talking. I watched the side of his face pull tight when he called us a team. He said the DA couldn't prove a thing. Not the way he needed to in court. And that the cops were just fishing for one of us to get scared.

I never said a word back to him about it. The only time he turned to look at me was when we split up to go home. He made a fist and put it out in front of him to connect with mine. "When we win the city championship, they'll have to write a bigger story about Black and White," he said.

I had to finish an essay for Ms. Sussman's class that night. Everybody had the same topic: How do you want people to remember you? I wrote that people should remember I was a good person. That I watched out for my family and friends and never bothered anybody. And that I tried my best at everything I ever did. It looked all right on paper, but I kept thinking about the stickups. So I started another essay. I wrote about being remembered for doing more good things than bad. And that I was lucky to have family and friends who cared about me. I put my name at the top of it and chucked the first one into the garbage.

I wasn't going to lunch because I didn't know what to say to Eddie's mother. But the next day, I passed her in the hall. We were on opposite sides of the white line that runs down the middle of the floor. There were lots of kids between us. So all we had to do was turn our heads and keep on walking.

Casey had us working on our fast break at practice. We'd move the ball all the way up the court without taking a single dribble. A kid standing under the basket would pretend to snap down a rebound, slapping the ball between his hands. He'd turn and hit a second kid running at half-court with a pass. In one motion, that player would zip the ball to the third kid streaking up ahead of him, and he'd lay it in. When it all worked out, you could hear the ball pop off kids' hands, one-two-three. You could close your eyes and know if they did it right by the sound.

Coach hadn't made a Friday speech since I got arrested. But before we went in to get changed, he called us over to the bleachers.

"I know it's been a rough couple of weeks for us as

a team," Casey said. "But we're all going to get through this season together. Everybody's going to learn something from it, including me. I just want you to remember, we didn't get to be a team because we're all wearing the same color uniform. We did it by working together and by sticking up for each other. So in the locker room, on the court and in school, stay focused on supporting each other. That's what being a team's all about."

It was a good speech, and some of us even started talking it up before we got back inside to change. Too bad that it had to be about Eddie and me, and not about winning the playoffs.

Eddie was the first to finish getting dressed. He leaned over to me and said he had to meet his father somewhere. He dropped a hand on my back, and he bounced.

Ms. Torres called that night to tell me I had been indicted. She said that if I agreed to cop a plea, she could get me home inside of two years. And that if I would give up the shooter, she could do even better for me. I told her to take the plea. My mother stared me down, and started drumming her fingers on the kitchen table.

WHITE

I studied the diplomas on Golub's office wall. He graduated from St. John's before he went to law school at the University of Connecticut. He talked about the case with my dad, and how he would get me off. The two of them went over all the holes the state had to fill in. The DA didn't have a gun, or a witness who said I was the shooter. Sidney Parker couldn't pick out my picture. And the woman who identified me wasn't positive.

The two of them talked about me like I was completely innocent. It didn't bother me to hear Golub talk that way. He was my lawyer. He was getting paid to believe in me. But I could hear in my dad's voice what he knew about the gun. I hated making a liar out of him, and I knew how angry he was.

"But can we trust Marcus not to claim you were there?" Golub said. "When the noose gets tight around somebody's neck, they're liable to say anything to save their own skin."

"And even if he did, who'd believe him?" my dad sneered.

"We'll worry about that when or if it happens," Golub answered.

On the way home, I thanked my dad for everything he was doing for me. But he just said, "Do you know how much money this is costing me and your mother?"

That night, I was doing sets of push-ups when Rose marched into my room. She said she just couldn't believe that me and Marcus could really do something so crazy.

"How could you point a gun at someone?" she asked.

"I don't know," I answered her, with my stomach flat against the floor.

That was about the biggest confession I had made to anyone.

Rose went on about me and Marcus going to jail, and how it would ruin the rest of our lives. I told her that my lawyer was on top of things. That I'd beat the case and play in college next year.

"If that bus driver wasn't so sure it was Marcus, this wouldn't be happening," I said.

"I guess that would have made everything all right," she said, kicking me in the ass.

On Saturday, it got all the way up to fifty-five degrees, without any wind at all. When it's cold for a long time, any little bit of sun feels like summer. I knew the Circle would be packed with players. By one o'clock, it would be prime time. That's when the older guys, who partied late on Friday night, would get out of bed and fill the courts. Me and Marcus had made every Saturday at the Circle for almost five years straight. We worked our way up from the bottom of the pile to the top. It killed me to think about not playing on a day that nice. But everybody there would be asking me about what happened. Besides, the cops might even be watching the park undercover, trying to show we did everything together.

By two o'clock, I was bored out of my mind and decided to go out. I wore heavy jeans and a pair of Timberlands. That way, no matter what, I couldn't wind up on a basketball court.

I walked around for maybe fifteen minutes, until I couldn't take it anymore. I turned around all at once, and headed for the Circle. I was cursing myself all the way there for being so stupid. But if I couldn't play, I at least had to see what was going on without me.

I jumped the little fence that separates the sidewalk from the grass, so nobody would see me coming. Then

I poked my head around the corner of one of the buildings. Probably every guy who ever had a beef in that park checked the place out the same way. The Circle was mobbed. Somebody had just made a shot to win the game. Half of the players were walking off of the court, and a new crew was coming on. I looked over every part of the park twice; Marcus wasn't there.

When I got back home, my mom had a sour look on her face and said there was a message on the answering machine for me. We had stopped picking up the phone, in case it was a reporter or St. John's. Until everything calmed down, my dad wanted Mr. Golub to do all the talking. And so did I.

Before I hit the playback button, my mother rushed upstairs. She didn't want any part of hearing what was on that tape again.

"Eddie, it's Rebecca. My parents saw the article in the paper and freaked out. They won't let me go out with you tonight. Don't call back here or anything. I'll call you tomorrow afternoon when I can get out of the house. We can do something then. I promise. Bye."

I explained everything to Rebecca after the story came out. That it was all a mistake. How after the cops decided it was Marcus, they went looking for somebody close to him. She was worried for me, and I was relieved that she didn't treat me like a criminal. But I didn't really know her parents, and wasn't surprised by their reaction.

The next morning, the phone rang just after eleven o'clock. My mom and Rose were at church, and my dad was working overtime. I didn't want Rebecca to get the answering machine again, so I picked the phone up on the second ring.

"Eddie Russo, this is Steve Jenkins, the coach of the basketball program at St. John's," the deep voice said.

"Good morning, Coach Jenkins," I answered slowly.

He said that hearing back from my lawyer was fine, but that he really wanted to talk to me or my parents. He asked me how I was holding up under the pressure, and if I was still going to school every day. I told him that I was on track to graduate. And nothing would stop me.

"Once you sign that letter, and commit to St. John's, you're a member of our family. If you ever need somebody to talk to, you can come to me or one of the school guidance counselors. We're always going to be here for you," he said. "But remember, a felony conviction is serious business, and would cost you this scholarship."

I told him how much I appreciated everything, and that my lawyer had it all under control. And I'd be ready to start in the fall.

When we were finished, I felt like I had just walked through a minefield without taking a single bad step. I was so pumped up that I ran around the house practicing layups and jumping off the balls of my feet. But when I finally started to come back down, I felt sick. And I hated every lie that had come out of my mouth.

On Monday, I was all geared up for practice. The starters scrimmaged against the scrubs. And I made sure our side was going all out. I hit my first six shots and was really feeling it. My next jumper fell short off the front lip of the rim. So I charged the basket and grabbed my own rebound. I jammed the ball home over Preston, and shot him a look like he didn't even belong on the court with me.

The ball kicked loose between a dozen legs. There were a bunch of arms just reaching for it. I hit the floor and hauled it in. It cost me some skin off my right knee and elbow. But it was worth it. I was setting the tone and everyone on my squad was following me. It was flowing good between me and Marcus, too. The starters never let up, and we just crushed them.

Casey watched without saying a word. When he finally blew the whistle for us to stop, he said, "That's the way to get it done, boys!"

I tried to give Marcus a pep talk on the way home. I started out with the playoffs and worked my way over to how the case would blow up in the DA's face. But the second I quit talking, Marcus cleared his throat.

"Eddie, I don't think taking the case to trial is going to work for me," he blurted out. "Parker knows it was me. And I don't think I can pretend it wasn't. I don't want to screw this up for you. Maybe your lawyer is just smarter than mine. Ms. Torres doesn't think there's a thing she can say to make me look good. I need to take whatever she can get me."

I drop-kicked my book bag halfway down the block. I felt like Marcus was just giving up. Then something snapped, and I just went off on him.

"Whatever she can get for you! What about me, my brother? You want to plead guilty. But that's only going to hurt my case. Do you get some kind of points from the DA for that?" I yelled at him.

Before the last word had left my mouth, Marcus exploded.

"You lousy little shit!" he screamed, wrapping both of his hands around my jacket collar. He drove me back against the side of a brick building. And I felt the air pop out of my lungs when I hit.

"We got into this mess together. But it's just me paying for it. And I haven't complained one fucking inch about it," he seethed, with his face pressed up against mine. "And all you want to know from me is how clean *I* can keep *you*."

I didn't move a muscle, or say anything. I just tried to look into his eyes. But he was so close that I could barely make them out. Then Marcus loosened his grip, and stepped back.

I felt lower than the curb—and stupid, too. I looked around to see if anybody on the street was listening. There were a couple of people who turned their heads, but they all just kept walking. I caught my breath, and took a step closer to Marcus.

"I know I've been seeing it all my way," I told him. "It's just been hard, all right?"

We didn't talk for the rest of the way home. But I listened to the sound of his footsteps. They never slowed down or picked up once. He just kept the same steady pace. Right before we split up, I gave Marcus a pound and said, "Black and White through thick and thin."

He nodded his head as he pulled his fist back from mine. "That hasn't changed from my side one time," he said. "Not one time."

That night, Mr. Golub called. I heard the sound of his voice on the answering machine before my dad picked up. It was dry, without any emotion. So I knew that I had been indicted by the grand jury. Dad held the phone to his ear and listened to him talk. Every couple of seconds, he gave Golub an "all right" or "okay." When they were through, my dad broke the news.

It was like when my grandpa had been sick for a long time, and everybody knew that he was going to die. Nobody was shocked. We were all pretty much prepared for it. It was the same with getting indicted. I was surprised how well my mom took it. She shook her head and her eyes got wet. But she didn't fall apart. I tried not to react to it, because it didn't matter much. I was going to face a lot worse before it was finished. I just wished Marcus would fight it like I was.

Casey spent half of our next practice at the blackboard, diagraming all the plays he wanted to run that Friday. It felt more like school than basketball. Everybody had to take notes on where to go for every play. We already had it all in our notebooks at home. But Casey wanted us to write it all out again.

"From your fingers to your brains," Casey said. "We'll do it on paper, then walk it through on the court."

We hardly broke a sweat. But it was one of the toughest practices we had all year. We walked around each other in circles, one step at a time. Me and Marcus did a slow dance together through every offensive set. We even had to pass an invisible ball back and forth.

And after a while, my arms started to get heavy.

On the way home, Marcus froze in his tracks. He stood in front of me, face-to-face, and told me that he was still going to take a plea.

"You're just playing the cops' game," I said.

"It's not a game for me anymore," said Marcus.

"No, because you're giving up. You're quitting on me, and it's making me look worse," I told him.

"Listen, it was *your* gun, and *your* mistake," he came back.

"And I asked *you* to hold it that night, but *you* quit on me then, too," I said, turning away from him.

It all stopped as fast as it came, and we just walked. But I knew from the sound of his voice that nothing I could say would make a difference.

After Marcus left, I wondered how it would feel to be free of this whole thing, or at least tell everyone the truth. I stood on the corner of my block and looked out into the traffic. Then I pulled up everything I'd been thinking about and feeling. I opened my mouth wide to scream. But not a sound came out.

I was watching TV in the living room when Rose came downstairs. She made me turn it off and started an introduction using her hand as a microphone.

"Ladies and gentlemen, Long Island City High School

presents Senior Night," she said out loud. "We'd like to acknowledge the parents of our senior athletes for all the contributions they've made."

My mom and dad started down the stairs, arm in arm. Mom was wearing a maroon dress with a blue-and-white bow. Dad had on his black suit that he only wore to funerals and weddings. When they reached the bottom, Rose pretended to snap pictures.

Senior Night was usually the last home game of the year. But once we clinched home court advantage for the playoffs, the seniors on the team voted to have it before our first playoff game. Then the gym would really be rocking that night.

The lights in the gym get completely turned out, and everything is pitch black. A white spotlight comes on, and each senior player walks his parents out to center court. Then the player gives his mother a bouquet of roses, and everyone applauds. My mom had been looking forward to Senior Night since I was a freshman. It was a way to say thank you to her in front of everybody.

My dad fidgeted with his suit. He kept running his finger between his neck and his shirt collar, trying to breathe. "How am I supposed to sit at a basketball game in a monkey suit?" he said, before he pulled off his tie to watch TV.

- - -

Marcus showed up at school the next day wearing his suit. I saw him walk into English class and did a double-take. He said that he was going down to the DA's office with his mother later on. His lawyer was going to be there, too, to read over the plea before he signed it.

He took a deal to be home in nineteen months. He said it could even get shortened if he didn't get into anything stupid while he was locked up. The state was giving him three weeks to report to jail. Marcus laughed and said that was just enough extra time for us to win the city championship. Casey knew all about it, and cleared Marcus to miss practice that day. That way he could still start in the playoff game on Friday.

All through class, I watched Marcus out of the corner of my eye. My stomach was twisting into knots.

Kids were still reading their essays in class. Ms. Sussman hadn't called on either me or Marcus yet. There weren't that many kids left to go. I knew that I'd be on the spot soon.

There were just five minutes left in the period when she called my name. I started to read as fast as I could. I didn't want to hear myself with Marcus sitting there that way. But Ms. Sussman stopped me in the middle of the first sentence. She told me to stand up while I was reading, and to slow down. So I had to go back to the beginning.

"I'd like people to remember me as somebody they could depend on. No matter what happens, I'm always right there. I'm not the kind of person who walks away when things get tough. I don't care if it's crunch time on the basketball court or the last play of a football game, I'm willing to put myself on the line. . . ."

B**L**A**CK**

Connelly pulled me out of science class. He just walked in while some kid was giving an answer and yelled out my name.

"Let's go!" he snorted to me.

Connelly kept two steps behind me. I peeked back and thought his knees were going to buckle from all the weight. I heard his breathing and heavy footsteps follow me down a flight of stairs to the front desk.

Jefferson was there talking with my mother.

"You have to sign him out," Connelly said to her as he wiped the sweat from his forehead.

Jefferson walked us outside and told my mother, "I know he's made some mistakes. But that's what adolescents do. Marcus is the type of young man who's going to learn from what he did wrong. He's going to pick himself back up and succeed. And one day, other kids from this neighborhood are going to look up to him for that."

My mother let out a long breath and said, "It's going to be a test for him, every day from now on."

Then Jefferson turned to me and said, "You don't know how lucky you are to have this strong woman in your corner."

I told him that I already did.

"No, you only think that you know," Jefferson came back. "You haven't seen enough at your age to really understand what it means. When you become a father one day, you'll see better. You'll understand everything your mother's done for you."

Ms. Torres met us at the DA's office on Union Turnpike, a few blocks from the Queens courthouse. She looked over the plea and gave me the okay to sign it. I pushed the paper down hard against the desk. I started out using big letters. But by the time I got to the end of my name, the letters were less than half that size. I picked the pen up off the paper and everything inside of me felt more settled. It was finally over.

I had three weeks before getting shipped upstate. After that, I wouldn't see my mother or sister for close to two years, except through a piece of glass in a prison visiting room. I wouldn't be running with Eddie, either. I'd be standing on my own. I'd be doing my time with adults, who could be locked up for anything. And I knew I'd probably have to fight to show them I wasn't anybody's herb. Deep down, that had me shook.

The school guidance counselor gave me a note to bring to all my teachers. They could write down what I did for them in the first half of this semester. Then when I got into a jail school upstate, I could finish classes. I could get my diploma, or take the GED exam.

The next day, I saw Eddie before English class. He was waiting for me to say how it all went with the DA. I could see how anxious he was about it. But I wasn't in the mood to replay the whole scene for him.

"So?" Eddie asked.

"It's over for me." I kept it short.

Two girls from class came up to us, and asked me how long it was going to be before I had to go to jail. Eddie looked at me like I'd been talking it up all over school. But the girls said there was a piece in the newspaper about me pleading guilty.

Casey met the team at the locker room door before practice. He pulled me off to the side and told me to chill in his office. He told everyone else to dress warm and run laps around the school for the next twenty minutes. Casey said he didn't know what was going on, but the principal wanted to see us both.

Ms. Randolph was on the phone with some kid's parent, and pointed to the two chairs in front of her desk. She said the kid's name right in front of me, and what he did in class to get suspended. I remembered the kid from the tenth grade, but I didn't want to hear a damn thing about anybody else's troubles.

The second she put down the phone, Ms. Randolph started talking to Casey and me. She said her part like she was reading it off the wall behind us, and the words weren't really hers.

"The Queens Superintendent of High Schools saw the story on you in the newspaper today. He called to remind me that with your conviction you are to be removed from any extracurricular activities while you're still here," she said, raising her cheeks to add some sympathy to it. "Not that I necessarily agree with it, but I must remove you from the basketball team."

When she was finished, she pushed her chair back, like I might attack her. But I had a good hold on myself. Anyway, I wanted to cry more than I wanted to pound somebody.

"What? What did you say?" Casey called out in shock. "He's free to walk around the streets until he starts serving his time. But he can't play high school basketball? That's insane!"

"You have to understand. Marcus has pled guilty to a violent crime. What if there's a scuffle on the court, and even in self-defense, he injures someone," she said with a straight face. "There could be a lawsuit against the Board of Education. Mr. Casey, you more than anyone should be sensitive to what can go tragically wrong in these situations."

Casey flew up from his chair and said, "Are you comparing Marcus to that animal who killed Jason Taylor? Is that what you're doing? You weren't even at this school back then."

"I am not comparing Marcus to anyone," Ms. Randolph shot back. "Don't put words in my mouth, Mr. Casey!"

I had a sick feeling in the pit of my stomach that kept on getting worse. Maybe I didn't stab somebody to death because he was a different color than me. But I helped rob people at gunpoint, and almost got someone's head blown off. And now I was going to prison, just like that bastard who killed Jason.

When we got back upstairs, Casey held a team meeting. He was still steaming and his face had turned completely red. The sweat was pouring off kids from running laps. Eddie was looking at me in my street clothes and shaking his head. He probably had it figured out before anybody else. Casey turned to me and pushed his lips together. Before he could start, I told them all that I was off the team.

"Because I pleaded guilty, they won't let me play," I said. "I screwed up this season for everybody. I probably could have waited another two or three weeks before I took the plea. I'm sorry. I just didn't know about the rule."

"You don't have to be sorry to us, my brother," said X, shifting his eyes over to Eddie. "You got caught out there and now you're paying the price. At least you're man enough to stand up for it. Some guys will never have that in them."

Most of the team started clapping after X had his say. But Eddie just stood there with both hands in his pockets.

The principal said I couldn't stay to watch practice or sit on the bench for the playoff game the next night. My teammates said they would clap loudest for me when I walked out with my mother for Senior Night. And they'd tell kids around school to do the same.

I thought the only time I wouldn't be with the LIC team was when I graduated and had a place to play in college. But I left Eddie and everyone else in the gym, and went down the back stairs alone. My mother was pissed as anything over it. She said they were treating me like a convict already.

But that night she ironed her best dress, and Sabrina's, too.

"People at Senior Night are going to know that your family is still proud of you. The principal can't make all your hard work for that team just disappear," my mother said, snapping her fingers.

The news about me being off the team traveled slow. The whole next day at school, kids kept coming up and wishing me good luck in the game. It was like getting kicked in the ass, over and over.

Rose found me in the library. She wanted to tell me what kind of raw deal she thought I got from the principal. I told her it didn't really matter anyway. My life had already changed, and I was going to have to deal with whatever people put in my way from now on.

She apologized for the way her parents were talking about me at home. And for them thinking that I put all of this onto Eddie. She hugged me tight, and everything hard inside me melted down a little.

Eddie didn't say much to me in English class, except that he couldn't believe the Board of Education pulled the plug on "Black and White." Ms.

Sussman still had kids reading their essays, and I was one of the last to go. I stood up and read out loud. I wasn't concentrating on anything but the words on the paper in front of me. I was sailing straight through it, without even listening to the sound of my voice. Then right before the ending, I missed a word and had to stop for a second. It was like waking up out of a daydream, and everybody's looking at you.

"In the end, I'd like people to say that I tried to be honest with them. I want them to remember the real Marcus Brown. Not the ballplayer or anybody else. That way they'll have a clear picture in their head about me, and not have to guess," I finished and sat back down.

In math class, the teacher had us working in groups of four. Eddie had his desk turned around to face me. We mostly talked about the game, and let the other two kids with us do all the problems.

"It's all on you tonight," I told Eddie.

Usually two hundred people showed up for a Friday night game. But for the playoffs and Senior Night, Eddie thought we'd get at least four hundred people in the stands. We were playing Aviation High School. They were the last squad to make the play-offs. During the first week of the season, we beat them by almost thirty points. But they'd got a lot better since then, and won just enough games to get in.

Eddie and me talked about our families being next to each other before they walked onto the court that night. We both knew that it was going to be tense.

"I'd rather face the DA and judge together than your mother," Eddie said.

Eddie met up with Rebecca after class. I was heading out the front door alone when Jefferson called me over to his desk. He reached into his pocket and took out twelve dollars.

"It's a six-dollar ride from the Ravenswood Houses to here. I want you to take your mother back and forth by cab tonight," he said, handing me the money.

I didn't want Jefferson's money. But I could tell right off that he wasn't going to take it back. So I closed a tight fist around the bills. I started to tell him how grateful I was. But Jefferson stopped me in the middle and said, "Every young brother needs a little help along the way. I'm just paying back what came down to me."

Sabrina was really excited about Senior Night. My mother made her a fancy red dress with lace skirts, one on top of the other. It was finished more than a month ago, and Sabrina had been trying it on every Friday night since. With her hair piled up high, she looked just like a princess in it. My mother had on a long black dress with heels. Around her neck, she wore a string of white pearls that my grandmother gave her before she passed away.

Both of them were watching the clock, and telling me that we were going to be late. I kept pushing them off. I ran for the phone the second it rang. A man on the other end said our cab was waiting outside. My mother smiled when I told her.

The driver must have been wondering why my mother and sister were dressed so nice, and I was wearing maroon sweats. Sabrina talked about being scared to walk out in front of the crowd the whole ride over. And by the time we got to LIC, the driver was going on to my sister about not being nervous. He even wished the team good luck.

There was still an hour before the game, and the players were just starting to warm up. The end of the first row was saved for the senior parents. I never left my mother and sister to walk over to Casey or the team. But once they started to run a layup line right in front of where we were sitting, everyone was coming up to us.

On Eddie's first run through the line, he took a few steps over. I got up to meet him halfway. He gave me a pound and nodded his head in my mother's direction. She pulled Sabrina in tight to say something, and Eddie moved forward on the line. I don't think either one of them looked the other in the face for more than a second. Every time Eddie came through after that, he was focused on the basket, with his game face on.

The stands filled up fast. Other parents moved into the seats next to us. Casey's wife was hugging everybody. Then Rose showed up with Eddie's mother and father, and took the last seats in the row. Rose and me kept looking at each other over everyone's heads. I wished that she was sitting right next to me. But there was no way.

Jefferson and Connelly were there, too. They were busy checking kids' IDs and making sure the crowd stayed cool. I made sure to catch Jefferson's eye, just to show him that I was glued to my family.

We were wearing our home whites. Aviation was dressed in green and gold. I could see myself out on the court, moving through the layup line. And every time somebody passed Eddie the ball, my hands started to twitch a little. The only times I ever watched the team play, I was sitting on the bench, waiting to get back into the game. I didn't know how I was going to handle sitting in the stands. The game hadn't even started, and I wanted to jump up out of my seat and take off running down the court.

After a while, the president of the senior council arranged us in order along the sideline. The ceremony was almost ready to start. Eddie and the other seniors came over to walk their parents across the court. The lights got turned way down, until it was almost black inside the gym. Music piped in over the PA system, and kids in the stands started to hoot and holler. Ms. Randolph stepped into the white spotlight and welcomed everybody to Senior Night. Then she handed the microphone over to Casey, who gave a speech from the heart.

"Our student-athletes invest a lot of time and effort in representing Long Island City High School," Casey said. "That added burden is also felt at home, where the parents of our student-athletes must work even harder to give their children support. Tonight we honor those parents."

The first family made their way out to center court. The senior council president handed our player a bouquet of roses. He gave them to his mother and kissed her with everybody cheering. The next family was already moving when Ms. Randolph planted herself in front of me.

"I told you that you couldn't be a part of any

extracurricular activities. That included Senior Night, Mr. Brown," she said. "Your family can go out there. But not you!"

"My son is walking with me!" my mother told her, flat out.

Ms. Randolph started to argue. But my mother's words turned me rock solid. I could have walked through a hundred Ms. Randolphs with her words running through my head.

Jefferson and Connelly were in the middle of it now. I looked back over my shoulder and could see Eddie handing his mother her bouquet. My mother started to move forward with me holding one hand and Sabrina the other. But Ms. Randolph blocked our way. I wanted to boot her across the court for disrespecting my mother like that. Jefferson tried his best to get Ms. Randolph to step aside.

That's when some black kids in the bleachers screamed she was a racist. Connelly stormed over and told them all to shut up. A girl oinked right in his face and called him a fat pig. Connelly lost it and jerked her hard by the collar. Some dude slugged Connelly in the mouth, and a bunch of kids piled on top of him. Jefferson rushed over to save his partner's ass, and everything in that corner of the stands just broke loose.

When the lights didn't come on, kids started throwing things in the dark. Casey's voice boomed over the PA for everybody to stay calm. Something hard whistled right past my ear. I turned my back to the crowd and shielded my mother and sister inside my arms. Sabrina dug her nails into my stomach.

"Don't let them hurt me!" she cried.

Eddie and his parents were standing in the spotlight out at center court. I knew that Rose was taking pictures from the first row. But I didn't see her anywhere.

The lights finally got turned up, but that didn't stop anything. Connelly had wrestled some kid out of the pack, and was beating the shit out of him. Jefferson had to hook Connelly around the throat and slam him to the floor to get him to stop.

Lots of people ran out onto the court, just to get clear of that mess. Eddie and his parents got swallowed up by that crowd. I lost sight of them. I saw Rose run past with tears coming down her face. If my arms were long enough, I would have reached out and held on to her, too.

Casey stayed on the microphone. He kept begging people to do the right thing, and most of them did. Then the cops showed up and cleared out the whole gym. They even had to separate Jefferson and

Connelly, who were pushing and shoving at each other now. There was blood running from Connelly's nose down to his chin. Jefferson's uniform shirt was ripped across the middle. Ms. Randolph was walking in a daze from one end of the gym to the other. And my mother was giving her lip every step of the way.

On the way out, I saw the broken glass on the gym floor. The case that held Jason's jersey got busted open. His uniform top was hanging loose, pinned up by only one shoulder. I reached my hand in through the sharp edges, and hooked it back on right.

The cops wouldn't let anyone stand out in front of the school, either. There was an ambulance parked outside and a bunch of black-and-whites with all their lights flashing. So we started walking home as soon as we hit the street. Sabrina looked like she just woke up from a nightmare. She was walking with the side of her face pressed up under my mother's arm.

My mother's steps were slow and even. Then she started to shake her head as we walked. She turned to me and said, "For better or worse, child, you'll find out everything you want to know about this world."

WHITE

Mom didn't stop crying until she found Rose. We were all standing in the middle of the court, looking at each other. I had seen my mom and dad every day for as far back as I could remember. Somewhere in my head, I had an outline of their faces. Maybe I'd been using that for too long, instead of really seeing them. They looked older and more scared now than I'd ever seen them before.

The cops only let the players, coaches, and refs stay in the gym, and moved everybody else outside. I lost sight of Marcus and couldn't spot him anywhere. My mother was holding on to her bouquet so tight that some of the roses got crushed. There were loose petals stuck to her dress and on the floor around her feet. I walked with my family over to the doors, and a woman cop pushed them through.

Casey was down on one knee, sweeping up glass off the gym floor. The principal was hanging over him. You could tell that they were arguing, but their voices

never got loud enough for anyone else to hear. When he finished with the glass, Casey stood up and walked right past her to a big aluminum trash can.

If it wasn't for Ms. Randolph, me and Marcus would be playing side by side right now. My parents and everybody else would be in the stands cheering. And Marcus's mother would have walked across the floor to get her bouquet. I wanted to tell her off in front of everyone. But the truth was that I was more to blame than anyone.

The refs gave us ten minutes to get loose again. Aviation was running a layup line with their coach out on the court watching them. Casey was still busy making sure everything was back together. Our guys were all taking jumpers, and we had a half dozen balls going up at the same time.

I was standing in the corner pounding the ball against the floor. First with my right hand, and then with the left. I guess I just wanted to feel like everything was still the same—that I could dribble without looking down at the ball, and that it would always come back up into my hand.

"Hey, White, you gonna play a big game for your boy out in the street tonight, or are you gonna turn your back on us, too?" X asked me with a real smirk.

"Just watch me," I answered him.

A security officer brought Rebecca and the rest of the cheerleaders back up to the gym. But the other coach said it wasn't fair that his pep squad couldn't get inside, and Casey agreed. The girls shook their pom-poms on the way out, and Rebecca blew me a kiss.

Right before we went out on the court, Casey pulled us together and said, "This is the part where we just play ball and all that other garbage can't touch us."

"No disrespect, Coach," X came back. "But how come it's always the black man that has to forget about all the bullshit."

Moses told X to let it go, and Casey stayed quiet for a few seconds until it passed. After Casey finished up, we put our hands together and shouted, "T-E-A-M!" But the sound of our voices barely carried out of the huddle.

The ref tossed the ball up at center court, and Big Andre won the tap. Preston ran down the loose ball and put it into my hands. I found X open down low. He took a tough fade-away jumper. But he hit it. The next time we had the ball, X forced up a shot with a defender all over him. He hit that one, too. I watched X run back on defense. It looked like every emotion in the world was racing through him at the same time. And he didn't have to hide or be ashamed of any one of them.

I needed to get into the flow. So I took the first

open shot I could find. The ball went halfway down into the rim, and then rattled back out. Before I could get my hands on the ball again, X took two more shots and missed them both by a mile. Then he got frustrated and smacked an Aviation kid—who had a clear path to the basket—hard across the arms. The refs whistled X for an intentional foul, and Casey got on him from the side-line about it. But X put both of his hands out in front of him to say that he had himself under control.

Half of the first quarter was gone and I didn't have a single point yet. We were down by a basket when I stole a pass. Preston was running alone ahead of me. I never once thought about giving up the ball. I ran right by him to the hoop and got my first two points.

Every play we ran was out of sync. Without the ball in Marcus's hands, we were a step behind on every-thing.

The kid Andre was guarding knocked Moses flat with a blind screen. Moses screamed at Andre all the way back up court for not letting him know it was com-ing. Then X missed another shot he should have never taken. The first quarter ended with the score tied 14–14.

When we got back to the bench, Casey didn't say a thing about strategy. Instead, he said we should clear our minds and try to focus more. He told X not to put so much pressure on himself. Then Casey pulled me off to the side.

"Eddie, this is your team now," he said, with a tight grip on my shoulder. "It's up to you to keep them all together."

I stepped back onto the court, and all of a sudden, I started to cry. For a second, I just lost control. Marcus, the cops, the bus driver, my grandpa—they were all fighting to get out. I shut my eyes. They were stinging from the salt. And I hoped it looked like I was wiping away sweat, instead of tears. Then I raised my arms and felt the air flowing through my chest. I looked up at the scoreboard, and just shook it all off.

I made a basket to start the second quarter, and then I caught fire. I hit five straight shots. But Aviation was making shots, too, and we were winning by only four points. Then the other coach brought a player with fresh legs off the bench to run with me. He was some kind of track star with long arms. His face looked a little like Marcus's. And that got into my head. He tried to stay within two feet of me, with his face up in mine. He was going all out every second to keep close. I could feel his breath on my skin.

It was almost impossible to get the ball with that kid

guarding me. It would have been different with Marcus on the court. And Preston wasn't a slick enough passer to find me when I did get free. I didn't get another shot off for the rest of the half. We went back to the locker room with only a two-point lead—36–34.

Casey was as calm as could be, and went over what the other team was trying to do to us. But it was our own mistakes that kept the game close, and everybody knew it.

"You got to put a lock on that trigger finger, X," Andre said. "You can't take all those tough shots."

"White was on a roll out there, just get him the ball," said Moses.

"These guys can't beat us," I said, heading for bathroom. "We're just better than them."

I ran the cold water in the white sink, and splashed it onto my wrists and neck to keep cool. That's when X followed me inside. I could see his face behind mine in the mirror. "You just find a way to ditch your black shadow out there, before he follows you home and climbs into bed with you," X told me.

We got back onto the court to warm up, and the refs were covering Jason's case with a blanket. They didn't want anybody to get cut on the broken glass hanging off of it. When they were finished, Casey put two fingers to his lips and touched the outside of the blanket before he came back to the bench.

"Play like you know you can," Casey told us. "That's all anyone can ask of you."

The track star got a good rest during halftime, and was ready to go all over again. He wasn't even part of their offense. When they had the ball, he just stayed close to me. That way I couldn't get a head start on him going back the other way.

No matter what we did, we couldn't pull away from them. We would go up by three or four points. Then they'd come right back and take the lead on us. All I had to do to swing the whole game around was get my hands on the ball. But I couldn't.

I kept running harder and harder. My black shadow started to lose a step. I even got away from him one play and made a basket. That's when the Aviation coach pulled him out of the game, and sent in another kid to take his place. This one didn't look anything at all like Marcus, except that he was black, too. He wasn't as fast as the first kid. But he was fresh, and followed me everywhere. Three minutes later, when that kid started to slow down, their coach brought another player off the bench to run with me.

We went into the fourth quarter down by four points. If the stands had been filled with people, no one would have believed their eyes, not even Aviation's fans. My black shadow came back into the game, and locked me right up again. I didn't touch the ball on offense for the next four or five minutes. Nothing went right for us. We were losing by six points late in the game. I got the ball in the corner, and my black shadow stripped it from me. Before he could take off the other way with it, I tackled him around the waist with both arms.

The two refs, in their black-and-white-striped shirts, pointed at me and blew their whistles. I raised my hand high to the scorer's table, and one of refs called out my number for the foul.

I couldn't watch the clock ticking down. But when the kids on the Aviation sideline started hugging, I knew the time was running out. I didn't care about the score anymore. I just wanted to get off one last shot. My black shadow didn't let me near the ball until the buzzer sounded. We lost 60 to 49. And I walked off the court with the ball in my hands.

Back in the locker room, Casey told us to put the game aside for a while and try to enjoy the weekend. He said that he'd save all the speeches for Monday. Nobody argued with him. Kids were just sitting in front of their lockers, stunned that we got knocked out of the playoffs so early.

I was pissed as hell. I didn't want to be anywhere around those guys. I couldn't believe that a kid with nothing going for him but two good legs could stop me. I got dressed and headed down the back stairs. I almost expected to see Marcus waiting outside. But he wasn't there. My dad was waiting for me. Rebecca and the other cheerleaders were there, too. The Aviation squad had come down celebrating. So they already knew.

BLACK

I woke up early the next morning and the sun was out full. Sabrina was too scared to sleep alone. She spent the night with my mother in her bed. The two of them were still asleep under the covers. I got dressed and grabbed a ball without making a peep. Then I headed down to the Circle.

It wasn't even eight o'clock yet. The first handful of players usually don't show up until after nine. But I was glad to be out there by myself. I found a flat piece of ground where I could put the ball down and it wouldn't roll off. Then I went out to the center of the court and started to stretch. I closed my eyes, leaning all the way back. For a second, everything was black. Then the orange light came pouring underneath my eyelids. I could feel the warm sun on my face.

I was a million miles away from the gym the night before. My mind was clear and focused on everything in front of me. I flipped the ball through the rim with my right hand, and caught it in my left.

I kept going back and forth between hands, putting up little shots. I had a good rhythm going. And as soon as the ball hit my hand, it was back up in the air again. I started to move around the court, making shots. I'd take off with a burst of speed, then throw on the brakes. I was going fast and slow at the same time, moving inside and out. I worked up a real sweat that rolled down my face and dripped to the ground.

I didn't expect to see Eddie. There was just too much going on for him to play out here. Other guys started showing up one by one. When we got enough bodies, they chose up sides. I heard my name get called first. After that, it didn't matter to me. I figured out the sides on our first trip up court. I saw who was turned towards me, and who was facing the other way.

It was an okay game. A lot of players who are just so-so show up early to get their licks in before the Circle gets too tough. But I wasn't holding back an inch. I was blowing by kids like they were standing still. Nobody on the other team wanted to guard me. My squad won the first three games, and I didn't slow down a beat. The next team was coming onto the court when I saw Moses and X walk into the park. I was waiting for them to say something about the night before. But they both sat at the end of the bench, looking at me like they'd let me down for everything.

I thought that maybe something else had jumped off after I left. That maybe something bad happened to Eddie or Casey. It went right by me the first time Moses said the team got beat. I had to reach back and put the words to the look on their faces.

I couldn't believe it. But it didn't seem important enough anymore to stress about, either. Win or lose, nothing was any different for me. Only the playoffs were over.

I walked onto the court and made the first three baskets of the new game.

My squad had point-game at 14–6. That's when I saw Rose at the edge of the park. She was standing between buildings, watching me play. I told X to take my spot, and walked off. The kids on my team made a fuss about me leaving and were calling after me. Rose put a hand out in front of her for me to stay. But I didn't pay attention to any of it. I grabbed Rose's hand and we walked out of the Circle together.

Rose asked about my mother and sister. I told her they got through the night in one piece. After we got past what Ms. Randolph did, and that the team lost, we didn't mention either one of those things again.

"I just wanted to come out and see you play," she said.

We went around the block one time, then turned up towards Steinway Street. I held on to Rose's hand all the way, until she pointed to show me something in a store window. After that, I just settled for walking with her shoulder next to mine.

Rose said she didn't think her parents would let her take the bus upstate to visit me. I told her I'd have to write her letters instead. She smiled at that, and said she'd answer them all. Then Rose asked me if I thought Eddie would go to jail, too.

"He's innocent until somebody proves different in court," I said. "That can be hard to do sometimes."

On the way back, Rose turned inside a flower shop, and I followed in behind her. She smelled lots of different flowers. And I put my nose to every one she did. Rose bought a dozen red roses. The salesman wrapped the stems in silver paper. Rose handed them to me with the water still dripping out from the bottom. I carried them all the way home for her.

On the corner of Rose's block, I tried to hand her back the bouquet. But she just laughed at me and said, "They're for your mother, Marcus. To make up for the ones she didn't get last night."

Rose kissed me good-bye and started for her house. Then she turned back around and caught me watching her from behind. And the sunlight shined in her eyes when she smiled at me.

My mother loved the roses. But I wouldn't take credit for them, and told her that they were from Rose.

Most of that night, I thought about Rose. I thought about what it would be like to hold her tight and kiss her for real. I dreamed she was lying in my arms, soft and warm.

My mother said that I should go to church with her and Sabrina. I really didn't want to, but I didn't want to let her down anymore, either. I hadn't been to church since the Christmas I started high school. That's when my mother told me I was old enough to make up my own mind about going, and old enough to stay home alone on a Sunday morning.

Reverend Hawkins was the only preacher I ever knew. He had been there since I was born, and even baptized me. He remembered my father growing up, too. Sometimes he'd tell stories about the kids who hung out on the church corner in the old days. My father was one of them.

I got two phone calls from my father since he'd

left. Both of them were on my birthday. The first time, my mother just handed me the phone. She whispered who it was to me, so my sister wouldn't hear. My father had the deepest voice I ever heard. I told him about playing ball and junior high. Before I knew it, he was saying good-bye.

Two years ago, he called again. Only I picked up the phone myself. He said, "Marcus, this is your father." He told me he could tell how I was growing by the sound of my voice. I talked about getting a scholarship and turning pro one day. He said he wasn't surprised I was going to be somebody. He never said out loud he loved me, so I didn't go there, either. But the call still felt good, like he was right there with me.

Reverend Hawkins had passed away since the last time I went to church. The new reverend was from Guyana. His accent was thick, and I couldn't understand half of what he said during the service. Maybe a lot of people couldn't, or it just took more practice hearing him. I mostly paid attention to the light coming through the stained glass windows. The same sky could be red, yellow, or green depending on where you looked. I hardly ever prayed. But I asked God to look after my mother and sister while I was away upstate. Then I put in a word for Jefferson, and everything he did for me.

After the service, my mother needed to go food shopping. So we walked down to the C-Town supermarket. Sabrina still got a kick out of seeing the big plaster animals on the roof. They had a white chicken with red feathers, and a black-and-brown cow staring down at you. There used to be a giant pig, too. But it got blown off the roof in a storm, and the store never fixed it.

Sabrina ran to get her own cart to push. She was making car noises with it, and racing up and down the aisles. I was going slow, pushing the cart while my mother dropped groceries into it. Then I challenged Sabrina to a race. She was ahead of me, but I was going to let her win from the start. She turned the corner too fast and almost ran into some old man. I was far back enough to look like I had nothing to do with it. But my mother threw a fit at the both of us anyway, and made Sabrina get rid of her cart.

We turned down the last aisle, and came out by the checkout lines. I was the first one to see it coming. They were heading towards us at the same speed we were moving to them.

"Sweet Jesus, I don't want this today!" my mother cried up to the ceiling.

Eddie's mother was pushing the shopping cart. Eddie and his father were walking a step or two behind her. Everyone just froze where they were for a second. It was like the negative to some picture that somebody put away and forgot about, with us in black and them in white.

We were maybe ten feet apart from each other. I looked Eddie in the face, and then my mother. Before anybody could move, my mother asked Eddie, "Isn't that my son's jacket you borrowed? From when yours got stolen that night?"

Eddie looked down at the jacket over his chest and arms. His father moved over to stand in front of his mother.

"Make sure to return it real soon," my mother said. "Marcus won't be with us too much longer. He's going to prison, you know."

Eddie put his hand up around the zipper. But my mother grabbed Sabrina by the arm and rolled her cart away. Eddie brought his eyes up and stared at me, like he didn't know what he could do. I wanted to say something, and even started to move my lips. But I couldn't find any words that made sense.

I put my hands in my pockets and followed after my mother.

The rest of the day, I could see that speech she gave Eddie flying around in my mother's head. She was doing housework with a real attitude. The words were going back and forth inside of her. Sometimes her lips would move without making a sound. Only this time, that speech was longer, and maybe somebody had something to say back to her. A couple of times, one or two of the words popped out of her mouth. But she'd jerk her body in a different direction to close the lid tight again.

I saw the scrub brush sitting in the bathroom, and thought about my one day cleaning toilets on Rikers Island. I could hear my mother working hard in the kitchen, and felt ashamed. I didn't want the next toilet I cleaned to belong to the state. So I picked up the brush and started at ours.

Both Jefferson and Connelly were missing from the front desk at school on Monday. I asked one of the other school safety officers what happened. He said the both of them were transferred to different office buildings run by the Board of Education, until all the charges got sorted out. Some kid at the game was charging Connelly with assault. Connelly was pressing charges against Jefferson for hitting him. For now, neither one of them was allowed to be around kids in a school.

I felt bad for Jefferson getting a rap like that, and

having to prove he didn't do anything wrong. Maybe he took an extra-hard swipe at Connelly. But that bastard deserved it. I wanted to go down to where Jefferson was and tell somebody in charge all the good things he ever did for kids. Then I'd probably have to say I was going to jail for pulling a stickup, and nobody would believe me anymore.

WHITE

All the way home from the supermarket, my mom was crying. She tried hard to hold it in, and lowered her head so we couldn't see how red her eyes were. My dad kept trying to make small talk with her, pretending that everything was okay. But every time mom tried to answer him, she broke out in a sob instead. I wanted to tell her that everything was all right. But it wasn't.

That night, my mom knocked on the door to my room. She spent a minute looking at all my trophies and posters up on the walls. Then she sat down at the edge of my bed, and told me how scared she was for me.

"Eddie, I don't care what that lawyer says. He could be wrong about everything. You could go to jail for a long time," Mom said, with her voice starting to crack. "You're still my baby, Eddie. I want you to have a good life. I don't want to see these things happen to you."

Dad came through the door as my mom started

bawling again. He got angry right away, and screamed at her for getting so upset. She tried to pull herself together, and started straightening up my room, and putting away my clothes. That's when she saw Marcus's jacket hanging on the doorknob to my closet.

She lost it.

"I don't want to see that jacket here again, Eddie. Get it out of this house, and give it back. I don't want to be responsible for having it here," she yelled through the tears, and ran out of my room.

My dad chased after her down the hallway, cursing at me for leaving the jacket out.

I took the jacket to school with me the next day. And I made sure that my mom didn't see me carrying it, either. I walked through the streets with it stuffed under my arm, and thought about all the good times me and Marcus had together. I wished that he was inside that jacket, walking next to me. I wished that I had never seen my grandpa's gun, and that we were a team again. But I squeezed that jacket inside my arm, and it was empty.

Most of the kids at school were just finding out that we had lost the game, and about the riot, too. They were coming up to me in shock, asking how we could lose. I told them that it was just a bad night for everybody, and that Aviation couldn't beat us again if we played them every day for a month straight. Then it hit me that Marcus would be sitting inside a prison cell before a month was up.

In homeroom, Ms. Randolph's voice came over the PA system, saying how proud she was of everyone who stayed cool at the game. She didn't say that there was a fight, or that the cops came. Instead, she just called it a "minor disturbance."

"I want to thank Coach Casey and the basketball team for reaching the playoffs again this year. They represented our school with dignity. I know that everyone is proud of them," Ms. Randolph said. "I also want to acknowledge the parents we honored at Senior Night. Without their support, our students would have to struggle much harder to achieve their goals. It's a pleasure to be part of giving something back to them in return."

I wanted to puke at all of that, because she didn't mean a word of it. She announced that I was the high-scorer for our team that night. And that I had played my last game for LIC and was going to St. John's next year. For the rest of the morning, kids talked to me like I did my part, and everyone else must have really screwed up for us to lose. I felt like a real heel nodding my head to that crap while I dragged Marcus's jacket around.

When I walked into English class, Marcus was up at Ms. Sussman's desk getting a load of work to do for after he was gone. I stood at his chair, waiting for him to come back. Everybody else was sitting down, copying the blackboard. I was standing out like a sore thumb. So I finally just hung the jacket over the back of his chair, and took my seat.

Marcus was halfway back to his chair when he saw the jacket. He stopped short, and looked like he was lost. For a second, Marcus turned his head towards me. Our eyes locked together. Then he turned away and fell right back into step. Marcus was already wearing a coat, and sat down with his back against the jacket.

After class, Marcus had his book bag in one hand and the jacket hanging loose in the other.

"How did they ever beat us?" he asked me.

"They didn't beat *us*," I told him. "They beat *me*. I was supposed to carry that game by myself. Instead, I got spanked."

Marcus asked me about Jefferson getting into it with Connelly. I didn't know a thing about it, and felt like I was at some other gym that night.

I tried to explain to Marcus about the jacket. But he

just waved me off. "Forget about it," Marcus said. "My mother's just on edge about everything right now."

I watched Marcus walk off to his next class. He carried the jacket out away from his body, like it wasn't a part of him anymore. I looked at him like he was already somebody different. Somebody I didn't have a handle on anymore. And I started to worry if *this* Marcus would ever give me up to the cops and say I was there.

Later on, I turned a corner and walked right into my mom and Ms. Randolph. They both saw me at the same time and stopped talking. Mom put her arm around my shoulder and kissed me on the forehead. Then she turned me to face Ms. Randolph.

"My son is really something," my mom said.

Ms. Randolph smiled without showing her teeth.

"I'm sure we'll all be talking about him for a long time," she answered.

Mom pushed me down the hallway, and told me not to be late for class. I stayed on Ms. Randolph's eyes until they got small and sharp, and she turned them back to my mom.

After math, me and Marcus went up to the gym for the final team meeting. I could hear balls bouncing and kids laughing from outside the heavy wooden door. They were already playing three-on-three. Everybody was smiling and ranking on each other with every shot that went up. There were boxes of pizza and sodas on the table in front of Casey's office. Big Andre was eating two slices at once, one on top of the other. He saw me and Marcus together and said, "Marcus, my man!" The two of them slapped hands, and pulled each other into a hug. Marcus grabbed an old ball out of the rack and started shooting on a side court.

I wasn't in the mood to play. Instead, I picked up a can of soda, and sat on the floor, up against the wall. I could feel the vibrations from out on the court running up my spine. I popped open the can and took a swallow.

The custodian came into the gym with his helper walking behind him. They took the blanket off of Jason's broken case, and started chipping away at the glass that was left around the edges. Marcus dribbled the ball in one spot, watching them work. Then the custodian pulled the white paper off a brand-new sheet of glass. The two of them lifted it up and fit it into the case. They rubbed out all the fingerprints on both sides, until it was clear and perfect. That's when Marcus went back to playing.

Casey stepped out of his office and blew his whistle. He walked over to the one section of the bleachers that was pulled out, and everybody followed. We all sat down. Then Casey climbed into the stands and sat right in the middle of us.

"For lots of reasons, this will be a season I'll never forget," Casey started out. "We learned what it was like to win together, and what it was like to lose. Nobody quit. Nobody went home. When it got tough, we walked out onto the court like a team. And when it was over, we walked off the court the same way. Even when they broke us apart, we stood up together and took what came. That's a team!"

Casey asked if anybody had something to add. That's when Marcus said what he knew about Jefferson. Kids hated Connelly's guts so much, they were just glad he was gone, even if Jefferson got caught up in it.

"Sometimes Peter's got to pay for Paul," Moses said.

"Then Peter must have been a black man," X said, looking right at me. "We always got to pay for somebody else."

Preston said that Peter and Paul were white, like everybody else in the Bible.

"Jesus was black!" X shot back at him. "He had woolly hair. Do you know a white man with woolly hair?"

"There's even a picture of black Jesus," said Andre. "My grandmother has one hanging in her house."

Casey just listened until all the talk died down. Then he said the gym would be open for another hour, and to take the food home that we didn't finish. On the way back to his office, Casey turned around and said, "Remember, seniors, I need your uniforms."

That really hurt. I thought if we had won the city championship, the school might let us keep our uniforms. I thought they might even retire my number. But now, some other kid would probably be wearing my uniform next year.

Marcus went over to his book bag and pulled out both of his jerseys. They were clean and folded, with the home whites on top of the road maroons. Then Marcus disappeared into Casey's office. He came back out a minute later without the uniforms. It was that easy for him. Marcus didn't play ball for LIC anymore. And Marcus wasn't the "Black" in Black and White anymore, either.

The jersey that I wore on Friday night was at home in a pile of dirty laundry. My road uniform was hanging in my closet. I just didn't want Casey to have to ask me for them.

Moses turned the radio up, and kids were playing games at almost every basket. I couldn't find a place to get comfortable. I didn't want to sit around and watch everybody else having a party. So I headed for the door.

The next night, my dad and I had to go down to Mr. Golub's office and make the last payment. Golub didn't get another dime after that, unless the case went to trial. Dad wanted me to be there to see him write out the check.

"Take a good look at what I'm spending my over-time money on," he told me. "This is the vacation we're not going to take this year."

Golub said the case against me was still weak. That after a while, the state might even drop the charges completely. It was a waiting game to see if I was going to crack, staring at all that time. The cops weren't going to quit, either. They had nothing to lose. They got to go home every night, no matter what. All they could do was get lucky and come up with somebody who said it was absolutely me.

Golub put a rubber band around my folder, and filed it away in alphabetical order. He said there was nothing left for him to do, except pick a jury if it came down to that. But that wouldn't be for another few months.

"We wouldn't want anyone who's ever been robbed

for one. We wouldn't even want people who've had trouble with high school kids in their neighborhood," Golub said. "And of course, we'd want more whites on the jury than blacks."

Dad said he was going to tell my mom that there wasn't any real evidence against me. And that the state would drop the charges by the summer for sure. Now I couldn't even tell her how worried I was. I had to pretend that everything was all right. I was as scared as I'd ever been in my whole life. And I couldn't tell my dad because he would have said that I deserved it.

My mom was always in my corner. I knew that she would stick up for me to the very end, even if a judge ever found me guilty. But I wondered if on the inside, she thought that I really did it, especially since Marcus had pled guilty.

I'd close the bathroom door behind me, and think how the prison cells on TV weren't any bigger than that. I even started leaving the door open a crack when I was in there, just to have a way out.

With basketball over, Rebecca wanted to start meeting up after school. I wasn't in the mood to scout any new talent. Besides, she had stuck with me through everything so far. And the more I thought about it, the more I knew I wouldn't want to see her with some other guy.

We were walking along the river on Shore Boulevard. All I could think about was the spot under the Hell Gate Bridge where I dumped Grandpa's gun. My heart was pounding and my palms started sweating the closer we got to it. I was holding Rebecca's hand when we reached the bridge. Maybe she could feel all of that inside of me. I stopped to look out at the water and thought I could see the exact spot where the gun hit. That's when Rebecca kissed me. She put her tongue all the way into my mouth, and curled it around my bottom lip on the way back out. A fire shot through me. But I wasn't sure what caused it. My eyes were shut tight and I reached both arms out around her. I held on until long after she was finished.

We crossed the street and started back through the park. When we got to the running track, I saw Marcus and Rose sitting together on a bench from behind. They were as close as you could get without being in each other's lap. They were talking, and Rose was squeezing Marcus's hand between hers. I swung Rebecca off to the side and changed direction in a hurry. No one but me saw anything.

I tried to push the picture of them out of my mind but couldn't. But by the time I got home, I could see them together. And it didn't bother me as much as I thought it would.

That night, Rose's cheeks were redder than I'd ever seen them. She did her homework in the living room, without saying a word to anyone. Later, she took Gotti out for a long walk.

My mom brought a basket of clean laundry up from the basement. She left it on the steps for me to carry upstairs the rest of the way. I bent over to pick it up, and my white home uniform was sitting on top. The 11 was staring me right in the face.

BLACK

There were less than two weeks before I had to report to the DA's office. Everything that was finally happening between Rose and me was going to get cut off cold. I didn't know how that would change things. When you keep a cover on your feelings for so long and they finally break free, it's hard to put them on hold again. Rose said that it was just time, like all the time we knew each other growing up. But I couldn't imagine not feeling her heartbeat now, and how warm she was in my arms.

I wanted to tell Eddie about Rose and me. I knew that when everything settled down, it would be a bump he'd get over. But that good one-on-one feeling we always had was gone. For now, I didn't want to put one more mountain between us.

Rose didn't tell her parents. Her father would have put her under lock and key. Her mother was already walking a tightrope over Eddie. Something like this would have sent her falling for sure. I was

worried that when they did find out, I would be sitting in a prison cell upstate. Then they would be knocking me down all the time to Rose, and I wouldn't be there to prove I was somebody different.

I couldn't hold it against them. When they let me into their house, they weren't thinking I was going to pull a stickup with their son and fall for their daughter. Up until last month, the Russos were probably patting themselves on the back for showing a black kid without a father how a family was supposed to be. But my mother was standing up taller now than they ever did, even if you stood them up one on top of the other.

My mother had it figured out about Rose and me from the beginning. I was glad, because I didn't want to hide anything from her ever again. She didn't connect Rose to her parents or Eddie. My mother didn't even care that Rose was white. But she told me that people were going to keep hammering us for crossing that line. She said that's when we'd find out how thick our skins really are.

I couldn't hang out with Rose around school because of her mother. So we'd walk up and down Steinway Street, and stay in the library on Broadway. When the weather was nice, we'd go down to Astoria Park and sit on the benches. Rose would take a second look at every white sanitation truck that rolled past. She was worried that her father's buddies would spot us and tell him that a black kid had his arm around her. I just played it off because I knew that she was under a lot of pressure.

In math class, Eddie turned around to see me marking off a calendar. I had a circle around my days left at home, and a big X from corner to corner on the ones after that. He was looking right at it. It didn't make any sense for me to pretend it was something else.

"I got to figure out how to make the best of these days," I told him.

Eddie shook his head and said, "School's the last place I'd be. I'd—"

He pulled up short on his words.

"I don't really know what I'd do," he finished, almost one word at a time. "Only you know how it feels."

I spent as much time as I could with my mother and Sabrina. I helped Sabrina with her math homework, and started doing more chores around the house. I made sure I was home for dinner every night. It was always important to my mother we ate as a family. Now I felt the same way.

"We'll always be a family. Time apart isn't going

to change that," my mother told us at the table. "We're going to take from this world everything that makes the spirit grow stronger. And that spirit will keep us from getting torn apart."

The things that were most important to me had changed. It used to be playing ball, and Eddie and me being big shots. Now it was my family. Soon there was going to be a wall between everyone I cared about and me. But that wasn't going to stop me from keeping focused on them.

I already missed seeing Casey every day. For the last fifteen years, Casey had coached eleven kids on the basketball team and forty kids on the football team. But I knew I wasn't just another player to him. When I handed in my uniform he told me he was still in my corner, no matter what. And that when I got out of jail, and college coaches called him about me, he would tell them that I was learning from my mistakes. He said I would be a leader on any team, and an example of how somebody could put their life back together.

I knew I'd always be tied to Casey through Jason. I'd never forget that Jason and me came from the same place, and wanted to do the same things. Jason lost his life, and I almost took someone's. Casey looked after the both of us as much as any coach could. Only I was still around to appreciate it.

I thought about Jefferson every day since he was transferred. I asked one of the officers at school if I could call him at his new post. But the officer said that Jefferson couldn't have any contact with students during the investigation. Things like that moved slow and would probably take another couple of weeks. So I asked the officer to tell Jefferson I'd see him again one day. And if Connelly ever came back, to tell him I said to go to hell.

I stressed, thinking my father would call on my birthday. Only I wouldn't be there to hear his voice. I didn't know what would be worse—my father finding out I was in jail that way, or him not calling for another two years and finding out from me after I got home.

I didn't ask for any money since I got out of Rikers. But for my last weekend home, my mother gave me twenty dollars and told me to spend it any way I wanted. It was impossible for Rose to get out at night. So I dumped any thought of playing ball at the Circle and took Rose to the Saturday matinee at Kaufman Studios. It was the first time we'd ever been to the movies alone. No Eddie. No cousins. It was just the two of us.

We walked all the way up to the theater and past

the parking lot where Sidney Parker got shot. I didn't want to cross the street to the exact spot. But I showed Rose where it happened. She wanted to get a clear picture of it. It wasn't something that I had to close my eyes to anymore. I could face what I did, and move on.

Rose picked out a love story, without any guns or violence. The theater was almost empty. We sat halfway back from the screen in the middle of the row, and shared a soda. I had my arm around Rose from the start. She leaned her head up against my neck, and stayed that way for nearly two hours. We watched all the way through the closing credits, until the lights got turned up.

On the way home, we stopped at the flower shop where Rose bought my mother's bouquet. I got her one red rose to remember the day.

"When you leave I'm going to press this inside a book," Rose said. "And I'm not going to open that page again until you get back."

That night, my mother went through the list of what she could mail to me upstate. She got a package together of things like toothpaste, socks, and underwear. Sabrina put her Walkman on the pile, and said she wanted me to have it. I never told her or my mother where it really came from. I held it tight in my hands and could almost hear that woman scream after we robbed her. I figured it belonged with me in jail. So I put it back on the pile and gave Sabrina a big hug.

The next morning my legs couldn't keep still. They were itching to play ball after missing out on Saturday morning. The Circle was always dead on Sunday. I shot the ball there by myself for twenty minutes. Then I jogged around to some of the other courts in the neighborhood, looking for a game.

The other yards were empty, too.

I headed back down 21st Street, ready to give up, when I heard a ball bouncing on the courts by the Department of Sanitation. I wasn't about to cross over until I saw for sure it was somebody worth playing.

Eddie had his back to me. He let a long jumper go from the corner. It went straight in, without even touching the rim.

I leaned up against a parked car, watching him. Eddie cut right and left with the ball. He hit shot after shot, wearing his maroon and powder blue Marauders. His stroke was as smooth as ever. But none of that mattered. I had his timing down from playing with him for so long. Maybe Eddie was carrying around too much inside him. He was a half step slower than usual. And it showed in every move he made.

I dribbled the basketball, crossing the street, and Eddie turned to see me coming. The D.S. was the first place we ever played together, and would probably be the last for a long time. I ducked through a hole in the fence. Eddie stood there with the ball glued to his hip.

"I was out looking for a game," I told him. "But I didn't think I'd find somebody this good."

"Yeah, I'm just good enough to get beat in the first round of the playoffs," Eddie came back with a straight face.

I tossed my ball off to the side, and put my hands out for Eddie to pass me the one he was holding. When he did, I pushed it right back at him and started playing defense. We weren't going hard in the beginning. And neither one of us said the score out loud after the first couple of baskets. So we didn't pay any more attention to it.

Eddie made an off-balance shot and threw me a smile. I got up tighter on him. And we both got more serious. I knew all of Eddie's moves and beat him to where he wanted to go on the court. When I was offense, I turned the corner on him every time. I pushed him to go faster and faster. But there was no way he could keep up, dragging everything around with him.

After ten minutes, Eddie needed a break. He was doubled-over, trying to catch his breath. I sat on the court with my palms flat against the ground behind me. Then Eddie followed. He took his hand off the ball and it rolled away. We were sitting face-to-face, with the sweat coming down the both of us. The rows of trucks parked outside the sanitation garage were quiet. There was hardly any noise from out in the street, either. And it felt like the only sound in the whole world was from our breathing.

There was nothing between us now, except for the line that separates black and white. Only I couldn't tell if it had been there from the beginning. Maybe it snaked its way through when we were too worried about saving our asses to see. I didn't know if it could ever get erased, or if we could find a way around it. I only knew that I wanted to try.

AUTHOR'S NOTE

I was inspired to write *Black and White* by several very real experiences in New York City. From 1992 to 1998, I taught adolescents who were awaiting trial on Rikers Island to read and write. The inequities of the criminal justice system, including who can afford the best lawyer and who can make bail, deem that the overwhelming majority of inmates on Rikers are either black or Hispanic. It's a truth you can never close your eyes to. It seeps deep into the subconscious of the young people held there, seeing only people who look like themselves being locked up. And on the days when they forget to ask *what's wrong with the system*, they sadly begin to wonder *what's wrong with us?*

Marcus: "But the main part of what goes on there [Rikers] started to sink in right away. It's black people, wall to wall. There are some Spanish inmates,

too. But everybody else is black. That whole first night, I kept thinking how if Eddie got arrested with me, his family would have bailed him out. Only I'd still be there. I couldn't beef about it. It wouldn't have been Eddie's fault. That's the way it is. We could be Black and White anywhere else in the world. But not on Rikers Island."

For two years, I helped coach a New York City high school (Aviation) basketball team. We arrived at Long Island City High School (Marcus's and Eddie's school) for a road game, and couldn't walk through the gym because there was a phys. ed. class still going on. Some LIC players opened a side door and took us up the back stairs to the visitors' locker room. One of those kids played a great game against us, catching my eye. Only the next time I saw him it was on the six o'clock news. LIC had gone upstate to play in a tournament. There was a lot of racial taunting coming out of the stands. Then suddenly, the whole gym exploded into a riot. In the spotlight on the news video, I could see that young man getting stabbed through the back with a chair leg. Tragically, he died right there on the court.

The seeds of that incident stayed with me for more than ten years, finally germinating in the character of

Jason Taylor, a former LIC team captain who suffers the same fate. His racially driven murder provides Marcus and Eddie with a reference point to evaluate their own growing divide.

Marcus on the stabbing: "People around my way said it was because of that natural hatred. That line between blacks and whites that can't get erased, no matter what. I just remember hating that kid's guts because of what he did. Not because he was white. And everybody I knew—no matter what color— hated him, too."

A few years ago, I was riding the G train from Brooklyn to Queens when an intoxicated homeless man with feces-stained pants went on a racially driven tirade, baiting whites, African-Americans, and Jews to fight each other. The passengers in that train car took everything he had to say, and probably learned something about how much heat they could stand without letting someone bring them to the boiling point.

I put Marcus and Eddie on that same train with their teammates to hear what this man had to spew. Their teammates find him hilarious, but our protagonists don't.

Eddie: *"I looked over at Marcus and he was looking right back at me. Other kids were howling. But not us. Maybe a month ago, we'd have been laughing, too. I kept thinking about being locked up with a nut-job like that and having to listen to his act twenty-four/seven."*

The protagonists' English teacher, Ms. Sussman, is based on my high school English teacher, Martha Sussman, whom I taught with when I started working in schools twelve years later. During my senior year, there was some racial unrest in my high school, and I remember Ms. Sussman going into the hallway and crying after breaking up two students who'd come close to fighting in class. That image of her crying stayed with me for a long time, and eventually found a place in the book.

Marcus: *"When she was done screaming, her eyes watered up. She went out into the hallway for a few seconds and pulled herself back together fast."*

The rewards of writing *Black and White* have been simple—letters, phone calls, and e-mails from teens who've found something in the novel they can identify with.

The writing process helps me, too. It gives me an outlet for everything that touches me so deeply, and gets me wound up tight. Without it I'd probably explode.

I think about Eddie, who said, *"I wondered how it would feel to be free of this whole thing, or at least tell everyone the truth. I stood on the corner of my block and looked out into the traffic. Then I pulled up everything I'd been thinking about and feeling. I opened my mouth wide to scream. But not a sound came out."*

I'm glad that's not my problem. I'm very lucky that I can channel what I've experienced and what I feel into books for young adults.

—Paul Volponi

AN INTERVIEW WITH PAUL VOLPONI

Oftentimes, readers will ask me questions about my writing. Here are some of the questions I've been asked by the readers of *Black and White*.

Why do you choose to write novels about young adults?

Teens make incredible protagonists. They have problems just as important as adults, but much less power to solve them. Their initial reactions to situations are usually very passionate and honest, and that makes me want to write about their world, which is really everybody's world.

Where did you grow up and how did it influence your writing?

I've always lived within two miles or so of Rikers Island in New York City. When I was growing up, strangers to the neighborhood would pull their cars over all the time and ask, *"How do I get to Rikers Island?"* My friends and I thought up a great response: *Rob a bank!* But when we looked into the eyes of these lost families going to visit loved ones in jail, none of us could ever say that punch line to their faces.

I also spent seven days a week on a basketball court, where the kind of code between teammates that keeps Marcus from ever thinking about giving Eddie up to the cops was ingrained in me early.

Astoria, Queens, is the central setting for *Black and White*, and I walk the same streets that Marcus and Eddie do in the story. The basketball courts next to the Department of Sanitation garage, the whirlpool beneath the Hell Gate Bridge, the supermarket with the big plaster cow and chicken on top, the strip of stores and library on Steinway Street, the movie theater and the parking lot where the gun goes off are all very real places. And some readers have told me they've gone out to follow in the protagonists' footsteps around Astoria as well.

Who were your favorite authors as a youngster, and did you like to read?

I liked Mark Twain because he commented on society and wouldn't give anyone or anything a free pass. Reading, however, was never one of my favorite things to do. Instead, I'd listen to people talk—on the streets, buses, subways, basketball courts—anywhere. That took the place of reading for me, and was how I collected stories. I also developed a strong memory from listening so close and could tell people the exact words they'd used in conversations from years before. But I really wish I'd read more as a teen.

My favorite books right now are *The Adventures of Huckleberry Finn* (Mark Twain), *The Grapes of Wrath* (John Steinbeck), and *Bury My Heart at Wounded Knee* (Dee Brown).

Why did you write Black and White, *and why did you decide to use two narrators?*

Despite the real-life inspirations, I don't believe I ever consciously chose this story. It somehow grew inside of me and simply demanded a way out. So if I didn't write it, I probably would have burst open one day.

Letting Marcus and Eddie each tell their own story seemed natural, and wasn't much of a decision for me at all. I just fell into the pattern of them narrating alternating chapters and never looked back. They each passionately believe in what they're saying and doing, so I never thought anyone else could convince us for them.

Why does the novel end without Marcus and Eddie throwing-down, or saying how they really feel about what happened, or about each other?

I didn't want to give them concrete feelings either way. There's a long road ahead for both of them, and I believe their feelings would change many times over. Imagine Marcus's first night in prison away from his family, or the first time Eddie really looks at himself in a mirror. With a revolving door of acceptance, denial, and anger to constantly negotiate, weighing them down with absolute feelings seems wrong. Also, I truly felt the story was finished at that point, and it was time to walk away from them both.

DISCUSSION QUESTIONS

■ Explain who you would rather have for parents—Eddie's mother and father, who protect him at all costs whether he's right or wrong, or Marcus's mother, who faces the truth head-on?

■ If Eddie had been the one identified by the shooting victim, do you believe he would have remained quiet about the identity of his partner, like Marcus did? Do you believe Marcus would have let Eddie take the rap alone?

■ How does the novel's opening scene, in which Marcus is running through the streets, foreshadow his changing relationship with Eddie, and the journey on which he is about to embark?

■ How do Marcus's and Eddie's reactions to the film *The Count of Monte Cristo* reflect what is going on in the book?

■ What is the symbolism in the following: Eddie's borrowing and returning Marcus's jacket, Connelly's and Jefferson's fight at senior night, and Eddie's tussle with his black shadow and poor play on the basketball court after Marcus accepts his plea?

■ At the end of the novel, Marcus heads off to prison and Eddie goes to college on a basketball scholarship. After all that has happened, would you say that one character is better off than the other? Why or why not?

■ Five years after the novel's conclusion, how do you picture Marcus's and Eddie's lives turning out? Where will they be, and what will they be doing? And who will have a closer relationship—Marcus and Eddie, Marcus and Rose, or Rose and Eddie?

■ In the novel's final paragraph, Marcus says, "There was nothing between us now, except for the line that separates black and white." Do you think the racial "line" was always there between Marcus and Eddie? Could Marcus and Eddie have ever gotten past this division?

WRITING TOPICS

■ Eddie's essay in English class seems far from the truth: *"I'd like people to remember me as somebody they could depend on. No matter what happens, I'm always right there. I'm not the kind of person who walks away when things get tough...."*

Rewrite Eddie's essay, *How do you want people to remember you?* for him to read to himself.

■ Marcus wishes he could apologize to the shooting victim, Sidney Parker: *"I wanted him to know how sorry I was. But there was no way to get through. No matter how hard I looked, it was just my reflection in that [blacked-out] window. And all I could see was my own black face."*

Compose a letter from Marcus, who is sitting in prison, to Mr. Parker, explaining his actions and feelings. What do you think Marcus would say by way of an apology?

■ Rose visits Marcus in prison, delivering a letter from Eddie, who is in the middle of his first college basketball season at St. John's. What does that letter say?

■ Compose a letter from Marcus's mother to Eddie's parents, describing her feelings about how they treated Marcus, whom they once called their "second son."

RECRUITING
VOLUNTEERS
IN THE CHURCH

RECRUITING
VOLUNTEERS
IN THE CHURCH

MARK SENTER III

VICTOR BOOKS®

A DIVISION OF SCRIPTURE PRESS PUBLICATIONS INC.
USA CANADA ENGLAND

Dedicated to the members of the Professional Association of Christian Educators whose ministries are dependent upon the effective use of volunteers.

Scripture quotations are from *New American Standard Bible,* © the Lockman Foundation 1960, 1962, 1963, 1968, 1971, 1972, 1973, 1975, 1977.

Library of Congress Cataloging-in-Publication Data

Senter, Mark.
  Recruiting volunteers in the church / by Mark Senter.
    p. cm.
  ISBN 0-89693-799-2
    1. Church work. 2. Voluntarism — Religious aspects — Christianity.
I. Title.
BV4400.S465 1990
254 — dc20
                                                        90-44571
                                                            CIP

---

1 2 3 4 5 6 7 8 9 10   Printing/Year 94 93 92 91 90

CONTENTS

85422

PREFACE

Without a doubt, the aspect of church ministry I was least prepared for in assuming the responsibility of the educational and discipleship ministries of Wheaton Bible Church in 1975, was the recruitment of volunteers to do the work of ministry on what we commonly referred to as "sanctuary square." Somehow it was easier, even then, to obtain workers for outreach ministries which took place in the community than it was to staff a ministry team which focused on people who came from Christian families and was primarily located in the church building.

Al Sloat and Doris Freese, two outstanding Christian educators, had preceded me at the church and developed ministries which had been described in appropriately glowing terms in evangelical periodicals. All I needed to do was maintain the best of these ministries while developing creative new strategies. Right? Wrong!

Just to maintain or create the required personnel, I quickly discovered that I needed a staff of over 400 people. To complicate matters, teachers and leaders started coming to me with comments like, "I thought you might like to select your own staff," and "It is about time for me to take a little sabbatical," and "I've just been staying as a favor to Doris." All of these and dozens of other comments added up to two words, "I quit."

Suddenly I had to do something I had never done before — recruit people I did not know to do the educational/discipleship ministries of our church. Through several years of struggling I

7

developed and used the ideas described in this book.

In the early 1980s I wrote *The Art of Recruiting Volunteers* based both on my experiences and the accounts of many of my colleagues. In order to merge the different sources into one narration I created Jeff Thompson and Walnut Heights Bible Church to act as a case study for these recruitment strategies.

As we enter the decade of the 1990s many aspects of volunteer ministries in the local church have changed, yet a majority of the ideas of the original book remain applicable. At the same time, some of the questions *not* addressed in the original book seemed more relevant to its reviewers: "How do you select and interview potential volunteers?" or "What if we use all of these ideas and still can't get someone to volunteer for a specific job, what do we do then?" This book is a response to these questions and the new research that has been done about volunteerism in America. Thus, *Recruiting Volunteers in the Church* is both a revision and expansion of the original book. Two chapters have been revised while four have been added.

It is my prayer that the ministries of discipleship and education in the local church will be strengthened through the ideas presented in this book.

Mark H. Senter III
January 1990

INTRODUCTION

Volunteers Can Bring Renewal

Volunteer lay ministry in the church began nearly 2,000 years ago during the emergence of the New Testament church in Jerusalem and Asia Minor. Even a cursory reading of Acts and the Epistles of Paul represents the early church as a closely knit body of believers, helping and serving one another in the spirit of Christ's love: "This is My commandment, that you love one another, just as I have loved you" (John 15:12). In fact, in the Apostle John's account of the Last Supper, the "love commandment" is repeated three times (John 13:34; 15:12; and 15:17) after Jesus washed His disciples' feet to illustrate the servanthood that was the heart of His ministry. The concept of service within the church, the body of Christ, is restated emphatically in James 2:17: "Even so faith, if it has no works, is dead, being by itself."

In the modern church, the concept of volunteer service has almost died under the impact of cultural fragmentation, the exaltation of individualism, and heavy economic pressures on the average American family. Ironically, the problems of fragmentation, individualism, and economic pressure are best addressed through close fellowship and strong service-oriented volunteer ministry in the church. Ministry to others, taking time to share gifts and talents, and meeting others at the point of their need all have a way of bringing health and wholeness to the giver as well as the one receiving the gift. Scripture tells us, "By your standard of measure, it shall be measured to you" (Matt.

9

7:2). All in Christ's body need to be both givers and receivers, and the church was designed originally to allow that to happen.

Lay ministry within the body of Christ is neither automatic nor spontaneous. If it were, the dynamic of service would be functioning much more freely and visibly than is happening in churches throughout the world. Rather, it must be started and sustained by "spark plugs," people who can keep the engine running. Members of the congregation must be asked to serve, assisted in identifying their gifts, then put to work in appropriate ministry.

There's a word for this process: recruitment. Properly understood and employed, recruitment is an answer to renewal in the local church.

The story is told of a Sunday School convention in which a wild rumor almost turned the place upside down. The rumor concerned an unnamed but reportedly well-known church in the heartland of the U.S., a church that *always had a surplus of volunteer workers and, consequently, a fantastic Christian education program and body-life ministry.*

As the rumor went, trained teachers at this church were ready and champing at the bit to move from the "waiting list" to on-line teaching positions in new classes that continually blossomed as the educational ministry grew. Existing staff teachers seldom complained or resigned, even after ten or more years of service, and no one at the church could remember the last time anyone quit a volunteer leadership position in midyear. The sick were visited. Needs were met in the body. Home prayer groups and neighborhood Bible studies flourished. Visitation was done by gifted volunteers, while the church grew by leaps and bounds. The pastor's Sunday messages were profoundly spiritual and deeply moving to the congregation, because he had plenty of time to pray and meditate with the Lord in developing them.

No one was quite sure where this story originated, but it spread around the convention floor like wildfire. A church without volunteer staffing problems? Pastors and Christian education directors clamored to know more about it. Was a workshop on recruitment going to be held? Where? What time? Why wasn't it listed on the convention program?

Within hours, the rumor had escaped the confines of the convention. Major publishing house representatives with curriculum display booths on the floor phoned their home companies to break the exciting news. At least two publishers assigned researchers to locate this "dream" church and to do videotapes on its recruitment strategy. The editors of the *Wittenburg Door* pondered the news and quickly determined to give their first "Bronzed Door Award" to the rumored church (as soon as it could be found) because it so epitomized the renewal ideals the magazine advocated.

Other reactions were equally swift. A Christian magazine assigned investigative writers to interview the pastor of this amazing church. Christian radio and television stations vied in the race to be the first to feature this "miraculous solution" to the problem of volunteer recruitment.

Then, as suddenly as the rumor began, it ended. A workshop leader from the Sunday School convention embarrassedly confessed that his workshop had been so dull that he had injected the story about the church with no recruitment problems just to wake the people up. And wake them up it did! "After all," quoted the news section of *Christianity Today*, "it gave everybody hope for their own church."

Unfortunately, hope is not built on fanciful stories to illustrate an evangelistic point, but on an honest understanding of the facts and a reasonable course of action designed in response to those facts. There are, in fact, churches with excellent recruitment programs, but for the vast majority of the churches in America, recruitment is a serious if not desperate problem. Why?

Recruitment of volunteer personnel is perhaps the most unglamorous part of the educational ministry of the local church—and yet one of the most essential. Some educators see it as the "pits." Others accept it as potential. But for both pessimist and optimist, recruitment adds up to a lot of hard work.

When I became a pastor of Christian education after eleven years of youth ministry, my greatest shock was in the area of recruitment of volunteer staff. For the first time I had to reach out beyond my immediate circle of friends to fill staff positions which had an annual turnover. A big turnover.

A slow panic set in. About 4:30 one morning I awoke with the awesome sword of staffing responsibilities hanging over my head. In those nagging hours between sleep and full consciousness, I wondered whether the pressure I was feeling was worth the satisfaction I would experience if and when the task was accomplished. Would this kind of ministry really meet the spiritual and social needs of children, youth, and adults in the church? There was only one way to find out.

The process had begun some months earlier when, over a period of several weeks, a number of teachers had resigned for various reasons. The holes in the staff were growing and my greatest hang-up was that I had no plan or system with which to recruit volunteers for staffing ministry positions. I needed nearly twenty teachers immediately, if not sooner, and I saw no way of filling the positions.

A workshop on recruitment at a Sunday School convention provided little help. A professor from a small college gave a bone dry and hopelessly abstract picture on the art of recruiting in the local church. It seemed apparent to me that he had never felt recruitment pains similar to the ones I was experiencing. I needed practical, how-to-do-it stuff, not theory.

A phone call halfway across the nation to a colleague-turned-professor proved to be the turning point in my recruitment pilgrimage. Patiently, he explained what he had done in the three churches he had served as pastor of Christian education. A pattern began to emerge. Workable ideas began to fall into place.

The panic wasn't over. So far, I had simply outlined a few ways to channel my panic energy into a hopeful approach to solving the problem. In fact, it took over two years for me to feel really comfortable and confident with the process that eventually worked well enough to staff a Christian education program using the abilities of over 400 people in ministry to children, youth, and adults.

My uneasiness over recruitment was relieved somewhat when I began realizing that I was not alone with my burden. A trip to the West Coast a year and a half later allowed me to visit five of the best-known churches in the nation. Recruitment was a problem everywhere!

As recently as two weeks ago this same problem raised its head as I talked with one of my friends about her son, the pastor of education in a rural town church in the Midwest. "His biggest problem," said June, "is getting enough people to staff their Sunday School and youth activities."

Large church or small, professional educator or lay superintendent, rapidly growing congregation or dwindling numbers, the challenge appears to be the same: How can we recruit Christians to join in changing the lives of people within the context of the local church? This manual has been written in answer to that question. It is designed to provide a practical system of recruitment and materials which are easily adaptable for use in any congregation.

This manual is designed as a tool to assist church educators in overcoming the obstacles faced in recruitment. Actually, it is a whole set of tools which can be used singly or in combination to bring real life and success to volunteer "harvesting" and thus to expanding the ministry of the local church.

Perhaps the most useful way to present these tools is to simulate a "real-life" situation in which the reader can "observe" as a new pastor of Christian education struggles with real problems to develop a successful recruiting program for his church. Though the people and events are fictional, the situations, problems, and solutions will be recognized by many as a composite drawn from the experiences of many pastors, churches, and Christian education leaders.

ONE

The Problem

Jeff Thompson, twenty-six-year-old graduate of Ormsby Seminary, former star benchwarmer of the University of Michigan
basketball team, swung his '84 Datsun into the staff parking lot
of Walnut Heights Bible Church and pulled up next to a brand-
new white Oldsmobile. He assumed it was the pastor's car.
Grabbing a battered briefcase, he stepped out into a brisk, chilly
spring wind to get a quick look at his first church—or rather the
first church to offer him the kind of job he'd prayed for: pastor
of Christian education at a growing fellowship.

Nestled at the base of a hill once covered by black walnut
trees, Walnut Heights Bible Church was no mean architectural
feat. Jeff could tell that the complex of buildings had been
designed by someone familiar with foot traffic patterns and noise
transmission problems common to larger churches, while the
simple lines and soaring steeple of the church proper communicated a quiet elegance—pure white outlined against a robin's
egg sky. The surrounding neighborhood was another story. Older homes, once lovely, now displayed peeling paint, overgrown
hedges, cracked windows here and there, and ugly lawns still
yellow-brown.

"Beauty is in the eye of the beholder," Jeff told himself as he
headed for the church office, breathing a quick prayer as he
walked. Jeff was ushered into his coworker's office by Peggy, the
pastor's slender, blond secretary, who put down two cups of
coffee and left quietly.

15

Herb Wilcox stood and extended his hand. A rugged-looking man in his early fifties, the pastor could have been called handsome except for the slightly oversize nose which threw his features out of balance. Older members of the congregation teased him about it now and then, but he took it in good humor. "Big enough to smell the will of God, small enough to keep out of other people's business," he'd say.

"Good to have you on board, Jeff," Pastor Wilcox said warmly. "Is Rita happy with the house you found?"

"Yes, sir," Jeff replied, slipping out of his topcoat. "I'm sure she's going to love it here, as soon as she gets to know a few people."

"I'm glad to hear that. Let's get right down to business, Jeff. I'd like to have a word of prayer with you and a chat before I show you your new office."

The two men prayed brief but fervent prayers before sitting — the senior pastor behind his desk, his new assistant in one of the overstuffed chairs in front of it. Herb Wilcox lowered his head and peered at Jeff over the top of his glasses.

"Scripture says, 'confess your sins to one another,' " the older man began. "I want us to start with a clean slate so the Lord will bless our work together. To be honest, you weren't my first choice for the job — I wanted someone more experienced. But we could not afford to pay the salary of a seasoned educator. So the church board asked if I could 'live with you' as pastor of Christian education, and I said I could.

"You see, ten years ago when I first came here, this congregation amounted to a grand total of two dozen people. It's now over 600, because of the Lord's blessing, a lot of trousers with worn-out knees, and blood, sweat, and tears spent feeding and loving these sheep.

"I'm used to running the Christian Education Department out of my hip pocket," Pastor Wilcox continued, "with the help of my wife, Henrietta, and my former secretary, Alma. When Alma retired last year, Henrietta said she couldn't handle the work load herself. We had to have someone — and you're it.

"Let me level with you. My biggest apprehension is that some hotshot seminary graduate, still wet behind the ears, will be critical of my old-fashioned ways of doing things and alienate my people from me. I'm concerned that he'll want to use my con-

gregation as a guinea pig for raw, untested, speculative programs—that will hurt feelings, sow discord, and upset the
progress we've made over the years. I don't want that to
happen."

Jeff Thompson felt the palms of his hands beginning to sweat.
Yet there was a relief at the candor of the man he would now
call "pastor."

"I don't want that to happen either, Pastor Wilcox," he said
quietly. "But I have to confess I've come into this job with a few
apprehensions as well, and you've touched on one of them.
When I was on the University of Michigan basketball team, I
didn't get off the bench—but I supported the first string, encouraged them, and cheered them on to win. And they did win
that year, taking the Big Ten crown. I'm a team man, Pastor,
and I do my best to help the team win—whatever position I'm
given. But from that experience I learned one lesson: You can't
do much from the bench.

"I came here to work, to minister, to help build up the body
of Christ in this church. You're the senior pastor, and I'm under
your authority. You can keep me on the bench if you want or
you can put me to work where I can do some good." Jeff felt the
tension rising in his voice and paused to take a deep breath and
swallow.

"My greatest apprehension," the new pastor of education continued, "is that I might encounter a pastor so committed to the
'Lone Ranger' approach to church operation that he'd rather let
the church go the way of the dinosaurs than allow new people
and new ideas to minister life to the body.

"I've been trained in Christian education. I've brought a lot of
enthusiasm and a few ideas to this job. I believe with the Lord's
leading and your advice and experience I can do well at this. I
don't intend to oppose your views or experiment on the congregation. All I ask is enough freedom to serve the Lord, you, and
the congregation to the best of my ability."

A smile played around Pastor Wilcox's eyes. Perhaps he understood. Maybe he could remember his idealism as he arrived at
his first place of ministry. At least he was listening.

"That's fair enough, Pastor Thompson," he said. "I'm releas-
ing you to take authority and responsibility over our Christian
education program. But I would ask that every proposal for

change, every new approach to problems, be brought to me for my input. As far as your relationship with the church board and the Christian Education Committee is concerned, I expect you to sell your ideas to them on your own. I'll support you, but I don't want to be bulldozing a path in front of you.

"Now, Jeff—I suppose you have some questions for me, so fire away."

Jeff grinned and relaxed a bit. "You supposed right, Pastor. I've got hundreds of 'em."

"Well, shoot one at me and see if I can be of any help." Pastor Wilcox's sudden modesty was nearly disarming to the newcomer. In a flash of insight Jeff saw how this veteran pastor could have run the Christian education program out of his hip pocket for so many years.

"What do you think is the greatest need which Walnut Heights Bible Church faces in the educational ministry?" inquired Jeff. It was a question that he had asked a number of times during the weekend that he and Rita had candidated at the church; yet he knew that it would be an important starting place for discovering the pulse of the church from the man who knew the needs best.

"Recruitment!" was the unhesitating answer of the older man. "We've got to have more people and better prepared workers, or we are going to wear ourselves out."

First thing the next morning, Jeff stuck his head into his new colleague's office. Peggy, the pastor's secretary, had objected to the unannounced intrusion, but the self-confident newcomer assured her that he would only be with the pastor for a couple of minutes.

"Amazingly enough, Pastor, I found it! It was stashed in a Lay's Potato Chips box near the top of one of my piles."

"Good morning, Jeff," was the unenthusiastic response of the interrupted pastor.

Jeff never broke stride in his explanation. "During my internship year in Minnesota, Tim Johnson, my supervising Minister of Christian Education, had me write a paper on 'Recruitment: A Current Report.' If you would, I'd like for you to look it over and tell me if these are the same problems we are dealing with here at Walnut Heights."

Unsnapping his briefcase, he reached inside and handed Pastor Wilcox a report that looked like a seminary term paper. "I'd appreciate it if you'd let me know what you think."

As abruptly as he had entered, Jeff retraced his steps to the outer office. One hundred and six seconds had elapsed. Pastor Wilcox thumbed through the report and began to read.

* * *

Recruitment

For the purpose of this project, "recruitment" means the obtaining of suitable Christian leaders from the congregation who will meet children, youth, and adults at the point of their need and guide them into a growing maturity in Christ through the educational agencies of the local church.

There are several words which stand out as key in this definition and deserve greater amplification. "Obtaining" does not mean coercion, manipulation, or a life sentence at "hard labor" in the Beginner Department. "Obtaining" simply means plugging people who want to serve God into sockets of spiritual need. It is the natural way of drawing the spiritual current from one person and passing it along to another, less mature person. Sometimes this involves a need which can be met. At other times it means assisting a person in discovering latent spiritual gifts or natural talents. Usually "obtaining" means asking a Christian to accept a specific responsibility for a designated amount of time.

"Suitable Christian leaders" is a phrase which recognizes that not everyone is cut out to assist wiggly three-year-olds or obnoxious junior high students in discovering God's truths in the Bible. In fact, more people are not suited for any specific ministry position than are uniquely suited. Some are not really Christians; others cannot lead; and still others find themselves mismatched due to temperament, training, background, or any number of God-given factors. But the exciting part of recruitment of "suitable Christian leaders" is that God does not allow a ministry need to develop without providing a person to meet that need.

The "point of their need" takes into account that people are unique. Each person develops at his own rate and in response to various circumstances. Physical limitations, emotional stress, and family upheaval, as well as the normal transitions of life, rub the "point of need" raw—making the person receptive to the healing oil of a Christian's ministry. Everyone has a need to be loved by a godly adult and to be taught eternal truths appropriate for his or her age-level, and this is most effectively done in relationship to personal needs.

"Growing maturity in Christ" is a phrase adapted from Colossians 1:28: "We proclaim Him [Christ], admonishing every man and teaching every man with all wisdom, that we may present every man complete [mature] in Christ." The maturing process will only be complete when a person stands before God as an individual whose name is written in the Book of Life (Rev. 20:15). Until then, however, the maturing process continues and the church is God's practice field in which this maturing takes place. Other believers, then, are the instructors and coaches for this maturing process.

The "educational agencies of the local church" will differ from church to church. In renewal-oriented congregations, the "agencies" may be revised each year or two, but leadership is still needed even though the process of recruiting may take a more passive form. For most churches, however, Sunday School, children's church, choirs, club programs, and youth groups will constitute the primary agencies for which Christian leaders are needed.

Obstacles

Meanwhile, facing reality, we find that recruitment may always be a problem. It sounds so easy when definitions are laid out and theological jargon is spun into neat webs of logic. But when it comes to obtaining a chairman for the club committee, certain difficulties appear. Before we look at the recruitment process, we would be wise to look at the obstacles which impact the local church in its recruitment of volunteer ministers.

Always a Problem. Lest we become too discouraged with the apathy which is found in our society, let's remind ourselves that recruitment of volunteers has always been a problem. Ezekiel records the Lord as saying, "I searched for a man among them who should build up the wall and stand in the gap before Me for the land, that I should not have to destroy it; but I found no one" (Ezek. 22:30). The Lord Jesus in commissioning seventy-two of His followers to go out in ministry, reminded them that "the harvest is plentiful, but the laborers are few" (Luke 10:2). The history of the Sunday School movement portrays a constant picture of inadequately staffed mission fields. A review of the minutes of the Christian Education Committee from years gone by or a conversation with former Sunday School superintendents will quickly reveal that the recruitment problem is not a new phenomenon. Yet it has been further complicated by cultural obstacles as we approach the end of the twentieth century.

Changing View of Volunteerism. Our society seems to be modifying the way it views volunteerism. Perhaps the best example of this is the United States military. During World War II and the Korean War there was a draft, yet men "willingly" volunteered to serve in the armed forces. With the advent of the unpopular Vietnam War, young men and women ceased to feel the moral imperative to serve. The result was an "all volunteer army" which enticed men and women to enlist with promises of competitive salaries and outstanding benefits.

The church, caught up in the "pay-me-what-I'm-worth" cultural mentality, is finding itself more dependent on paid staff members and less on the volunteers who at one time were the backbone of the church's ministry. Though many of these paid staff members have become facilitators for assisting volunteers to serve more effectively, many paid professional staff have become nothing more than replacements for volunteer ministers.

Working Women. More than half of the women in the United States today are working at jobs outside the home. Many of these women are married and share some family responsibility with their husbands, but the bulk of family obligations still fall upon women. However, much of the volunteer "manpower" of days gone by was provided by women — primarily housewives. Women had more discretionary time and therefore could spend more time in service to the church or community. Women assumed most of the responsibility for the care of the home, often supervising the children in performing some of the household chores. This freed the men to serve part-time in volunteer capacities in the church. Now, with the high-pressured demands of society and economy, families have less discretionary time

21

and therefore guard it more jealously, leaving many of the responsibilities at the church untended.

Absentee Fathers. At the same time that mothers have been working more, fathers have been putting in longer hours pursuing the elusive dream of our culture's success syndrome. The suburban sprawl of homes surrounding the major cities of our nation have made commuting a way of life. In many families the father spends two to three hours each day traveling to and from his job. When added to an eight-hour plus workday and the possibility of a second job during the evening to make ends meet, the church has lost another potential volunteer. Hardly able to give his family enough quality time to keep it together, he is likewise unable to provide any kind of volunteer help with projects or ministry responsibilities at the church.

Success of Adult Classes. While these factors have been taking place outside church, there has been a change in the philosophy of Christian education within the local church. The postwar baby boom has grown up to be the dominant generation within the church. With this has come an emphasis on adult continuing education. Adult Sunday School classes have taken on a very important role in the church, not only for teaching biblical truth but also for providing the basis for social relationships and spiritual intimacy. The midweek service has declined in importance because of hectic schedules of members of the congregation. Sunday School classes, on the other hand, have increased in importance, providing much of the spiritual support and encouragement which was previously received at a midweek service. Consequently, adults tend to be less likely to volunteer for church service opportunities at a time which would take them away from their own Sunday School classes.

Social Isolation of Teachers. In contrast to the rising social importance of the Sunday School class is the tendency of teaching responsibilities to isolate children's Sunday School teachers from fellowship with the church family. In much the same way that mothers at home encounter frustration over lack of conversations with friends and other adults, teachers may lose contact with their church peer groups. As a result, a teacher may choose to teach a class for only one year and then return to his or her adult class to reestablish some of the friendships which have been "sacrificed."

"Me" Orientation. One of the legacies left to the church by the Vietnam War generation and its concurrent protest movement is the phrase, "I've Gotta Be Me!" The narcissism of the protest movement and drug culture of the 1960s has become an accepted part of life in our culture. Activities in the church have been significantly devalued. The pleasure or satisfaction of the individual has become the standard by which every activity is measured. Thus, if a need for volunteers in the Christian education program is announced, a typical response of the "me" generation, as author Tom Wolfe called it, is "What will I get out of it? What will I have to give up?" rather than "How can we as a church get this task accomplished?

Lack of Theology of Service. In our consumer-oriented society individuals most frequently judge the value of an activity by the personal benefit derived from it. For many, a sense of gratification is derived from receiving the most benefit with the least effort. This worldly attitude has invaded the church to the extent that the value of one's quiet time may be judged on the amount of "blessing" one has gotten out of the devotions. Christ's example of washing His disciples' feet and the lesson of servanthood it embodies seem to have been forgotten.

The "gimme" mind-set has carried over into volunteer ministry in the church. Frequently, a parent will choose not to teach Sunday School until his or her child is old enough to be enrolled in the program. To make sure that the child receives a good Sunday School education, the parent will make a commitment. But the commitment is not to service, it is a commitment to protect one's own interests.

Project Orientation. Long-term commitments may be a thing of the past. Today, people tend to be project oriented. There is a great desire to be able to get into a job, get it done, and go on to the next thing.

The YMCA has discovered in its use of volunteers that many people prefer to volunteer fifty hours of service over a four-week period of time rather than spread it over six months or a year. We've developed a sort of immersion psychology. A businessman is more likely to be willing to commit to a short-term experience of selling Christmas trees for the YMCA, than to teaching a skill to senior citizens once a week for a year. The latter apparently ties up too much time and limits other "project type" commitments that the volunteer might want to make.

The impact of this mind-set on the educational program of the church is clear. A person would generally rather volunteer as a day camp worker or teacher in Vacation Bible School (and exhaust himself/herself in one week of ministry), than make a year-round commitment to teach in the Sunday School program.

Fears. There are many fears associated with taking a volunteer ministry position in a local church. One such fear is the "I'll-never-get-out-of-it" phobia. It is based on the myth of the faithful lady in the Beginner Department who has been teaching for the past twenty years without so much as a year's sabbatical leave. There is no way that the average young adult wants to get locked into a situation like that.

A second fear is the "What-if-the-kids-go-wild?" phobia. Of all the people I have interviewed for teaching positions in childrens' educational programs, this is the most commonly expressed apprehension. Parents may have difficulty in handling their own children, and they wonder how in the world they will be able to control, not one or two, but eight or ten children in a confined classroom area.

The "What-if-they-know-more-than-I-do?" phobia is a third major fear. This is felt many times by the new Christian who is aware of the possibility that children (especially older ones) who attend a Christian day school and thus have been exposed to teaching from the Bible on a daily basis, might be attending the class. The possibility of being embarrassed before all the children of the class sometimes causes discomfort within the potential teacher. Similar fears keep some gifted adults from volunteering to teach adult Sunday School classes.

It Is Someone Else's Job. One of the greatest obstacles to recruitment in the local church is that the responsibility is so freely passed along to other people. The senior pastor expects the pastor of Christian education to do it. The pastor of Christian education expects the recruitment committee to do it. The recruitment committee expects the department superintendents to do it. The department superintendent expects the Sunday School cabinet to do it. The Sunday School cabinet expects the Christian education pastor to do it. The buck is passed from person to person and from group to group. There is very little "ownership" of the responsibility and, therefore, the task too often falls on the already overloaded shoulders of one or two key people.

Vacuum of Prayer. Jesus told His disciples to pray that the Lord of the harvest would send forth workers into His harvest fields (Matt. 9:38). The same need is evident today—the people of the local church need to be praying that God would send forth workers through the teaching and evangelistic programs of the church. Yet too many prayer meetings tend to become more like the hospital auxiliary, unemployment bureau, or counseling center listing the troubled individuals and marriages in need. The importance of these need areas is undeniable, but prayer for them must not overrule fervent intercession for church needs and programs that minister health to the entire body.

In "The Marva Collins Story," the television version of a preparatory school's efforts to provide quality education to disadvantaged black children on the West Side of Chicago, Marva asked a discouraged youngster, "How do you eat an elephant?"

"One bite at a time!" was the child's timid response.

One bite at a time can turn an obnoxious responsibility into a palatable, if not tasty, feast.

*   *   *

Wednesday, Pastor Wilcox invited Jeff to lunch at a local restaurant. Over hot roast beef sandwiches, the senior pastor casually remarked, "That report of yours on recruitment—very interesting stuff."

TWO

Who Does the Recruiting?

Jeff Thompson, the lanky new pastor of Christian education at Walnut Heights Bible Church, squirmed uncomfortably in his chair in the waiting room, pushed his glasses back on his nose with a nervous gesture, and shuffled once again through the sheaf of papers in his manila folder. Two months had flown by since Jeff had joined the "real world" of church ministry. The soft rhythmic clatter of the secretary's electric typewriter punctuated the morning with that "getting-things-done" atmosphere that Pastor Herb Wilcox demanded of all paid staff.

Abruptly, the door to the pastor's office pushed open, and Pastor Wilcox's head poked out, gray eyes twinkling over his granny glasses. "Come in, Jeff," he said. "Let's have a look at what you've worked up. And, Peggy, bring us some coffee, please — and hold all calls during our conference time — excepting my wife, of course."

"Yes, Pastor Wilcox." Like Jeff, the secretary was a relative newcomer and hadn't yet earned the privilege of using the more familiar "Pastor Herb" form of address.

Jeff settled in the overstuffed chair in front of the pastor's desk, smiling his thanks as Peggy handed him a steaming cup of coffee. Pastor Wilcox flipped open Jeff's manila folder, sipped his coffee, and tossed an absentminded "thank you" after his departing secretary. Running a hand through his still thick, wavy, gray-blond hair, the older man mused over the top page, lost in thought. "We've run our education program by personal

26

touch for so long, I can hardly believe there is any other way of doing it."

"There may not be," affirmed Jeff.

Pastor Wilcox cleared his throat and began to read from the paper in front of him. "Educational staff—39 Sunday School teachers, 18 children's church leaders, 20 children's club leaders, 8 youth group sponsors, 8 home Bible study leaders, and 7 committee members and officers. Total—100 volunteer staff members." The pastor let out a low whistle. "Is that all?"

"No, sir. That doesn't include the nursery workers. They're on a separate list—volunteers rotate from month to month."

"You've really done your homework," Pastor Wilcox commented. "Is this a list of current volunteers?"

"Not exactly," Jeff explained. "We'll be losing about a dozen by next fall—four of the ladies are pregnant, six families are moving out of town, and two of the men will be working Sundays. And I'd like to recruit eight more to reduce class sizes."

"So, you'll need to recruit about twenty new volunteers." Pastor Wilcox picked up his pen and began to scrawl a note. "I'll just tell Henrietta we need to 'lean a little' on a few old-timers. We'll get your recruits."

"Please, sir," Jeff offered. "Let me try it my way. I'll have to break in sometime, and it might as well be now."

Pastor Wilcox's eyebrows lifted a notch. "Do you know what you're getting into, Jeff? It's going to take you ten phone calls to find one volunteer. And, because you're new, the people you phone are going to toss questions at you for half an hour before letting you go. That's five hours of phone calls to get a single volunteer, and even then your recruit may be a washout when you speak face-to-face with the person. We're looking at a solid month's work to fill twenty volunteer positions."

"Maybe six weeks," Jeff admitted. "I agree, that's a lot of work—especially when I'm planning to organize a father-and-son canoe trip, participate in summer youth camp, and take a week of vacation with my wife, Rita. If I had to do it all myself, it might never get done—at least not right, anyway."

The senior pastor peered at him over his glasses. "I suppose you have a trick up your sleeve?"

"In a way." Jeff laughed. "I just believe recruitment is everybody's responsibility. I plan on asking for help."

Pastor Wilcox reddened. "I just offered help—and you refused. I really don't understand this at all!"

"No offense intended, Pastor," Jeff said gently. "I realize I was hired to take the recruitment problem off your shoulders, and that ironically I need your help at the same time—as well as assistance from other leaders in the church. But I wanted to know what the Bible had to say about recruiting—so I went back to the drawing board, so to speak.

"It's all in that folder right on your desk." Jeff pointed. "Take your time, Pastor Wilcox. I plan to give copies to members of the Christian Education Committee, and the adult Sunday School teachers too."

Puzzled but curious, the senior pastor turned back to the report on his desk as his young "wet-behind-the-ears" seminary graduate assistant slipped quietly from the room. He began to read the report.

* * *

Recruitment and the Holy Spirit

Though the task of recruiting workers for the educational program may seem overwhelming and at times awesome, the responsibility does not lie with pastors of Christian education alone. The One ultimately in charge of providing workers is the Spirit of God. In fact, three of His major activities in the life of a believer are related to voluntary Christian service.

1. *Filled to Serve.* Following Christ's resurrection, the disciples were told to remain at Jerusalem until they received the Holy Spirit who would empower them to serve as bold witnesses for the kingdom of God (Acts 1:4-8). Later, as Paul writes to the Ephesian church, he reminds them that they are to be filled with the Holy Spirit. This filling will in turn produce a willingness to submit to or serve one another (Eph. 5:18-19, 21).

Perhaps this is why new Christians frequently volunteer to accept teaching positions or work in club programs. The realization of what Christ has done in their lives has so filled them with a sense of joy and responsibility that they are eager to share this news with other people.

2. *Gifted to Serve.* Earlier in this same letter, the Apostle Paul speaks of spiritual gifts that have been given to the church. These gifts have come in the form of uniquely equipped individuals who are able to prepare God's people for their responsibility of building up and strengthening the Christian community (Eph.4:11-13). Though the variety of gifts is better described in 1 Corinthians 12–14, the same emphasis holds true in Paul's letter to the Ephesians: Gifts are for edifying or building up the body of Christ.

A strange mind-set has infected the church in recent years related to the use of spiritual gifts. Instead of accepting gifts as a means to serve other Christians, many people in the local church have assumed a showcase mentality, placing their spiritual gifts on display for other people to see, they fail to touch them. There is much more talk about spiritual gifts in some churches than there is of using them for serving the body of Christ.

The object of spiritual gifts, to build up the body of Christ, was evident in the early church as it was built up in both numbers (quantity) and in spiritual maturity (quality). Today, the Holy Spirit is just as anxious to produce these same results in the local church through the ministries of Spirit-filled and gifted people.

3. *Fruit to Serve.* A third major function of the Holy Spirit is that of producing fruit. The fruit of the Spirit, listed in Galatians 5:22-23, is love, joy, peace, patience, kindness, goodness, faithfulness, gentleness, and self-control. The description of these qualities of Christian living as "fruit" is most fitting. A tree does not bear fruit so it can proudly proclaim that it has grown apples or pears on its branch. Instead, bearing fruit is a process natural to a healthy tree. The fruit is enjoyed, not by the tree itself, but by someone else who has picked the fruit to eat it, to be nourished and strengthened by it.

Fruit is enjoyed most when it comes as a gift. Somehow, our society has reversed that concept. Besides making the possession of the gift more important than the use of the gift, some Christians are writing books about the various fruit of the Spirit as if to proclaim the intrinsic value of the fruit itself. It seems to have been forgotten that the fruit has to be shared, consumed to fulfill its purpose.

The entire context of the passage about the fruit of the Spirit is that of Christian service. "For you," states the Apostle Paul, "were called to freedom, brethren; only do not turn your freedom into an opportunity for the flesh, but through love serve one another" (Gal. 5:13).

The Holy Spirit will be doing His job of recruiting long before the summer recruitment drive begins. The Holy Spirit has always filled certain believers for service; He has gifted them in ways to delight the perceptive pastor or superintendent. At the same time, He has given people within the congregation fruit which they need to give away. These assurances should encourage leaders involved in recruiting volunteers in the local church.

Pastor—Creates Consciousness

In most churches it is the pastor's responsibility to promote a climate in which service is an essential element of Christian living. In some churches, depending on the size, personality, and personal preferences of the pastor, the senior minister may be deeply involved in the recruitment process or occasionally active in the ongoing task. But no matter what the size of the church, the pastor has a vital role in the recruitment process by preaching and teaching from God's Word. In many ways, the teachers of the adult classes within the church share this same responsibility.

There are five primary ways in which the pastor can establish a climate of service through a teaching and preaching ministry.

1. *Teach Service.* Scripture is filled with the mandate to obey God and serve mankind in both the spiritual and physical realms. From Genesis 2, where God places Adam in the Garden of Eden to work it and take care of it, to the Book of Revelation where the churches are told by the messenger from God to repent, the concept of physical and spiritual service dominates Scripture. Thus it becomes the pastor's responsibility, in proclaiming the whole counsel of God, to teach the importance, not only of hearing the Word but of "doing it" as well.

2. *Model Service.* Though it is difficult for the senior pastor to be deeply involved in the educational program, there are many ways to model Christian education before his congregation. A pastor may discuss variety in approaches that teachers may take to a given lesson. One may volunteer to give a devotional, lead

a game time, or explain a hobby in the club program of the church at least once or twice a year. Camp, Vacation Bible School, or some aspect of the music program may provide an opportunity to model commitment to Christian service above and beyond the primary commitment of preaching. The more people see "live" examples of Christian service and not just hear verbal teaching, the more they will be willing to follow this example.

One note of caution. "Modeling" does not mean taking over the responsibility. The ownership and thus the responsibility for the various educational ministries could easily slip onto the shoulders of a pastor merely attempting to model what he was teaching. This would only serve to frustrate both the pastor and ultimately the educational staff.

3. *Illustrate Service.* A senior pastor once commented, "The last person to speak to me before I go on the platform is likely to get quoted." It was not that he would go to the pulpit unprepared, for he was extremely articulate and spoke without notes. He was, however, wise enough to make use of fresh illustrations even if he had not previously planned to do so. Therefore, from time to time, the Christian education pastor would feed him appropriate information just before a given service so that he, in turn, could share the joy of the educational ministry through current illustrations of what God had been doing.

This desire to know and to share what has been happening should be widely understood throughout the church. In many churches the only reason volunteer group leaders phone the pastor is to discuss or report something negative. People in educational ministries should share the positive experiences of their ministry with their pastors—testimonies about what God has been doing in their departments. Pastors can then find ways to share this, whether from the pulpit, in small group discussions, or with the church board. Any way it is done, the affirmation and encouragement which come as a result of successful accounts of ministry will make the process of recruitment easier throughout the church.

4. *Feature Service.* A pastor who is a vital part of the recruitment process will frequently provide opportunities for people to testify as to what has been happening in their areas of ministry. Testimonies can be a vital part of the congregational life as

people share the joys and sometimes the agonies of ministering within a fellowship. The Christian Education Committee and board members need to be exposed to the life-changing events which happen as a result of the policies and financial support which they have provided. Congregational business meetings can be turned into times of celebration as the harvest from a year of labor is surveyed and then dedicated to the Lord.

5. *Stimulate Service.* In most churches the pastor is the person who is most attuned to the spiritual gifts which have been granted to the church. He can watch the gifts bud, bloom, and mature in the lives of his parishioners. As he sees these gifts as well as the fruit of the Spirit mature, he can use his influence to stretch an individual in growing. It is much like a high school football coach who sees potential in the spindly form of a freshman quarterback; the trained eye of the coach sees confidence, ability to throw accurately, a quick sure hand, and agility amid the rush of opposing linemen. The coach will then refine this raw talent and work to bring it to maturity. Similarly, the pastor, because of trained sensitivities, has the opportunity to single out and develop leadership from within the congregation to recruit the best people for service within the local church.

Pastor of Christian Education—Guides the Gifted

The pastor of Christian education has the potentially most rewarding position within the church staff. It is an opportunity to work with the congregation in order to discover its spiritual gifts and ministry preferences. Then he or she has the privilege of providing places of service to these people whom God has prepared for ministry. For the CE pastor to accomplish this task, six distinct functions must be handled in either a formal or informal manner.

1. *Understand People-Needs.* Before the CE pastor can begin recruiting and placing workers, one must understand the needs of the congregation and which of those can be met through the Christian education ministry. A distinction needs to be made at this point. When we speak of needs, we are not referring to positions which need to be filled (though that must be kept clearly in mind). Instead we are talking of the "people-needs" which are crying out for help, support, and teaching.

People-needs may refer to the sparks that are ignited when a certain class of junior high boys comes together. They may refer to the basics of our faith which a new believer desires to learn and understand. People-needs may refer to a challenge from a loving adult which will result in a vibrant Christian witness on the campus of the local community college. Whatever these people-needs are, the pastor of Christian education has the responsibility to know them before he or she can effectively recruit people to meet those needs.

2. *Discover Gifts of Believers.* A person with a knowledge of people-needs and no knowledge of how to meet those needs will be frustrated. Most ministers have experienced this at one time or other because their sensitivity to needs far exceeds the recognition of spiritual gifts within the congregation. Thus it becomes the responsibility of the pastor (or director) of Christian education, and in some cases the superintendent of the Sunday School, to be constantly watching for the manifestation of gifts, even in embryonic fashion, among the parishioners.

The recognition of gifts also implies personal conversations *with* people, discussing their inclinations for service, and *about* people, discussing the emerging manifestations of gifts which may have not been discovered by the Christians who possess them.

Perceptive pastors and Christian leaders find that the Holy Spirit provides gifted people to meet every spiritual need which He desires to have met at a given time. The problem of recruitment comes, not because of a lack of appropriate people, but because we have not activated the resources which God has provided in the local church.

3. *Connect Gifts with Needs.* This is not a rush process. Nor is the task accomplished in one short recruitment push in late summer or early fall. The introduction process is as delicate as that of introducing your daughter to your best friend's nephew who has just returned from his second year in college. You want to create the opportunity for a relationship to develop without pushing so hard as to destroy the possibility.

It's almost as if the pastor of Christian education is merely a spokesman for God, a provider of information, and a resource for people who desire spiritual development.

4. *Interview Volunteers.* It is very important for the pastor of

Christian education to interview volunteers before placing them in ministry positions for two primary reasons. First, the pastor needs to have as thorough a knowledge of the volunteer staff as possible to wisely place each person in need-meeting positions. Second, the CE pastor needs to understand the expectations and fears of the volunteer in order to assure her that her expectations will be met and that support will be available to handle those aspects of the ministry which generate apprehension.

5. *Assign Workers.* When the needs of individuals in the congregation and the gifts of the volunteer are clearly understood, no one in the congregation is better equipped to assign the person to a job than the pastor of Christian education. He may choose to solicit the assistance of a church committee to broaden his insights, but since he is functioning as the executive director of the Christian education program he is ultimately responsible for the placement and (if necessary) the removal of volunteers in ministry. Any system which removes the responsibility of placement from the CE pastor is either compensating for deficiencies in that pastor or tying his hands. Neither should ever occur.

6. *Cultivate Continued Gift Development.* Once a person has been placed in a ministry, that does not end the relationship between the pastor of Christian education and that volunteer. In fact, in some ways the relationship needs to grow stronger as the pastor of Christian education continues to assist his or her coworkers in developing and perfecting their gifts and ministry preferences. A note of encouragement after a firsthand classroom observation, an article on an area of interest relating to one's spiritual gifts, the suggestion of a workshop to attend or resource person to be sought out, are all ways which can contribute to the development of a Christian education worker.

The implications of the Christian education pastor's responsibilities are twofold. First, one needs to be out among the people discovering needs and gifts, asking questions, making observations, listening, supporting. The pastor of Christian education who expects to work from the office and dictate orders, write creative bulletin announcements, and develop programs on paper will rarely succeed in recruitment.

Second, the CE pastor should remain in the same church for several years, at least. No matter how hard he works, he will

34

never be able to discover the needs of the people in one or two years. Gift potential is similarly hard to detect on a one-shot basis. Insights are gathered slowly and pieced together as a person matures, not only in his spiritual life but also in his physical and mental capacities. Putting all of this together, the pastor of Christian education who succeeds in recruitment will become most effective when he has spent a number of years discovering needs, identifying gifts, and introducing the people who possess them.

Christian Education Committee—Monitors the Ministry

The Christian Education Committee need not be actively involved in the recruitment process except on an informal or task-related basis. As individuals, the committee members will probably want to participate in the recruitment process, but they are not the ones who are primarily responsible for the task.

In fact, if the Christian Education Committee members become active in the recruitment process it can become a negative reward system. By this I mean a person can be asked to do one job (serve on the CE Committee) and when he does a good job as a committee member he is "rewarded" with a second job, that of recruiting new volunteer staff members. This negative reward system frequently assures that neither one of the jobs will be done well and that frustrations may set in as the committee members feel overwhelmed by the responsibilities placed on them.

There are, however, specific responsibilities which the Christian Education Committee can and should shoulder as a group and as individuals.

1. *Monitor Needs and Personnel.* One of the responsibilities of the Christian Education Committee is to know what is happening in the education program. Because the volunteer staff members are so vital to the ministry process, it is important that the committee members know the concerns and joys of the ministry.

Prayer should be a vital ministry of the committee. As they pray for needs to be met through people they should also assure their volunteer staff that specific prayer requests are being remembered each time the committee meets.

2. *Continually Look for Gifted People.* The Christian Education

Committee is the eyes and the ears of a CE pastor. Just as he is looking for gifted people and unmet needs, the committee should be doing the same thing. The use of specific gifts should be encouraged by committee members; ideas of which person should be sought to meet a specific need should be passed along to be acted on by the pastor of Christian education through the channels he has set up.

3. *Individually Plant Seed Thoughts.* A person does not cease to be a committee member once she leaves a committee meeting. Her function merely changes. Instead of making policy she becomes an advocate for Christian education. One of the best ways to do this is by planting seed thoughts in the minds of people who attend the church.

A seed thought is an idea or suggestion made at an appropriate time in a loving manner. "Have you ever thought of teaching?"/"You're really gifted with adults."/"What do you think your ministry is going to be during the coming year?"/"You are really skilled with your hands. Have you ever thought of working in our Media-Resource Center?" These and many other comments might be dropped into a conversation laying the groundwork for someone to approach that same person at a later date with a specific ministry in mind.

4. *Approve Financial Resources.* Recruitment is usually made much easier when the recruiter can assure a volunteer that the church has provided resources to assist in equipping new teachers and leaders through training workshops and seminars.

Adequate equipment and supplies either purchased by the church or reimbursed from the Christian education budget let a new teacher know that he or she is considered important by the leadership of the church. The Christian education budget should make room for curricular material and also for equipment, supplies, awards, supplementary materials, honorariums for outside resource people, and a multitude of variations within these categories.

5. *Affirm Existing Staff.* Two primary factors will encourage a teacher to continue with his teaching responsibility — achievement and affirmation. Achievement means that a person feels as if he is doing a good job. This feeling may be based on the fact that he has done everything that is in his job description as a teacher of fourth-grade boys during a given year. It may be based

on the fact that one or more of his students have made a profession of faith during the time he was their teacher. It may be based on the nonverbal cues given by students in class.

The second important factor is that of affirmation. People need to be patted on the back while doing the Lord's work. Some churches provide a recognition dinner at the end of the year to which all of the teaching staff are invited free of charge. Other Sunday Schools recognize certain individuals as teacher, superintendent, or club leader of the year as a way of affirming outstanding work.

By whatever means it is done, the Christian Education Committee should be among the most aggressive "affirmers" in the church.

Department Leaders and Teachers—Sharing the Satisfaction

To avoid the negative reward system, as in the case of the Christian Education Committee, the teaching staff should not be made primarily responsible for recruitment within the Christian education program. However, there is nothing quite so compelling as the person who is excited about his or her ministry opportunities and wants others to share in the joy of ministry. Thus the department leaders and teachers have the following responsibilities.

1. *Share the Satisfactions of Teaching.* The more people in the church hear about the joys of ministry both from the pulpit and from the teaching staff, the easier it will be to find volunteers to be part of this ongoing ministry. Though it may sound crass, everybody loves a winner—person, ministry, or program. As a teaching staff talks about the lives that have been touched through the educational ministry of the church, people will want to become part of that ministry.

2. *Direct People to the Pastor of Christian Education.* There is a tendency for the sincerely interested volunteer to become a recruitment and placement committee all combined in one. Despite any advantages there may be in capitalizing on a person's enthusiasm to recruit others to work with them, the pastor of Christian education needs to retain the responsibility and control of placement. It is quite possible that as he interviews a person recently recruited by an excited teacher, he will discover

this person's talents might be better used somewhere else in the church. The insight that the CE pastor can provide may insure a longer and more meaningful period of service to the body of Christ.

It is the responsibility of each teacher to direct new recruits to the pastor of Christian education who will, in turn, place people in ministry situations which will maximize the use of their spiritual gifts.

3. *Work to Make the Teaching Team Effective.* If each Sunday School teacher is working only for himself and is not attempting to be part of the teaching team to which he has been assigned, isolation will occur. The only factor which would keep the teaching team together would be their common concern for the children they teach. Consequently, there would come a drifting apart and a lack of mutual support and encouragement.

By contrast, the teaching team members who work together and support one another find that there is little turnover in their departments. Consequently, there is no need to recruit new workers as often for those departments. Also, a loving family atmosphere is created which becomes attractive to new or potential teachers.

Personnel Committee — Contacts the Congregation

A Personnel Committee may be formed either as an ad hoc committee which serves for a limited period of time to survey the congregation or as a standing committee which is constantly assisting the pastor of Christian education in the recruitment process. The committee should be composed of people who are gifted in interpersonal relationships and are willing to take the time to talk with people — on the phone, face-to-face, in informal settings, or by personal appointment.

The responsibilities of the Personnel Committee, however, are fairly straightforward. They include the following.

1. *Survey Every Active Member of the Church.* For the most part this will mean making phone calls to the adults in the church on a systematic basis. The object of these phone calls is merely to discover what area of ministry people foresee for themselves in the coming year.

Contrary to what might be imagined, most people greatly

appreciate a phone call and are willing to talk about the needs of the church and their own areas of interest.

2. *Explain Needs to Interested People.* If a person is to effectively explain the needs of the education program, the CE pastor, director of Christian education, or the Sunday School superintendent will need to provide that information to Personnel Committee members. With that in hand, the Personnel Committee members can be on the lookout for specific types of people who can meet specific types of needs.

3. *Direct Pastor of Christian Education to Contact Interested People.* Once the interest has been discovered, that information needs to be passed along to the pastor of Christian education as quickly as possible so that appropriate interviews may be set up prior to the waning of the initial interest. Thus the committee members need to touch base with the CE pastor at least once a week and, at times, more frequently than that.

Membership Committee—Challenges the Committed

As people join the church there is a tendency to merely put their names on the church roll; they then do nothing more than show up for church and drop a few dollars in the offering plate. Many churches recognize this problem and require candidates for membership to go through a formal membership process during which they are informed of the needs within the church that could be met by their gifts and talents. Thus the Membership Committee has the following responsibilities in the recruitment process.

1. *Interview Applicants.* As individuals on the Membership Committee interview applicants for membership, certain characteristics, talents, and areas of interest tend to emerge in the conversation. These impressions may then give the committee members opportunity to ask further questions.

2. *Information Regarding Past Service.* Indicators which may provide clues leading to the recruitment of new members as volunteer staff include the areas in which they have previously served both inside the church and in the community. A list of these experiences and any related training should be noted.

The fact that a person has served in a position does not necessarily indicate current interest. It is wise to ask the question, "Where do you see yourself ministering as a member of this congregation?" The question is broad enough to allow potential members to start a new direction in ministry or continue on a proven path of service.

3. *Forward Information to Pastor of Christian Education.* It is important that this information be fed as rapidly as possible to the person most knowledgeable about the recruitment process. Though there may be no immediate openings in the education program, the CE pastor needs to begin the process of building a relationship with these new members in the areas of their interests and to assist them in developing their spiritual gifts.

Conclusion

It is obvious that the recruiting of volunteer staff in the local church is everyone's responsibility. But not everyone has the same responsibility. Just as the various gifts within the body of Christ complement each other to make a healthy and well-developed body, so the various functions within the recruitment process are necessary so the educational ministries of the church are adequately staffed at all times.

If the CE pastor has to do all the recruiting on his own, the job may never get done, or he might find himself so burned out and "people tired" that he will lose the joy and satisfaction of seeing people volunteer to serve.

With this larger picture in mind, we can go on to look at specific areas of recruitment and some of the tools which can be used to make recruitment of volunteers in the local church an effective and happy process.

*   *   *

Pastor Herb Wilcox sipped his now cold coffee and shook his head. "Lord," he prayed, "if that young man You've sent me can handle something this complex, I am grateful. If he can't, please give him a hand. Amen. But for me to use the pulpit to advertise his program — that's another story, Lord. I'll have to think about that one."

THREE

Recruitment Calendar:
A Game Plan

The honeymoon was over. The first six months of Jeff's ministry had been an unexpected joy. The people of the Walnut Heights Bible Church had responded with enthusiasm to the creative ideas and spiritual insights of their resourceful young pastor of Christian education.

The Winter Institute of the Bible attended by eighty-seven adults for four consecutive Wednesday nights in the freezing cold weather surprised even Pastor Wilcox. The Volunteer Ministry Recognition Dinner had been another well-received innovation. Abandoning the traditional potluck dinner in the church fellowship hall, for which members of the congregation showed little enthusiasm, Jeff persuaded three church businessmen to pick up the tab at a luxurious restaurant.

Other successes were in the works. Vacation Bible School was staffed and organized with a week remaining before the public school year was to close. More registrations for summer day camp had poured in than any of the staff could remember. Even Winifred Doyle was pleased because Jeff had personally painted her classroom the pale sunshine yellow she had selected.

So, the honeymoon was over. All of these accomplishments were merely a prelude to the major organizational and recruiting tasks Jeff now faced. Thelma Packsma had resigned from the four- and five-year-old department because of summer plans. Gloria Benner, department leader of the junior teaching group, was expecting any time now and did not intend to resume her responsibilities until the baby was out of diapers. That was only the tip of the iceberg.

Rick and Marian Fantozzi decided to move to Michigan; Johnny Banks returned to school; Henry and Debbie Forcash wanted to take a sabbatical after eleven years in the Junior High Department; and so the saga continued, seemingly with every ring of the phone. It was as if everyone had waited for the breaking in of the new pastor of Christian education to bail out en masse.

It was time for Jeff to develop and implement his game plan, preceded by a great deal of prayer. "With men it is impossible, but not with God," he found himself repeating, "for with God all things are possible."

The telephone was his deliverance. Calls were placed to seminary buddies, former professors, the Christian education director under whom he had interned, and four or five people who were only names on publicity pieces for Sunday School conferences. The phone seemed to become part of his ear as he asked repeatedly, "How in the world can I recruit all the volunteer staff I need for this summer and the coming school year?"

People talked. Ideas gelled. Bits and pieces began to come together.

Gradually a strategy developed—a game plan. The game plan wasn't perfect and had to be revised and amended from time to time, but at least it was a start on a systematic approach to recruiting volunteers. Gradually, Jeff began to feel it was going to work. The anxiety began to subside, and he told his wife, "I finally feel the Lord's giving me a handle on this job."

The following calendar is a summary of Jeff's game plan. It isn't the plan Jeff implemented in those early months of ministry, but reflects the surviving elements of his strategy with the "wheat separated from the tares." (Later chapters will explain in detail how each element of the plan works.)

RECRUITMENT CALENDAR

PURPOSE
To outline a year-long, step-by-step approach to the recruitment of volunteer workers.

OUTLINE
September
1. Time and Talent Campaign (see chapter 4)
   a. Letters
   b. Brochure
   c. Publicity in bulletin and church newsletter
   d. Messages from pastor
   e. Service features during morning worship service focusing on specific ministries
2. Continue meeting with *ad hoc* recruitment group but conclude meetings by midmonth (see chapter 7)
3. Begin Teacher Aid Program training for junior and senior high students who want to teach
4. Promote training program
5. Follow up on registration cards (see chapter 5)
   a. Phone call
   b. Set up interview
   c. Ask to attend training program
   d. Place in departments when appropriate
6. Follow up on new membership Ministry Questionnaires (see chapter 6)
7. Rhoda's Band (see chapter 8)

October
1. Time and Talent campaign (see chapter 4)
   a. Have faith promise responses put on computer printout.
   b. Have computer print address labels for each person who responds.
   c. Send letter of appreciation to each person not presently involved in the education program, asking them to call the Christian education office for an interview with the CE Pastor.
   d. Phone all new volunteers who do not respond to the above letter (c.) and schedule appointments with the Pastor of Christian Education.
2. Follow up on registration cards (see chapter 5)
   a. Phone call
   b. Set up interview
   c. Direct to January training program
   d. Place in departments when appropriate

3. Follow up on new membership Ministry Questionnaires (see chapter 6)
   Follow steps b., c., d. from number 2 above
4. Promote training program
5. Service feature on club program (see chapter 9)
6. Begin work on volunteer recognition dinner
   a. Establish means of paying for dinner
   b. Secure speaker

November

1. Follow up on registration cards (see chapter 5)
   Follow steps in number 2 above
2. Follow up on new membership Ministry Questionnaires (see chapter 6)
   Follow steps b., c., d. from October #2
3. Feature church-time ministries in a bulletin feature and Sunday service interview (see chapter 9)
4. Service feature on early childhood ministries

December

1. Time and Talent campaign (see chapter 4)
   a. Complete appointments with new volunteers with CE Pastor
   b. Send letter to all new volunteers and new members inviting them to attend an educational training program in January
2. Follow up on registration cards (see chapter 5)
   Follow steps from October #2
3. Follow up on new membership Ministry Questionnaires (see chapter 6)
   Follow steps b., c., d. from October #2

January

1. Hold educational training program for all volunteers and new members not already involved in the educational program
2. Publicize educational training program (see chapter 9)
   a. Bulletin insert
   b. Church newsletter
   c. Pulpit announcements

3. Follow up registration cards (see chapter 5)
    a. Phone call
    b. Set up interview
    c. Direct to April training program
    d. Place in departments when appropriate
4. Follow up new membership Ministry Questionnaires (see chapter 6)
    a. Set up interview
    b. Direct to April training program
    c. Place in departments when appropriate
5. Service feature on youth ministries
6. Establish committee to plan volunteer recognition dinner

February
1. Placement of newly trained volunteers (see chapter 10)
    a. Observation in departments
    b. Establish permanent substitute teachers for departments
    c. Place teachers where appropriate
2. Follow up on registration cards (see chapter 5)
    Follow steps from January #3
3. Follow up on new membership Ministry Questionnaires (see chapter 6)
    Follow steps from January #4
4. Select director for VBS and/or day camp
5. Service feature on children's ministries (see chapter 9)
6. Secure restaurant for volunteer recognition dinner

March
1. Prayer support month in Christian education (see chapter 8)
    a. Distribute prayer sheets to all adult classes on a weekly basis
    b. Use the services of the church to expose people to need for prayer support for the various educational ministries
        —joys
        —needs
        —requests
2. Follow up on registration cards (see chapter 5)
    Follow steps from January #3
3. Follow up new membership Ministry Questionnaires (see chapter 6)

Follow steps a., b., c., from January #4
4. Summer staff recruitment
    a. Select departmental superintendents for VBS and/or day camp
    b. Send out letter to all volunteers from last year's VBS
5. Publicity on VBS and/or day camp
6. Rhoda's Band (see chapter 8)

April
1. Establish *ad hoc* recruitment group by midmonth (see chapter 7)
    a. Purpose: To recruit staff for summer and fall ministries
    b. Meet weekly with committee members for reports and assignments
    c. Interview all personnel recruited by committee
    d. Continue meeting until all positions are filled
2. Hold educational training program similar to that in January
3. Follow up on registration cards (see chapter 5)
    Follow steps from January #3
4. Follow up on new membership Ministry Questionnaires (see chapter 6)
    Follow steps from January #4
5. Recruit club leaders for all clubs
6. Send out Christian education evaluation letter to superintendents (see chapter 11)
7. Present Christian education media presentation in evening service (see chapter 9)
8. Complete plans for volunteer recognition dinner

May
1. Continue meeting with *ad hoc* recruitment group until positions are filled (see chapter 7)
2. Training program for club leaders
3. Follow up on registration cards (see chapter 5)
    a. Phone call
    b. Set up interview
    c. Ask to attend training program in fall
    d. Place in departments when appropriate
4. Follow up on new membership Ministry Questionnaires (see chapter 6)

Follow steps b., c., d. from May #3
5. Publicity on summer ministry
6. Training for VBS/day camp personnel
7. Hold volunteer appreciation dinner

June
1. Continue meeting with *ad hoc* recruitment group until positions are filled (see chapter 7)
2. Follow up on registration cards (see chapter 5)
   Follow steps from May #3
3. Follow up on new membership Ministry Questionnaires (see chapter 6)
   Follow steps b., c., d. from May #3
4. Rhoda's Band (see chapter 8)

July
1. Continue meeting with *ad hoc* recruitment group until positions are filled (see chapter 7)
2. Follow up on registration cards (see chapter 5)
   Follow steps from May #3
3. Follow up on new membership Ministry Questionnaires (see chapter 6)
   Follow steps b., c., d. from May #3

August
1. Continue meeting with *ad hoc* recruitment group until positions are filled (see chapter 7)
2. Publicity on recruitment (see chapter 9)
3. Service feature during morning worship service
4. Message(s) from pastor on ministry through Christian education (see chapter 2)
4. Follow up on registration cards (see chapter 5)
   Follow steps from May #3
4. Follow up on new membership Ministry Questionnaires (see chapter 6)
   Follow steps b., c., d. from May #3

FOUR

Time and Talent Search

Jeff managed a quick "hello" to Peggy and ignored her look of surprise as he barged into Pastor Wilcox's office without knocking. She still was not used to the impetuousness of the former college athlete and big man on campus. Herb Wilcox, half-dozing in his swivel chair, sat up with a start, straightened his necktie and managed a patient if slightly annoyed smile. "What can I do for you, Jeff?" His voice held an edge of uncertainty, understandably evoked by his assistant pastor's brash entry.

"Pastor, I need your help," Jeff began. "You know this Time and Talent Campaign we've been discussing; I think it would be great if you would kick it off from the pulpit."

Herb Wilcox took a deep breath and stared out his office window at the big broadleaf oak tree next to the nursery building. "I appreciate the energetic approach to your job, Jeff—I really do. But, you were hired to run the Christian education ministry, and I thought you were going to take the recruitment responsibilities off my back. Frankly, I can't see how that's being accomplished with you tossing the ball back to me."

Undismayed, Jeff pushed his glasses back onto his nose and continued. "Sir, it's just that the congregation needs to know you're behind it, that it's not some flash-in-the-pan idea I cooked up to see if we could get some nibblers to try it out. They need to know how important it is and why."

The senior pastor swiveled his chair around to face his young colleague. "Have you considered the possibility that the Sunday worship service might be too valuable in the spiritual feeding of the flock to sacrifice to a commercial or series of commercials for any special project?"

"Yes, sir—I have," Jeff said. "I know how they need to be fed, and I have a tremendous respect for your sermons. But they need to know more about feeding each other too. All I ask is that you think about it, sir."

The problem, Jeff decided on his way home, was that his senior colleague of seven months didn't have an adequate understanding of what a Time and Talent Campaign was all about. To work right, it had to be a concentrated exposure of the congregation to biblical teaching about the use of natural talents and spiritual gifts in the local church. They needed to know there were varied opportunities for each person to make a commitment for service for the coming year.

Actually, there was a second more subtle problem. An inadequate understanding on the part of the church decision-makers of the biblical concept of every believer serving had caused the concept not to be emphasized in teaching. Though the CE Committee had enthusiastically endorsed the Time and Talent Campaign, the church board had to appropriate the extra funds for printing and postage costs. They also would field the flack that was bound to come from the Harley Jenkins faction within the church for tampering with the morning worship service. Thus, Jeff had a low-key campaign to launch, starting with Pastor Wilcox and concluding with key members of the church board.

The minicrusade began with Jeff casually raising hypothetical questions in private conversations with Pastor Wilcox and—later—two influential board members:

● "What needs do we have that are going unmet?"
● "To what extent are these needs a result of insufficient personnel?"
● "To what extent do you think our people are aware of the biblical teachings about stewardship as it applies to the use of time and talents as well as financial resources?"
● "Do you think that biblically sound sermons on the subject would assist the board in ministering to the needs now going unmet?"
● "Who would be the best person in the church to address these subjects?"

These questions obviously steered the discussion in a specific direction. In actual conversation, however, it wasn't so easy to toss them out so cleanly, or lay them end to end. But, each time Jeff was able to weave some of the questions into dialogues. In fact, his persistently suggesting Pastor Wilcox as the ideal voice to present these thoughts to the congregation tended to cement staff relationships and raise the board's opinion of their pastoral team. In a private meeting in his office, Pastor Wilcox told Jeff the idea was sound, and he would cooperate wholeheartedly.

The following month, the series of messages began, drawn from the gift passages in 1 Corinthians 12–14. Pastor Wilcox emphasized that every believer is gifted, and that every gift provided by the Holy Spirit is designed to be given away.

The Time and Talent series was well received by the congregation, and a respectable number of people began ministering within the church for the first time. However, as the pastoral team evaluated the response, two weaknesses became evident.

"The messages just weren't that practical," admitted Pastor Wilcox. "They were Bible-based but not well related to life — at least not the lives of our people." It was an honest confession — and he was right. The illustrations used were about other churches in different times. What was needed were current illustrations from the lifeblood of Walnut Heights Bible Church.

The second weakness was identified by Jeff's wife, Rita. "The girls in my Bible study group don't know how to respond to Pastor Herb's messages," commented Rita one night at the dinner table. "They're too fuzzy — too abstract. Most don't know what actual needs might be met through their services in the church. Some of the girls are feeling really guilty for not volunteering and frustrated because they don't know what they'd be volunteering for."

As Jeff thought about Rita's comment, the truth was apparent. He wasn't one to volunteer carte blanche for something that vague either. He wanted a fairly clear picture of what was involved before he'd commit himself. How could he expect others to blindly go for something still so much up in the air?

From these two observations, a thoughtful, mature, and highly successful Time and Talent Campaign emerged the following year. Dynamic Sunday morning messages presented the biblical basis for Christian service while Sunday evenings Pastor Wilcox laid out specific areas of ministry within the church fellowship. The following items proved to be the primary ingredients in the commitment drive:

1. Biblical messages, appropriately illustrated from the body life of Walnut Heights Bible Church, on a Theology of Service.

2. Personal testimonies from people who had experienced the joy of serving.

3. Slide features of ministries which deserved to be highlighted.

4. A list of all known service opportunities and who to contact for more information.

5. A commitment brochure printed and mailed to every person who attended the church during the previous year.

6. A definite Commitment Sunday, publicized well in advance, when commitment brochures would be collected and ministries would start functioning.

The following outline is a description of the Walnut Heights Time and Talent Commitment Campaign as it developed in the years that followed. Also included are samples of materials used to raise the awareness of the congregation in the area of use of talents in serving.

TIME AND TALENT COMMITMENT CAMPAIGN
Outline of Steps

WHEN?	BY WHOM?	WHAT?
During winter months	Church Board	• Examine and adopt the concept of a Time and Talent Commitment Campaign. • Adopt a theme for drive. • Establish a budget for drive. • Set dates for drive.
During spring months	Photographer	• Take color slides of the activities of the church in which volunteers participate (focus on close-up pictures — no more than two or three people in a picture). • Take similar black-and-white pictures which can be used in the brochure.
	Pastor of Christian Education	• Create a Time and Talent Commitment brochure and lay it out in rough copy. • Select a prayer chairman who will organize special prayer meetings for the actual dates of the Time and Talent Commitment Campaign.
Early summer	Editor: Church newsletter	• Announce dates of the Time and Talent Commitment Campaign in the fall (see page 56).
	Pastor of Christian Education	• Compile a list of known service opportunities in the church and the name of the person to contact for more information about those ministries (pages 57–61).
	Pastor	• Plan the major themes of messages. • Discuss themes with the CE pastor to allow him to coordinate service features and testimonies with messages.

WHEN?	BY WHOM?	WHAT?
Late summer	Pastor	• Write a letter to the congregation which will introduce the Time and Talent Commitment Campaign and provide the brochure as a means of response (pages 64–65).
	Pastor of Christian Education	• Finalize brochure and have it printed. • Secure volunteers to stuff letters and brochures into envelopes. • Put together a slide-tape presentation (preferably programmed with two projectors and a dissolve unit) of volunteers in action to be used during the drive. • Select and contact volunteers from the previous year to testify of the joy of Christian service during the drive.
	Prayer Chairman	• Organize prayer groups and meeting times. (It is desirable to do this in conjunction with the existing structure within the church.)
Last week before drive	Pastor of Christian Education	• Mail letters from pastor to congregation. • Confirm various elements of drive. • Announce Time and Talent Commitment Campaign from the pulpit and through the bulletin. • Recruit volunteers to tabulate the commitment responses so that the information will be readily available throughout the rest of the year. (A computer printout may be quicker and more useful.)

WHEN?	BY WHOM?	WHAT?
		• Identify all unfilled volunteer ministry positions in the church.
		• Notify prayer chairman of existing ministry needs.
	Prayer Chairman	• Distribute information about existing ministry needs to prayer groups.
		• Distribute names of existing volunteers to prayer groups for praise and intercession.
During drive	Pastor	• Preach sermons on Time and Talent Commitment.
		• Use testimonies and slide presentations in the services.
	Pastor of Christian Education	• Distribute lists of known volunteer service opportunities.
		• Distribute additional Time and Talent Commitment brochures at the church services during the drive.
During drive	Prayer Chairman	• Keep in contact with all prayer groups and notify them of answers to prayer as volunteer ministry positions are filled.
	Editor: Church Newsletter	• Feature article on the Time and Talent Commitment Campaign (see page 62–63).
	Bulletin	• Insert one-page articles concerning service into the bulletin (see pages 66–67 for examples).
	Elders	• Collect commitment brochures on Commitment Sunday (the last Sunday).
First week after drive	Pastor	• Send form letters to people who responded, thanking them for

WHEN?	BY WHOM?	WHAT?
		their commitment to ministry. Two letters should be used, one going to those who are continuing in ministry and the other going to those who are new to volunteer ministry (see pages 70–71).
	Pastor of Christian Education	• Look through commitment brochures to discover people volunteering for ministries where help is needed immediately. • Set up interviews for each person who is new to the volunteer ministry of the church (see chapter 5). • Begin process of getting all of the responses listed (manually or by computer) according to the areas of ministry for which they volunteered.
Following weeks	Pastor of Christian Education	• Continue interview and placement process until all new volunteers have been placed or directed into more productive areas of ministry. • Notify current volunteer leadership (superintendents, head usher, club leaders, etc.) of volunteers for their areas of ministry.

EARLY SUMMER NEWSLETTER

NEWSLETTER

Walnut Heights Bible Church

2315 Walnut Road, Wheeling, IL 60090
708-555-1234

COMMITMENT CAMPAIGN ANNOUNCED

"Hands of Time . . . and Eternity" is the theme of the Time and Talent Commitment Campaign scheduled for the last three weeks in September. The announcement was made by Board Chairman Jonathan Honeycut following the June board meeting.

The Time and Talent Commitment Campaign will include: (1) messages by Pastor Herb Wilcox related to the theme; (2) special prayer meetings asking the Lord to prepare the hearts of the congregation for a new year of service; (3) special features in the church services focusing on the various ways in which needs are being met through Walnut Heights Bible Church; and (4) a special service of commitment when each member and active attender of the church will be asked to present time and talents to the Lord.

"It is our aim," commented Pastor Wilcox, "to have every person in the congregation make a commitment of time and talent, no matter how great or small, for the coming year as a result of the "Hands of Time . . . and Eternity" Commitment Campaign.

SERVICE OPPORTUNITIES HANDOUT

Service Opportunities

The number and variety of opportunities available at our church make it possible for everyone interested to find a niche to use their time and talent in the Lord's service. Consider this list carefully and then contact the person designated as contact person in your area of interest.

A. **Pastoral**

Shepherding Ministries. Monthly contacts with an assigned group of people. Contacts may be made at church, at home, or on the telephone. Hospital visitation, and/or notifying pastors of individuals with needs. *Contact:*

Adult Class Officer. Elected positions in all Sunday School classes. Encouraging class members, planning events, choosing curriculum, and planning the direction of the class in terms of teaching and support functions. *Contact:*

Counseling: Lay/Certified. If you possess a degree or experience in long-range counseling, the pastoral staff would be interested in possibly making referrals to you. *Contact:*

B. **Evangelistic**

Jail Ministry. Visiting inmates, leading Bible studies, counseling, encouraging men in the county jail. *Contact:*

Neighborhood Bible Studies. Reaching out to neighbors through an evangelistic Bible study. *Contact:*

2:7 Discipleship Training. An opportunity to learn how to apply Christian principles in your life and pass them on to others. *Contact:*

Church Visitor Visitation. Visit people new to our church in their homes and welcome them to Walnut Heights Bible Church. *Contact:*

C. **Teaching**

Sunday School (all ages). Always looking for new and additional teachers and substitutes. Commitment is on a yearly basis and curriculum is provided. *Contact:*

High School Core Group Leaders. Meet during the week with a small group of high school students and involve them in Bible study. *Contact:*

Day Camp Counselors. Day camp meets for one to two weeks each summer. Activities, Bible studies, missions, and taking trips to various places make up each day's activities. A counselor is in charge of a small group (up to ten) of children from one age-group.
Contact:

Awana Council-time Leader. People who enjoy giving object lessons, and/or short talks to boys and girls. Age-level varies from K-8. Involvement varies from one week to two months.
Contact:

Women's Bible Studies. There are many women's Bible studies meeting throughout the week. They are always looking for teachers who would be willing to come in for a specified time and lead their studies.
Contact:

D. **Christian Education**
(Administrative and Support Ministries)
Long-range planning. Individuals with vision, educational insights, and knowledge in the area of planning.
Contact:

Christian Education Committee. Meets monthly to establish policy, make and review decisions, and help determine direction for the CE program for all ages.
Contact:

Sunday School Department Leader. Responsible for leading a group of teachers in working together in effective teaching of a specific group of children.
Contact:

Awana Club Director. Same type responsibilities as above, except meets on Wednesday evenings under the Awana format.
Contact:

Sunday School Age-Group Coordinator. Oversees and evaluates children's area Sunday School departments. Assists in recruitment of teachers and encourages leaders and teachers in their ministries.
Contact:

Day Camp Director/Assistant Director. Works in planning the program, all parts and pieces of curriculum, and in training counselors and junior counselors.
Contact:

Media/Resource Center Technician or Worker. Helps keep the Media/Resource Center in good operating condition, helps teachers find needed materials, willing to try new mediums of expression for teaching, and discuss them with teachers.
Contact:

Missions Education. Various opportunities for planning banquet programs and teaching children about world need.
Contact:

Librarian. Assist in cataloging books, suggesting new books and services, serving as "check-out" librarian on Sundays.
Contact:

E. **Counseling**
Shepherding Ministries. See letter "A."
Phone Shepherds. Make telephone contact with new people who attend our church. Help answer their questions or refer them to someone who can. Training provided.
Contact:
High School Core Group Leader. See letter "C."
Jail Ministry. See letter "B."
Lay/Certified. See letter "A."

F. **Preaching**
Rescue Mission Work. Giving a Bible message to men and women on skid row.
Contact:

G. **Children** (Coaching and caring type ministries)
Sunday School. See letter "C."
Quizzing. Encouraging children to learn and memorize an entire book of the Bible each year. Compete with other teams from the area in answering questions on the material covered.
Contact:
Graded Choirs (Primary 1 and 2, Middler 3 and 4, and Junior 5 and 6). Pianists and directors.
Contact:
Nursery worker. Care for babies and toddlers during morning and evening programs.
Contact:
Weekday child care during women's Bible studies.
Contact:
Special Education. Work with "special" children during the Sunday School hour.
Contact:

H. **Youth**
High School Core Group Leader. See letter "C."
Summer/Spring Missions Project. Go on a trip as a sponsor to various mission fields. Work with students in helping them understand the meaning and significance of the missions activity in which they are involved.
Contact:
Junior High/High School Sunday School Teacher. See letter "C."
Camp Counselor for Junior High or High School. Same as counselor under letter "C."
College Ministries. Teach a Sunday School class, lead and assist in a weekday Bible study. Invite college students into your home.
Contact:

I. **Visitation**
Cradle Roll Visitor. Visit parents of newborn babies, give them literature, and find out if and where they are involved in our church.
Contact:
Outreach Leader in Sunday School. See letter "B."
Transportation. Often people in our congregation need rides to doctor's appointments, events, and church services.
Contact:
Work with the Elderly. This could be many things from teaching crafts in the monthly meetings to bringing meals to a shut-in.
Contact:

J. **Caring**
Women's Prayer Groups. There are several groups of women who gather weekly to pray for specific ministries in the church.
Contact:
Membership Committee. Interview individuals who wish to join our church. Make phone contact with people who indicate interest in joining.
Contact:
Deacon/Deaconess. See letter "A."
Transportation. See letter "I."
Work with Elderly. See letter "I."
Nursery Worker. See letter "G."
Weekday child care. See letter "G."
Office Help. All kinds of office work: Collating, photocopying, typing, going over computer printouts, sorting church newsletter mailings, etc.
Contact:
Single Adult Ministries. Being willing to help fix a car, repair something in a house, invite singles into your home for dinner and fellowship.
Contact:
Deaf Ministry. Learn to sign, sign services, teach signing to others.
Contact:

K. **Additional Opportunities that don't fit under existing headings**
Stewardship and Finance Committees. Financial and budget planning.
Contact:
Public Relations. Writing news releases, planning promotion strategies, making posters, etc.
Contact:
Audio Committee. Help operate the church sound system.
Contact:
Choir.
Contact:

Communion Committee. Set up for, and get elements ready for Communion observance.
Contact:
Social Committee. Help set up punch, coffee, refreshments, various meals, for various social functions at church (i.e., annual meeting, Good Friday breakfast, mission banquets, going-away receptions, etc.).
Contact:
Greeters/Ushers.
Contact:
Cassette Ministry. Duplicating tapes, recording, selling, etc.
Contact:
Assist in parking cars on Sunday mornings.
Contact:
Assist in snow removal.
Contact:
Senior High Handbell Choir.
Contact:

LATE SUMMER LETTER

Walnut Heights Bible Church

2315 Walnut Road, Wheeling, IL 60090
708-555-1234

Dear Friends:

A successful vacation, it has been said, is a period of relaxation when your self-winding watch runs down. Digital watches have nearly made the definition obsolete, but I trust that your busy summer has not made the idea of a vacation obsolete in your life. I hope you have been refreshed in your body and spirit.

With the summer vacation period coming to an end, it is our opportunity and responsibility as a church to set the hands of ministry in motion once again. Of course, many of these ministries have continued without losing a second during the summer, but now we need additional hands to keep up with the growth anticipated this fall.

Just before our Lord commissioned His 12 disciples and sent them out to minister (Matt. 10), He made one observation and instructed His followers to take one course of action. "The harvest is plentiful," He said, "but the workers are few. Therefore beseech the Lord of the harvest to send out workers into His harvest" (Matt. 9:37-38).

This is the most appropriate time of year for me to make a similar request of you. First, please *look* at the opportunities available to us as a church to meet needs in our community. Then *look* at your own gifts, abilities, and time commitments and ask yourself, "Where can I fit into ministry *this year?*"

Then *pray* that the "Lord of the harvest" will "thrust forth workers" to do His work in our community. Be assured that He does have the people to accomplish the ministries that He has in mind.

Our "HANDS OF TIME . . . AND ETERNITY" brochure accompanies this letter. It is designed to help you examine your time and talents and then make a year-long commitment to ministry in our community. Please look at it carefully and consider it prayerfully.

On the last Sunday morning of this month, please bring your "HANDS OF TIME . . . AND ETERNITY" brochure to church filled out as a commitment of your time and talent to the Lord. A special offering will be taken during the morning worship service at which time you will be able to present your time and talent as a living sacrifice to the Lord.

If you have any questions, please call me. May I assure you that I will be standing with you in prayer.

Sincerely,

Herb Wilcox

Herb Wilcox
Pastor
Walnut Heights Bible Church

HW/pb
Enc.

TIME AND TALENT BROCHURE

INSTRUCTIONS FOR COMPLETING THE TIME AND TALENT BROCHURE:

1. After prayerful consideration of God's Word and His leading in your life, complete this "Hands of Time . . . and Eternity" brochure.

2. Circle all numbers which describe the areas of ministry and the age/sex of people to whom you wish to minister.

3. Be sure to both sign and print your name, address, and phone number before returning the brochure on Commitment Sunday, September 25.

4. *Each person* should complete a "Hands of Time . . . and Eternity" brochure in order to distinguish among ministry preferences within families.

5. Tear off the front panel of the brochure, and transfer the areas of ministry that you have circled in the brochure to the panel which you have detached. Then post it in a location in your home where you will be reminded to pray for that ministry daily.

6. Bring the completed brochure to church on Sunday morning, September 25, and place it in the "Hands of Time . . . and Eternity" offering plate at the conclusion of the service as a celebration of your commitment to serve.

7. If you are unable to attend church on Commitment Sunday, please drop your brochure in the mail during the following week.

Thank you for your willingness to be used by God.

Walnut Heights Bible Church

2315 Walnut Road, Wheeling, IL 60090

312-555-1234

HANDS of TIME . . .

AND ETERNITY

Ours are the hands of time. Ours is the touch of eternity. The question that each of us at Walnut Heights Bible Church must ask ourselves as we consider the lives of people with whom we are in contact is as simple and yet complex as the lives we lead: "WHAT CAN I DO WITH MY TIME AND MY TALENTS TO HAVE AN ETERNAL IMPACT ON PEOPLE THIS YEAR?"

A time and talent commitment is one way to answer this question. God has graciously given us a growing church. Now we must be careful to commit ourselves to the ongoing ministry needs of our church and its worldwide outreach.

A time and talent commitment is:

. . . *A STEP OF FAITH*—Faith that God in His graciousness will see fit to accept our gifts and talents and use them for His glory.

. . . *A PROMISE TO SERVE*—Serve in a capacity compatible with our gifts and talents.

. . . *A CONFIDENCE OF BLESSINGS*—Blessings that only God can provide to those who are willing to say yes to His direction.

. . . *AN ANTICIPATION OF IMPACT*—Impact on people, young and old, rich and poor, sick and well, who need to be touched by the hand of God.

The Apostle Paul stated simply, "It is God who is at work in you, both to will and to work for his good purpose" (Phil. 2:13). As you examine the possibilities of service at Walnut Heights Bible Church this year, be assured that it is God who is guiding your desires and your pen as you write down your preferences for ministry in the coming year.

FRONT SIDE

By God's Grace and under His guidance, I have committed myself to _____ ministries with _____ (age/sex) at Walnut Heights Bible Church during 1983-1984

Yes! I am interested in investing my time and talents in ministry . . . (Please circle the number that most closely describes the: A. *MINISTRIES* and B. *PREFERENCES* of the age and sex with which you would like to be involved.)

A. MINISTRIES

CARING MINISTRIES

Visitation
1111 Newcomers
1112 Telephone Visitation
1113 Shut-ins
1114 Sick
1115 Nursing Homes
1116 Hospitals

Special Assistance
1211 Elderly
1212 Handicapped
1213 Special Education
1214 Alcoholics
1215 Counseling
1216 Overnite Accommodations
1217 Cooking

WORSHIP MINISTRIES

Worship Services
2111 Usher
2112 Greeter
2113 Parking Lot Attendant
2114 Information Booth
2115 Nursery
2116 Sanctuary Decorations

Music
2211 Adult Choir
2212 Youth Choir
2213 Special Vocal Music
2214 Instrumental Music
2215 Song Leader
2216 Accompanist: Piano
2217 Accompanist: Organ
2218 Accompanist: Guitar

SUPPORT MINISTRIES

Administration
3111 Typing
3112 Filing
3113 Telephoning
3114 Assembling
3115 Bookkeeping
3116 Mailing
3117 Mimeographing

Communication
3211 Editor
3212 Writer
3213 Slide Presentations
3214 News Gatherer
3215 Photographer
3216 Paste-up
3217 Cassette Production
3218 Cassette Sales
3219 Proofreader
3220 Poster Maker
3221 Art Work

Transportation
3311 Youth Activities
3312 Special Events
3313 Van Available
3314 Station Wagon Available

Maintenance
3411 Landscaping
3412 Carpentry
3413 Cleaning
3414 Electrical
3415 Plumbing
3416 Painting
3417 Lawn Mowing
3418 Equipment Repair

Library
3511 Librarian
3512 Reviewing Books
3513 Cataloging
3514 Material Preparation
3515 Committee Member

Audiovisual
3511 Librarian
3512 Projectionist
3513 Filing
3514 Material Preparation
3515 Committee Member

DISCIPLING MINISTRIES

Sunday School/Children's Church
4111 Teacher
4112 Substitute Teacher
4113 Department Leader
4114 Department Secretary
4115 Children's Church Leader

Youth Work
4211 Sponsor
4212 Small Group Leader
4213 Home Available
4214 Pool Available
4215 Boat Available

Camping
4311 Resident Camp Director
4312 Resident Camp Counselor
4313 Stress Camp Leader
4314 Family Camp Committee
4315 Day Camp Director
4316 Day Camp Counselor

Club Program
4411 Boys Club Leader
4412 Girls Club Leader
4413 Committee Member
4414 Special Speaker

Specialized Ministries
4511 Vacation Bible School
4512 Christmas Program
4513 Drama
4514 Puppetry
4515 Refreshments
4516 Athletic Coach
4517 Family Life Committee
4518 Special Education
4519 Hearing Impaired
4520 Home Bible Study

MISSION MINISTRIES

Foreign Missions
5111 Missions Committee
5112 Correspondent
5113 Missions Conference
5114 Woman's Missionary Fellowship

Local Evangelism
5211 Neighborhood Bible Study
5212 Neighborhood Canvass
5213 Jail Ministries
5214 Outreach Projects
5215 Personal Work

B. PREFERENCE FOR MINISTRY

Age
6011 Preschool
6012 Grade School (K-6)
6013 Junior High (7/8)
6014 High School
6015 College/Career
6016 Adult—Married
6017 Adult—Single

Sex
6111 Male
6112 Female
6113 Male and Female

Your Signature _____
Name _____
Address _____
City _____ State _____ Zip _____
Home Phone _____
Business Phone _____

BACK SIDE

SAMPLE BULLETIN INSERT

Hands of Time...and Eternity

Has it ever occurred to you what the digital watch is doing to our language? Phrases like "a quarter after 2" or "watch out for that boat approaching at 2 o'clock" will mean very little without the slow moving hands of a clock as a point of reference.

But even with digital watches, time still remains our most precious natural resource. The question each Christian must ask is, "What can I do with my time to make it count for eternity?"

Each of us has in our hand certain talents and gifts which can be used for God's glory. Each of us is limited by a multitude of demands on our time and energies. Thus each person in our church is encouraged to stop and ask himself/herself, "Where will my time and talents best be used for God during the coming year?"

In the "Hands of Time . . . and Eternity" Commitment brochure you will find five areas of ministry.

Caring Ministries put you in contact with people who are new to the church or need special care because of age, illness, or special circumstances.

Worship Ministries are related to the public services of the church.

Support Ministries refer to those essential tasks which take place behind the scenes without which communication, transportation, and maintenance would break down.

Discipling Ministries are the leadership opportunities for a person to have face-to-face contact with people who are willing to be taught the living and written truths of God.

Mission Ministries focus on the outreach of the church in the local community and around the world.

As you consider the opportunities presented in the brochure, please be in prayer that God will direct you in how you should use your hands for time and eternity.

CHURCH NEWSLETTER—
DURING DRIVE

NEWSLETTER

Walnut Heights
Bible Church

2315 Walnut Road, Wheeling, IL 60090
708-555-1234

COMMITMENT SUNDAY SET

Sunday, September 23, has been designated by the elders of Walnut Heights Bible Church as "Commitment Sunday." During the morning service, all members and regular attenders of the church will be called on to present their "Hands of time . . . and Eternity" Commitment brochures as an act of worship and service.

In commenting on the nature of the service, Pastor Wilcox observed, "The objective is to experience a celebration of Christian service. The worship service will climax as each person places his/her commitment brochure in the offering plates passed by the elders of the church. The congregation will then rise to sing 'Lead On, O King Eternal,' and together dedicate itself to a year of Christian service."

The areas of service at Walnut Heights Bible Church include, but are not limited to, caring ministries, worship ministries, support ministries, discipling ministries, and mission ministries. "Hands of Time . . . and Eternity" Commitment brochures are available in the church bulletin, in the lobby of the church, and in the church office until Commitment Sunday.

Instructions on How to Follow Up on "Hands of Time . . . and Eternity"

Commitment Responses

1. Recruit a group of volunteers to sort out the commitment brochures (or cards), placing the brochures of those already involved into one stack and those seeking to become involved into another stack.

2. Mail response letters to everyone who has responded — one letter to those who are already involved (p. 70) and another letter to those seeking to become involved (p. 71). These should be mailed within the week following Commitment Sunday.

3. Responses should be grouped according to the categories of response in order to have a handy reference list for recruitment purposes as needs arise. The easiest way is to have this done on computer (thus the numbers on the brochure).

4. Distribute copies of the computer printout to key people who will need the information for recruitment purposes during the year.

Tabulation Sheet Time and Talent Commitments

Walnut Heights Bible Church

CHILDREN'S CHURCH LEADER – PRESCHOOL	PHONE # AS OF 07-APRIL 90		
000127-02 Ball*Carolyn*Mrs 432 R _ _ _ _ Rd Wheeling, IL 60090	Home (708) 555-4321	Bus. (708) 555-6789	[1]Level A
000133-02 Bucknel*Agnes*Mrs 334 F_ _ _ Prospect Heights, IL 60070	Home ( )	Bus. ( )	Level A
000096-01 Cling*Stephen*Mr 805 D _ _ _ Wheeling, IL 60090	Home ( )	Bus. ( )	Level B
000137-02 Cooper*Lura*Mrs 732 W_ _ _ Wheeling, IL 60090	Home ( )	Bus. ( )	Level A
000142-02 Cunningham Shirley*Mrs 1946 C _ _ _ Ln. Wheeling, IL 60090	Home ( )	Bus. ( )	Level A
000143-02 Ebersol*Terry*Mrs 618 L _ _ _ Ave. Wheeling, IL 60090	Home ( )	Bus. ( )	Level B
000013-02 Lawrence*Mary Anne**Mrs 533 W_ _ _ Ave. Buffalo Grove, IL 60090	Home ( )	Bus. ( )	Level A
000023-02 Neighbor*Marjorie**Mrs 3S605 W_ _ _ Ave Palatine, IL 60067	Home ( )	Bus. ( )	Level B

---

[1]Level Refers to present involvement: A — Presently active; B — Not presently involved

FOLLOW-UP LETTER to people presently involved.

Walnut Heights Bible Church

2315 Walnut Road, Wheeling, IL 60090
708-555-1234

Dear Coworker:

Thank you so much for responding to the Time and Talent Commitment for Walnut Heights Bible Church. You were one of _____ people or families to so respond. Isn't it great to be among so many concerned people!

I realize that you are already involved in the ministry of our church in discipling people. Thank you for reconfirming your commitment. It means a lot to me.

Your brother,

Herb Wilcox

Herb Wilcox
Pastor
Walnut Heights Bible Church

HW/ma

FOLLOW-UP LETTER to people not presently involved.

Walnut Heights Bible Church

2315 Walnut Road, Wheeling, IL 60090
708-555-1234

Dear Steward of God's Time and Talent:

Thank you so much for responding to the ministry aspect of the stewardship program. You were one of _____ people to so respond. Isn't it great to be among so many concerned people?

The question now comes, "How do I turn my commitment into action?" Here are the steps you should take:

1. Since we prefer all new Christian education personnel to understand our philosophy of learning, we encourage you to attend our Christian Education Training Program which will begin on Sunday, October 7, at 9:30 A.M. in room 110.

2. We would like to interview you so we can get to know you more personally. Please call Pastor Jeff Thompson or me and set a time when we can get together.

3. Even though we may not be able to immediately place you in a ministry position, there are usually openings due to unforeseen circumstances after the first of the year. Please be patient in your willingness to serve. We will use you and your gifts as soon as possible.

Thank you so much for your response on Hands of Time . . . and Eternity Commitment Sunday. It means a lot to the leadership of the church to know that you are committed to serve Jesus Christ.

Your brother,

Herb Wilcox

Herb Wilcox
Pastor
Walnut Heights Bible Church

HW/rb

FIVE

How Can I Volunteer?

"What does a person have to do in order to teach Sunday School around here?" blurted Rosemary Wilson to a rather stunned Jeff Thompson one Sunday after the morning service. He couldn't believe what he was hearing. In the first place, he would have never suspected that the shy, red-haired legal secretary would be interested in teaching Sunday School. Second, he'd never before seen Rosemary with sparks in her eyes and such animated gestures. It was obviously a case of blind bypassing of a potential recruit—a thought that brought a blush to his cheeks.

"Am I supposed to knock one of you pastors down and hold you there until you tell me I can work with those boys and girls? I've signed registration cards from the pew rack three different times, and nobody has ever bothered to contact me!"

"Well—consider yourself contacted," Jeff said, trying to pick up the ball. "I'm sorry, Rosemary. I honestly don't know why you haven't been called. But I will check on it."

Rosemary's mood mellowed and it appeared as if tears might well up in her eyes. "You can't imagine how difficult it is for a person like me to build up enough nerve to write a note to you, Pastor Jeff, much less ambush you after church. But I really do want to teach."

Jeff repeated his apology and made small talk with Rosemary, seeking further to help her feel needed.

"The registration cards," thought Jeff, after the Rosemary incident, "I wonder who looks at them after they're collected on Sunday mornings?"

A little checking turned up a procedure established somewhere back in antiquity in which the church secretary was responsible for looking at the cards on Monday morning. She then sent welcome letters to those who checked the "Visitor" box on their cards, sent Christian education fliers to those who checked the "Christian Education" box, and made a list of all the prayer requests and illnesses. The final step was to place a report of all this on Pastor Wilcox's desk for him to see Tuesday morning. The cards were then placed in a storage case and slipped into the cupboard above the photocopying machine.

Jeff looked back through the registration cards over the past seven weeks, and sure enough, three times Rosemary Wilson's cards had two checks by the words "Christian Education." The first check was Rosemary's; the second, Jeff recognized, was the ink of the church secretary's pen. Three times she faithfully sent out the Christian education flier to an "obviously absentminded" parishioner, checking off the card indicating the follow-up had been done. The problem was, the list on Pastor Wilcox's desk—of potential Christian education workers—wasn't reaching Jeff.

Immediately the system was changed. On Tuesday mornings when Jeff walked into his office, a list of those indicating interest in Christian education awaited him, complete with phone numbers. Generally the phone calls required no more than 25 minutes to complete before he left the office at the end of the afternoon. True, most people merely wanted information about the Christian education program, but at least one or two every week wanted to become involved in the ministry to children, youth, or adults. A recruitment tool had been rediscovered, after almost remaining buried in an old bureaucratic ritual that wasn't making the right connections.

Out of curiosity, Jeff began logging his Tuesday phone calls. It wasn't long until an interesting trend began to emerge. A growing number of people whom Jeff had talked with on the phone were expressing appreciation to the young pastor for his warmth and helpfulness. Some of these, in turn, later began volunteering for the educational outreach ministry which touched so many lives for Christ. Courtesy had blossomed into a means of building up the very ministry that had generated seemingly fruitless initial inquiries. "Fruit needs time to ripen," Jeff realized. Courtesy and warmth had paid unexpected dividends.

In time the registration card was modified to make follow-up contacts easier to classify (see card on page 75) and more specific. Jeff soon discovered that he didn't need to make all the calls himself. A number of people from the church thoroughly enjoyed making this type of contact with people and were willing to accept the Tuesday follow-up as their primary ministry in the church. Log sheets were handed to Jeff by Wednesday night so he could be kept current with the contacts being made. Any person who could not be reached by phone got a letter on Thursday apologizing for not making phone contact, but expressing Jeff's desire to assist in any way possible if the person would give him a call at the church office (see letter on page 76).

Pastor Jeff had taken another step in meeting the needs of the recruitment problem. By not viewing people merely as potential workers, he'd gained rapport and established new relationships. From those relationships emerged a flow of individuals who wanted to join Jeff in the important CE ministry.

MODEL INFORMATION CARD
placed in pew racks

FRONT OF INFORMATION CARD

WELCOME TO OUR SERVICES

☐ A.M.
☐ P.M.

Date _____

Mr. and Mrs.
Miss
Mrs. _____ Phone _____
Mr.

Address _____
Street   City   State   Zip
☐ This is a new address

Please check: AGE:

☐ Visitor ☐ Regular Attender ☐ Member   ☐ 12-17
☐ Desire information about _____   ☐ 18-22
☐ Desire to volunteer my time and talent   ☐ 23-30
☐ Desire church membership   ☐ 31-40
☐ Would like to receive a visit   ☐ 41-50
☐ Special request (see back of card)   ☐ 51-60
WALNUT HEIGHTS BIBLE CHURCH   ☐ Over 60

BACK OF INFORMATION CARD

Special request _____

_____

_____

Notes of information _____

_____

_____

Reservations desired for _____

_____

_____

75

LETTER to people not successfully contacted in two phone call attempts.

Walnut Heights Bible Church

2315 Walnut Road, Wheeling, IL 60090
708-555-1234

Mrs. Darlene Baltz
650 XYZ St.
Wheeling, IL 60090

Dear Darlene:

Thank you for your registration card indicating an interest in volunteering your time and talents. I'm sorry we were unable to reach you by phone.

Please call the church office at 555-1234; we will be glad to discuss your interest in serving the Lord or to answer any questions you may have.

Sincerely yours,

Jeff Thompson

Jeff Thompson
Pastor of Christian Education

JT/rb

LETTER to persons wanting more information.

Walnut Heights
Bible Church

2315 Walnut Road, Wheeling, IL 60090
708-555-1234

Mrs. Susan Johnson
221 ABC Drive
Wheeling, IL 60090

Dear Susan:

It was a joy to talk with you on the phone this morning. I trust that the information we discussed was helpful to you.

As I promised, I am enclosing two items: Our "Opportunities for Service" list and a Time and Talent Commitment brochure. I have passed your name along to the person whose name I have circled on the "Opportunities" sheet.

He is a busy person, like yourself. If he doesn't call you by the end of the week, please feel free to call him. His phone number is provided.

Thank you for your interest in serving the Lord.

Sincerely yours,

Alice Walker

Alice Walker
Volunteer Phone Visitation
Worker

TABULATION OF
INFORMATION CARDS

CHURCH REGISTRATION CARD FOLLOW-UP SHEET

Date	Name	Age	Address	Phone	Registration Card		Church Response	
					Item Checked	Information Provided	Contact Assigned	Results

CHRISTIAN EDUCATION INTERVIEW

Interviewee _____

Address _____

Phone (Home) _____ (Work) _____

1. Background Information: (What has contributed to making you who you are today?)

2. Spiritual Life: (If you would die tonight, what kind of reception would you receive from God?)

3. Experience in Christian education: (What have you done to teach people about Jesus Christ?)

4. Area of Interest: (What types of ministry would you like to have this year?)

5. Greatest Apprehension: (What do you fear most about volunteering as you have?)

6. Desired Reward: (What personal satisfaction or rewards would you like to receive for ministering this year?)

Assignment _____ Date Available _____
Comments:

Interviewer _____ Date _____

SIX

Expectations of New Members

It was a ten-minute drive from Jeff's house to the church. This December morning he barely noticed four filling stations, two bowling alleys, and five traffic signals as he drove along. A thought had occurred to Jeff as he approached the two elm trees whose dark leafless silhouettes marked the two-mile point on his jogging route earlier that crisp winter morning.

Simply stated, the idea was this: "If we can give a packet of offering envelopes to new members of the church, why can't they be given a packet of service cards as well? After all, hadn't Pastor Wilcox made a strong point during the Time and Talent Commitment emphasis during October that stewardship encompassed not only financial aspects of the Christian life, but the use of one's gifts and abilities as well?"

The longer the idea lingered on his mind, the more exciting the concept became. By the fourth traffic signal, Jeff had the packet visualized. The box would be approximately the same size as the packet of offering envelopes, but the contents would be significantly different. The first item would be a tape of Pastor Wilcox's most moving sermon from the Time and Talent series preached during the fall. Also included on the tape could be testimonies from volunteers featured during that same period in the fall and the touching words spoken by Alice Clarkson as she received the Walnut Heights Bible Church Sunday School Teacher of the Year Award at the Volunteer Ministry Recognition dinner the previous May.

Next would come a set of ministry cards—one for each area of ministry of the church. They could be drawn from the list of opportunities for service developed during the fall (pages 57–61), and could include a brief description of the ministry plus the name and telephone number of the person to contact for more information. These could be printed individually in case one of the ministries was later dropped or changed. Then the whole list would not have to be reprinted—just that particular card.

In a separate color, a Ministry Experience Questionnaire could be included. The purpose of the MEQ would be to record the ministry background of each new member of the church. The questionnaire, as Jeff visualized it, would contain a checklist of formal training and seminars in areas related to Christian ministry, talents and skills, and a record of ministry experiences enjoyed over the years. No one would be forced to submit this to the church, just as new members were not forced to tithe. However, Jeff hoped every fresh batch of membership candidates would consider options and responsibilities for service along with the other privileges of church membership.

The last piece in the packet would be a preaddressed and prepaid Volunteer Service Commitment Card, a scaled down version of the Time and Talent Commitment brochure used during the fall. Each new member would be encouraged to fill out the card and drop it into the mail within a week after he or she had received the right hand of fellowship. Then these responses would be added to the list of volunteers tabulated after the Commitment Campaign held during the fall.

Jeff exploded into Pastor Wilcox's office, still wondering if that last traffic light had been red or green. The ideas came pouring out of him like water from a rainspout. Pastor Wilcox peered unimpressed at Jeff over the rims of his glasses. "Slow down, Jeff," he sighed. "If it's all that good, it will stand up to slower sifting. I like some of what I hear, but. . . . " The pastor's voice trailed off.

Jeff reddened impatiently. He should have realized by now that any of his creative brainstorms if presented too hastily and excitedly would meet with initial caution from his senior pastor. Pastor Wilcox had developed a response that Jeff learned to interpret as a cold-water treatment, or "slow-down-Mr.-Hotshot." The pastor would blandly say something like, "Oh, that's nice," which left Jeff wondering if he should drop the whole idea.

Undeterred, Jeff bided his time. At an opportune moment, two weeks after first sharing the idea, he brought it up again in a much more composed fashion. This time Pastor Wilcox seemed much more open. But there remained a distinct lack of enthusiasm for the idea which Jeff could not understand.

In his attempt to sort out why the senior pastor appeared to be dragging his feet on this potentially dynamite innovation, Jeff had lunch with Ernie Larson, the stocky, balding chairman of the Christian Education Committee. Ernie wore the loudest neckties Jeff had ever seen—but he was also one of the most perceptive and discerning men in church leadership.

"Could it be finances?" asked the chairman, after hearing Jeff out.

"No," responded Jeff, "if we get our printing done by Fred Cowan at Master Graphics (who had volunteered during the Time and Talent Commitment Campaign the previous fall) and the tape duplication through the church's cassette ministry people, the total cost to get the idea rolling would be under $100. Besides, the pastor has assured me that money won't be an issue on an otherwise good idea."

"How about the board?" the chairman continued. "Is Herb getting flack from them over your volume of innovations?"

"Negative again. I've raised that question with him several times in the last three months, and his feelings seem to be that almost every idea I bring up makes him look good for having recruited me."

"Maybe we should break down the problem into its component parts," Ernie suggested. "Let's see if we can discover where the holdup might be."

For the next half hour the two men picked over the details of Jeff's bogged-down brainchild. Almost all its main elements were timely retreads of ideas that Walnut Heights had already used, not really controversial. "What about the tape with the pastor's message?" Ernie queried.

Jeff shook his head. "That's Pastor Wilcox at his best," he said. "Why would he object to his own taped sermon?"

"I remember that message," the chairman said. "Maybe you're

overselling it, in terms of your enthusiasm for the whole project. Is it really *that* good, Jeff? Would Herb think it was all *that* good?"

"You might have something there." Jeff let his mind go back to the fall Time and Talent series. "I remember Pastor Wilcox telling me how rushed he felt putting those sermons together on such short notice. Come to think of it, he really didn't come across very enthusiastically. And he forgot to mention. . . . " Jeff blushed. "You're right, Ernie. We talked about the series later. I guess I was his worst critic, since it was my idea. And he agreed that he'd needed more time to work out the ideas.

"Pastor Wilcox must think I'm an amnesia case for not remembering my own criticisms! How could I have been so insensitive?"

In October the following year, after an outstanding series of messages delivered by Pastor Wilcox on the subject of the theology of Service, a Volunteer Service Packet was introduced, acquainting new members with service opportunities they had as parishioners in Walnut Heights Bible Church. A tape was included.

MINISTRY CARDS

1. SUGGESTED FORMAT:

TITLE OF MINISTRY:

Description of Ministry:

Schedule of Meetings:

Leadership Needed:

Person to Contact for More Information:

WALNUT HEIGHTS BIBLE CHURCH
2315 Walnut Road, Wheeling, IL 60090   708-555-1234

---

2. FORMAT ILLUSTRATED:

SUNDAY SCHOOL MINISTRIES/CHILDREN'S CHURCH MINISTRIES

Description: Each Sunday morning educational opportunities are provided from the cradle to the grave as human needs are focused on through the lens of the Bible. A map is provided on the back of this card in order to show class locations.

Schedule:
9:30 Sunday School (all ages)
11:00 Children's Church (through second grade)
7:00 Third Wednesday night of month—
Staff Planning/Training Meeting

Leadership Needed:

Department Leaders	Song Leaders
Teachers	General Officers
Secretaries	Adult Class Officers
Pianists	Visitors

Person to Contact for More Information:
Rev. Jeff Thompson (555-1234)

WALNUT HEIGHTS BIBLE CHURCH
2315 Walnut Road, Wheeling, IL 60090   708-555-1234

84

MINISTRY EXPERIENCE QUESTIONNAIRE

FRONT OF CARD

MINISTRY EXPERIENCE QUESTIONNAIRE

Name ————————————— Phone ————————————

Address ————————————————————————————
City   State   Zip

Answer each of these questions as fully as you feel comfortable.

1. What skills and talents do you have which might be used at Walnut Heights Bible Church?

————————————————————————————————

————————————————————————————————

————————————————————————————————

– –
(Fold to make 3″ x 5″ card)

2. What training have you had which might assist you in ministry at Walnut Heights Bible Church?

————————————————————————————————

————————————————————————————————

————————————————————————————————

3. What experiences have you had which might assist you in ministry at Walnut Heights Bible Church?

————————————————————————————————

————————————————————————————————

————————————————————————————————

BACK OF CARD

4. In what areas of ministry would you be most likely to serve during the coming year?

_____

_____

_____

- -

(Fold to make 3" x 5" card)

5. If you could do anything for God without fear of failure, what would that be?

_____

_____

_____

_____

_____

WALNUT HEIGHTS BIBLE CHURCH
2315 Walnut Road, Wheeling, IL 60090   708-555-1234

VOLUNTEER SERVICE COMMITMENT CARD

As a new member of Walnut Heights Bible Church, I understand that I have the privilege and responsibility of committing my time and talents to serve in the ministries of the church.

After reviewing the service opportunities provided in this packet, I would like to make a commitment to serve in the following capacities:

_____

_____

_____

_____

Signed, _____

WALNUT HEIGHTS BIBLE CHURCH
2315 Walnut Road, Wheeling, IL 60090   708-555-1234

SEVEN

Recruitment Group

"Growth is a problem, not just an opportunity," concluded Roy Mayfield, a slender retired schoolteacher and one of the age-group coordinators with whom Jeff was meeting.* A blessing, they all agreed, but yet a problem just the same.

The four age-group coordinators huddled with Jeff in his office as the sounds and scents of late spring drifted in through his partially opened windows. Several years had passed since the first Time and Talent Recruitment Campaign, and even with the success of the fall recruitment efforts, it had become increasingly evident that something else had to be done in the spring and summer months to keep the ministry fully staffed.

"It seems to me," continued Jo Williams, the grade school children's Sunday School coordinator, "that all we should have to do is get enough information to the people of our church for them to see the need and then respond. Our people have shown a real commitment to evangelism and discipleship. All they need is information."

A questioning look crept across Mary Ellen Watkins' freckled face. For two years now this tireless auburn-haired housewife had served as the early childhood coordinator for the church-time ministries, and consistently her area of ministry had been

---

*An age-group coordinator is a person assigned to assist the pastor of Christian education in the recruiting, training, and encouraging of teachers and department leaders in either Sunday School or church-time at a particular age-level (early childhood, children, youth, or adult).

the first to need replacements but the last to be staffed. At first she blamed herself. But as time passed and the same pattern repeated itself a second time, her fellow coordinators helped her see that she was doing everything the rest of them were in just as tactful and compelling a manner, yet with less satisfactory results.

"Maybe prayer is the key," Mary Ellen offered wistfully, half questioning and half commenting. "All the information in the world won't necessarily bear fruit without the prayer support of God's people. The verse about praying the Lord of the harvest to send forth workers into the harvest fields keeps coming to mind. That doesn't just apply to missionaries in West Irian. It's equally true right here in Wheeling."

For the next few minutes the discussion focused on reasons why people attending Walnut Heights Bible Church *should* be volunteering to minister to the new families who had been added to the Sunday School roles in the last few months and what the biblical norms were in the early church. Yet the fact remained: Departments were short of staff.

"What we need is revival," concluded Mary Ellen. "There's nothing else we can do except pray for it."

"Revival?" Jeff half mumbled. The very idea resurrected thoughts of his childhood church where "revivals" began on Sunday and concluded the following Sunday. That memory was a far cry from the idea of revival which Mary Ellen had been referring to, but the word had stimulated a brand-new train of thought.

"Revival," pondered Jeff, as the conversation continued around him. What *had* brought about certain periods of deepening spiritual insights and commitment during his childhood? Young Life ranch, was a good example. What had caused young people to respond to God? Was it emotion? Prayer? Oratorical skills? Suddenly the fog cleared in Jeff's overactive mind. A pattern emerged.

"The fact is," interjected the young pastor, as if he had been totally immersed in the conversation the entire time, "that we've tried each of the concepts that *should* have worked, and they have to a great extent. But, we're still short of volunteer staff. Perhaps the problem is that we're using these ideas piecemeal fashion instead of pulling them all together.

"The word 'revival,' which Mary Ellen referred to a few minutes ago," Jeff continued, "triggered some thoughts in my mind. Each spiritual awakening I know of combined the two elements we've mentioned plus one other. Prayer followed by Bible-based information and an invitation to commitment. It's in response to an invitation that people make decisions."

Suddenly, everyone was talking at once about how years ago such invitations were commonly given in evangelistic services, tent revivals, and church camps. "They still do it in many churches," Jo offered excitedly. "But some groups have learned to personalize it. Young Life, Campus Crusade for Christ, and Campus Life get into one-to-one discussions where the evangelist first earns the right to be heard, then shares the Good News with the person and asks for a decision for Christ."

"Where are you going with all of this?" interrupted Mary Ellen, impatiently.

Jeff grinned. "I think we should use the same pattern in our recruitment efforts. After specific prayer about who should be contacted and who should do the contacting, let's seek out people who have 'earned the right to be heard' by virtue of their ministry within the church, and ask them to evangelize on behalf of our ministry needs, one on one with other church members, then ask for specific responses—decisions."

Mary Ellen brightened and they all broke into spontaneous applause. The air of gloom vanished. A sense of excitement emerged as the five members of the leadership team refined the basic concept and hammered out a new recruitment strategy to help them deal with the spring personnel shortage.

From that discussion in Jeff's office emerged what came to be known as the Ad Hoc Recruitment Group. "Ad Hoc" was used to indicate the temporary nature of the group, for it would be brought together only when recruitment needs outran available volunteers and regular leadership couldn't come up with more.

The following procedures were developed, which proved their value repeatedly in subsequent years:

Daily Prayer

Jeff and his age-group coordinators prayed specifically for the best people as members of the ad hoc recruitment group. Then after the recruitment group was in place, continued in daily prayer for the specific ministry needs of the church.

Group Selection

After a potential group had been formed, Jeff would contact each person individually. Though each was approached in a manner consistent with how well Jeff knew the person, three steps emerged as normal procedures: a contact letter, a job description, and a personal discussion (usually on the phone).

Recruiter's Notebook

The easiest method for the members of the group to keep themselves organized and on top of the task was to have all the information they needed together in one place. So Jeff developed a notebook which was given to each member of the recruitment group, which was updated on a weekly basis. The book included:

1. A list of all ministry positions available.
2. The names of the people who had already committed themselves to ministry during the coming year or for the interim.
3. Ad Hoc Recruitment Group Report sheets to be used to log and report contacts.
4. Job descriptions for each of the ministry positions in the church.
5. A list of the people in the congregation along with their addresses, telephone numbers, and Sunday School class affiliations.

Weekly Breakfast

One of the most memorable traditions which emerged from the ad hoc recruitment group was the Saturday breakfast at a local restaurant. This particular time was chosen because most of the mothers in the group could call for "reinforcements" at home on Saturday morning, then they could slip out for an hour with a minimum of disruption to the family's schedule. Most of the group members enjoyed having breakfast together (at their own expense) away from the distractions of family and phone.

Normal Schedule

Soon the breakfast meeting became a very comfortable routine. Breakfast and fellowship were followed by a brief prayertime (yes, even at the back table of a busy restaurant). Reports would follow, with Jeff asking each person to comment on conversations with each individual assigned to group members at the previous breakfast meeting. Discussion concerning the remaining ministry openings came next, as Jeff updated his coworkers on the progress of ministry commitments and then focused on suggestions for the best people to approach to take responsibility for the remaining opportunities. Usually Jeff had some specific names in mind before breakfast, but invariably new names were tossed in which had never occurred to him. The breakfast would conclude after six to eight names were assigned to each group member for contact during the coming week.

Personal Contact

During the coming week, each group member was responsible for making the assigned contacts at his or her own convenience. The conversation usually included a warm greeting which identified the caller with Walnut Heights Bible Church, a transition statement about the opportunities for Christian service available during the coming year, and a personal invitation: "Where do you think you would like to minister in the church during the coming year?" The direct question (invitation) was the key to the whole process. Without it the process would, for the most part, fizzle, ending in a noncommittal "I'm just not sure." With it, each person contacted had prompting and encouragement to examine his or her own gifts, talents, and abilities and to zero in on an appropriate target ministry for the coming year.

From this point on, Jeff would follow the normal procedures for interviewing and placement of volunteer workers. But now there was a special group whose sole function was to support the work of Christian education, the age-group coordinators, department leaders, and others within the church by obtaining new volunteers to assist in ministry.

COMMITTEE MEMBER
CONTACT LETTER

Walnut Heights
Bible Church

2315 Walnut Road, Wheeling, IL 60090
708-555-1234

June 14, 1990

Mrs. Carolyn White
318 W _____ St.
Wheeling, Illinois 60090

Dear Carolyn:

I am sitting here staring at a stack of recruitment needs which we have both immediately and for this coming fall. For an optimist, this stack is quite a challenge. For a pessimist, the same stack is overwhelming. I must confess that I am an incurable optimist and so I believe we are going to be able to meet our recruitment needs.

Even the greatest optimist cannot do a job such as this by himself. For that reason, I'm writing to ask if you could work with me in an *ad hoc* recruitment group which will meet weekly through at least October. It will be the task of this group to contact by phone key people in the church, asking them to staff various positions in the education program. I am enclosing a job description of what we will need to do.

There is a very urgent need for our church, and I need capable people to serve with me in this crucial period of recruitment.

I will be in my office at 10:30 this Sunday morning. Please drop by and let me know if you would be able to serve with me.

Sincerely yours,

Jeff Thompson

Jeff Thompson
Pastor of Christian Education

JT/pb

RECRUITER'S NOTEBOOK
Sample Page #1

AD HOC RECRUITMENT GROUP

1990

WALNUT HEIGHTS BIBLE CHURCH

PURPOSE
1. To recruit a full staff of Christian education workers for positions beginning September 4, (199__).
2. To contact the people of our church (via phone or in person) in order to discover where they feel their gifts can best be used.

PROCEDURE
1. Pray every day for the right people to minister through the educational department of the church. The Lord will supply.
2. Meet with the group for breakfast once a week until either October 1 or the staff is recruited, whichever comes first.
3. Each person will be assigned to contact about eight people per week.
4. In contacting the people assigned:
   a. Ask where they would be interested in serving the Lord in the Christian education program this year.
   b. Inform them of the anticipated areas of need.
   c. Set up a tentative appointment with them on a Friday afternoon or a Saturday for interviews and answer any questions.
5. Report back to the group concerning the responses of the people contacted.

RECRUITER'S NOTEBOOK
Sample Page #2

SUNDAY SCHOOL
and CHILDREN'S CHURCH

Ministry Positions and Personnel
Walnut Heights Bible Church

CRIB NURSERY 9:30 A.M.
1.
2.
3.
4.
5.
TODDLER DEPARTMENT
(12-24 mo.) 9:30
1.
2.
3.
4.
2-3-YEAR-OLD
DEPARTMENT 9:30
1.
2.
3.
4.
4-5-YEAR-OLD
DEPARTMENT 9:30
1.
2.
3.
4.
1ST-2ND-GRADE
DEPARTMENT 9:30

CRIB NURSERY 11:00 A.M.
1.
2.
3.
4.
5.
TODDLER DEPARTMENT
(12-24 mo.) 11:00
1.
2.
3.
4.
2-3-YEAR-OLD CHURCH
11:00
1.
2.
3.
4.
4-5-YEAR-OLD CHURCH
11:00
1.
2.
3.
4.
1ST-2ND-GRADE
CHURCH 11:00

RECRUITER'S NOTEBOOK
Sample Page #3

CHRISTIAN EDUCATION AD HOC RECRUITMENT GROUP

Report Sheet—Week of _____

Date	Name	Address	Phone	Personal Information	Interest Area	Contact	Results

RECRUITER'S NOTEBOOK
Sample Page #4

WALNUT HEIGHTS BIBLE CHURCH

Christian Education Department
Job Description: Teacher

1. Length of Service: one year or until August 31 (whichever comes first). Commitment will be reevaluated at that time.
2. Basic Function: Creating an effective learning environment and guiding/involving learners in life-changing Bible learning.
3. Reporting Responsibilities: To the department leader who is responsible for the efficient functioning of the team.
4. Sunday Morning Responsibilities:
    A. Works with department team in setting up room to create an effective learning environment.
    B. Is ready to greet first learner who arrives and to involve him/her in meaningful participation.
    C. Guides Bible learning by:
       —selecting challenging Bible learning methods/activities
       —helping learners explore and discover God's truths
       —being well-prepared in the use of Bible stories, verses/passages, questions, comments that help to accomplish the Bible teaching/learning aim
       —encouraging learners to express ideas and feelings
       —helping learners apply Bible truths in ways that result in changed lives
    D. Evaluates learners' progress.
    E. Models the love of Christ and the power of God's Word in ways that are appropriate to the age-level.
    F. Shows love and concern for learners by getting to know them, accepting them where they are, actively listening to them and sharing their concerns/needs/joys.
    G. Affirms, supports learners.
    H. Keeps to time schedule worked out by department team.
    I. Participates with learners in large-group time and assists department leader as needed.
    J. Follows up on absentees.
5. Additional Responsibilities:
    A. Participates regularly in training/planning meetings.
    B. Required to attend one CE training conference each year.
6. Time Commitment Responsibilities: Most well-prepared teachers will spend a minimum of three-five hours each week in preparation and classtime.

EIGHT

Prayer Support

Mary Ellen's comment kept ringing in Jeff's mind: "The verse about praying to the Lord of the harvest," she had said, "doesn't just apply to missionaries in West Irian. It's equally true of the children right here in Wheeling."

There were people in the church whose primary ministry was in the area of prayer. The men's prayer group, for instance, met every Saturday morning to bring before God the needs of the church and to support the missionary family in intercession.

Miriam Kowalski, homebound due to age and frail physical condition, was one of the church's strongest prayer warriors. Undaunted by her afflictions, Miriam's prayer life had only been enhanced by her advancing age. Old-timers at the church claimed that she'd singlehandedly prayed the Campbells and at least a half a dozen other boys into the ministry during her years in Walnut Heights Bible Church.

There were other prayer groups as well. Most were small. Most were linked to a common age, interest, or cause such as the high school group, an adult Sunday School class, the Women's Missionary Society, and the Sunday School department leaders who prayed together at their monthly meetings. These were groups already meeting for prayer and, with proper information consistently channeled to them, they could become intercessors for the volunteer needs of the entire church.

Phone calls were made to those Jeff knew in each of these prayer groups. Each time the response was approximately the same, "No, we haven't been praying for volunteers to serve within the church mainly because we didn't know what the needs were."

Two methods of communicating ministry personnel needs to the prayer groups were set up. By each Wednesday, Jeff would put into the mail a current list of ministry needs as well as an update on the prayers that had been answered. The lists would also be distributed at the midweek prayer meeting so everyone could also participate in the recruitment process through prayer at home.

In case any group wanted to know more about ministry needs so prayers could be more specific, they would need to call someone for more information. Ordinarily, Jeff would have been happy to become the phone contact, but he was already overcommitted. It would be necessary to find another volunteer to fill the slot. Jeff knew just the right person; he called immediately.

"I'll do it!" Mary Ellen Watkins agreed. It seemed to be a case of the right person for the right job. After all, it was Mary Ellen's problem that had initiated this whole process of seeking prayer support. Now, not only would the early childhood coordinator's program be brought to the Lord's attention, but other program needs as well.

The system was ready to go. Jeff and Mary Ellen would review the needs each Sunday. Then the prayer group leaders would call during the week to be kept current with recruitment needs and answers to prayer. "It's very exciting," reported Mary Ellen, after the system was underway. "Those calls can become miniature revivals as we rejoice over what the Lord is doing in our church. It almost seems a shame that the children, who benefit the most from the new teachers and club leaders, are not actively involved in the prayers that the Lord is answering so beautifully. That's where the fun and action are!"

Again a light went on in Jeff's mind. Why shouldn't the younger members of the body of Christ be part of the exciting prayer life of the church? After all, wasn't it Rhoda, a young girl at the prayer meeting in John Mark's house in Acts 12, who roused the saints to rejoice over the fact that their prayers had been answered and that Peter, miraculously freed from prison, was standing at the gate outside? Of course children should be part of the recruitment prayer process!

Yet, children are different. For one thing, a child's attention span is significantly shorter than that of an adult. Another factor is that a child perceives needs directly connected with his own realm of experience much more easily than remotely related needs. Consequently, to pray for a teacher for his sister's Sunday School class would mean more to a second-grader than to pray for a chairman for the missionary committee of the church.

With these thoughts in mind, Rhoda's Band was formed for grade-school children in Sunday School. Three times a year — fall, spring, and summer — just before day camp (or whenever the needs arose), Rhoda's Band was called into action as one of the early arrival activities. Each edition of the Band lasted four weeks. The first week emphasized to the children the need for Rhoda's Band:

1. Pray *daily* that the Lord would provide *His* teachers and club leaders for ministry positions with which the children had contact.
2. Encourage adults (especially Mom and Dad) to pray with him or her for the Lord to meet that need.
3. Report back during the early arrival activity time as to how often the need had been prayed for by him or her and by others.

The remaining three weeks would then be spent hearing reports from the children about their faithfulness in praying the Lord of the harvest to send forth workers into their harvest field, reporting to the children concerning the people God provided in answer to their prayers, and praying together that God would meet these needs. Sometimes the members of Rhoda's Band were encouraged to write postcards to the people who had responded in answer to their prayers. Then new prayer assignments were made. Each new edition of Rhoda's Band lasted no more than four weeks so the idea wouldn't become trite or stale to the children.

At this point, prayer not only met recruitment needs, but had become a teaching tool. Children and adults alike were beginning to discover and delight in the faithfulness of God as He responded to prayers which Jesus Himself had commanded His followers to pray.

PRAYER SUPPORT STRATEGY

RECRUITMENT PRAYER SUPPORT STRATEGY

<u>Walnut Heights</u> Bible Church

Where we are:

1. For the past three years we have done nearly everything we could to recruit Christian education staff, including well over 400 phone calls, pleas from the pulpit, following up on stewardship responses, etc.
2. At the same time Sunday School has grown in attendance.
3. Consequently, we find ourselves constantly short of Christian education workers.

Where we should go:

1. Since it is the Lord's responsibility to thrust forth workers into this field of service (as to all fields), we must be involved in asking Him to provide workers.
2. We must continue doing everything possible to recruit Christian education staff while realizing that only God can provide them for His work.
3. We must mobilize as many people as possible to pray for the Christian education staff and their ministries.

What we will do:

1. Contact the following groups of people and ask them to pray *daily* for the staff needs of Christian education:
   Church Board
   Officers of Adult Classes
   Church Prayer Chain
   Sunday School Teachers
   Church-time Teachers
   Club Leaders
   High School Moms' Prayer Group
   Wednesday Night Prayer Meeting
   Weekly Women's Prayer Meetings
   Women's Missionary Fellowship Prayer Circles
   Saturday Morning Men's Prayer Group
2. Update the recruitment prayer requests by means of the Volunteer Staff Needs sheet by Wednesday and distribute to all of the above.
3. Questions about the personnel needs or concerning the activities of people to be recruited should be directed to Mary Ellen Watkins, the recruitment prayer coordinator.
4. Teach children to pray by creating Rhoda's Band – an early arrival activity for Sunday School children.

WEEKLY LISTING OF NEEDS

VOLUNTEER STAFF NEEDS
Walnut Heights Bible Church

Week of _____

"Beseech the Lord of the harvest to send out laborers into His harvest" (Luke 10:2).

Immediate Needs:

	No. Weeks Listed	Prayers Answered
SUNDAY SCHOOL (9:30 A.M.)		
CHILDREN'S CHURCH (10:45 A.M.)		
CLUBS		
OTHER NEEDS		

This sheet is to inform you of our education needs. Please keep them in mind as you pray each day.

CHILDREN'S PRAYER BAND

RHODA'S BAND INSTRUCTION SHEET
Walnut Heights Bible Church

PURPOSE
1. To teach children to pray that the Lord of the harvest would "send out workers into His harvest" (Matt. 9:38).
2. To obtain volunteer workers for the ministry of the church partially as a result of the prayers of children.

AGE-GROUP
Rhoda's Band of prayer warriors will be comprised of children in the third through sixth grades.

MEETING TIME AND LOCATION
At 9:15 A.M. on Sunday mornings in the Middler and Junior departments of Sunday School, for four weeks in a row, at three different times this year:
1. September 4, 11, 18, 25
2. January 8, 15, 22, 29
3. June 3, 10, 17, 24

LEADERSHIP
1. Mary Ellen Watkins will serve as the coordinator of Rhoda's Band and will be responsible to provide membership cards, prayer requests, and answers to prayer to the various Rhoda's Band leaders just prior to and during the dates listed above.
2. Middler and Junior Department leaders will appoint one teacher to be the Rhoda's Band leader in their departments.

PROCEDURE
1. Rhoda's Band leaders will announce and explain Rhoda's Band one week prior to previously listed dates, encouraging children to join.
2. On the first Sunday the leader will meet with children fifteen minutes prior to Sunday School and briefly tell the story of Rhoda's participation in prayer over adults' concerns (i.e., Peter), tell the needs for volunteer workers in the church, explain responsibilities of Rhoda's Band members (see membership card), and distribute membership cards.

3. On the following three weeks the leader will receive reports of prayer activity from children (five minutes), tell of answers to prayer and new needs (five minutes), pray for newly stated and not-yet-answered prayers (five minutes).

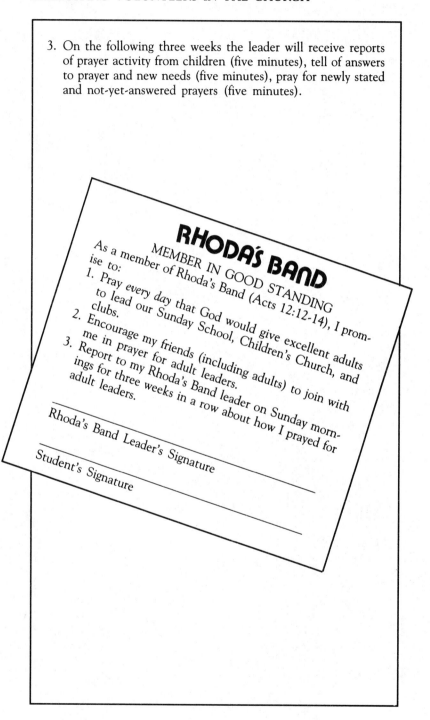

RHODA'S BAND

MEMBER IN GOOD STANDING

As a member of Rhoda's Band (Acts 12:12-14), I promise to:

1. Pray every day that God would give excellent adults to lead our Sunday School, Children's Church, and clubs.

2. Encourage my friends (including adults) to join with me in prayer for adult leaders.

3. Report to my Rhoda's Band leader on Sunday mornings for three weeks in a row about how I prayed for adult leaders.

_____
Rhoda's Band Leader's Signature

_____
Student's Signature

NINE

Publicity

There are some things a person does almost instinctively. Publicity was one of those areas for Jeff Thompson. Perhaps that's why his conversation over lunch at the regional Sunday School association meeting had seemed so unusual.

The conversation was triggered almost incidentally after a workshop on leadership development. As Jeff was leaving the room with four other men, one of them threw out to his colleagues what seemed to be a simple question.

"What do you fellows do to promote Christian education ministries in your churches?"

The question seemed straightforward enough, and Jeff waited for the others to start tossing answers to the man. No one spoke. Each person seemed to be waiting for his companions to open up first with ideas, insights, methods tested in the fire of experience. But the only sounds in those few seconds were their own footsteps on the gleaming hallway floor.

"We've tried a few approaches," Jeff finally volunteered. "They might seem old to you but they've worked for us."

As the group made its way to a nearby restaurant, the assistant pastor from Walnut Heights Bible Church shared his experiences and ideas about publicity as well as why he used each method of promotion. The response of the group surprised Jeff. His thoughts had seemed so simple, so logical, so obvious. Yet the ideas appeared refreshingly new to his colleagues.

"Pastor Thompson," said one of his new friends, "I think

you're the one to do the workshop presentation on publicity and recruiting at next year's regional Sunday School association meeting." Jeff was too surprised to respond.

The following year the CE pastor from Walnut Heights Bible Church had refined the random hash of ideas he'd shared with his colleagues the previous year and packaged them in a logical progression he felt would make sense to pastors with or without experience in the areas covered. The word had apparently made its way through the grapevine; over forty pastors and Christian education directors were present.

Publicity and Recruitment Workshop

The purpose for providing publicity as a part of the recruitment process is to maintain a high visibility for the ministries in which volunteers participate. Publicity stimulates and sustains a high level of motivation and interest on the part of congregation members in being involved. This includes the removal of false impressions or information.

Principles

1. *Keep the joy and responsibility before people.* The focus of each piece of literature or public statement about volunteer service should be positive and based on Scripture. Guilt and other forms of manipulation are not acceptable tools for securing workers. Such approaches are not scriptural, and they are counterproductive over the long run. The emphasis should be placed on sharing our gifts and talents with others in anticipation of the joy with which the Holy Spirit rewards those who are faithful.

2. *Publicize often.* Look for ways to place information about ministry before the people of the church. Don't wait for routine times such as late summer and early fall, when members of the congregation are anticipating recruitment plugs and may have developed a built-in resistance to the content of what is being said. Instead, publicize Christian education throughout the year, reporting frequently on what the Lord has been doing. At Walnut Heights Bible Church the pastors sit down together at least once a year to plan monthly times when visibility can be provided for the educational ministries of the church in one or more of the following: morning and evening services, bulletins, news-

106

letters, business meetings, and church board meetings.

3. *Prepare carefully.* Don't waste the time of the congregation with useless clichés and ill-prepared announcements. Respect the integrity of your people by putting as much time and care per minute of delivery into public announcements as your pastor places in the preparation and delivery of his sermons. This will allow people to gain confidence in the ministry before they make commitments to serve.

4. *Visualize meaningful elements.* If one picture is worth 1,000 words, one well-chosen illustration is worth at least 500 words. Statements convey knowledge whereas illustrations communicate feelings which frequently "hook" the motivational instincts of the listener. Testimonies of changed lives are perhaps the best source of meaningful illustrations.

5. *Use a variety of voices.* Though the pastor will usually be the most effective spokesman for recruitment purposes, even his influence will be diminished by overexposure. The pastor of Christian education, the education committee chairman, Sunday School superintendent, and club leaders might be other voices as long as they are gifted, or trained in basic communication skills. The mere fact of their positions, however, doesn't automatically "qualify" them to bring visibility messages before the congregation. In fact, unofficial and unexpected voices might be more effective at times. One pastor of a very large church invited his early childhood workers to bring one entire preschool department into the morning worship service during the announcement time and interviewed a couple of the children before putting in a plug for teachers of the department.

6. *Piggyback on success.* The best time to enlist new staff for ministry is immediately after God has accomplished some exciting results through service in the church. But this type of enlistment will not take place unless the people of the church know what's been happening. Tell them. Then ask for new volunteers. Church camp, rally day, high school ministry projects, and special family activities can serve as launching pads for renewed awareness of ministry potential.

Possibilities

In addition to the normal means of "making announcements" about ministry opportunities, the following methods should be considered.

1. *Interviews.* An interview can be rehearsed, and this may give effective but shy volunteers the confidence to share what God has been doing through them.

2. *Testimony.* In many churches testimonies of meaningful service are spontaneously shared within the time normally allowed for testimonies or body life experiences. Planned sharing in worship services is also effective.

3. *Skits or dramatic vignettes.* This means of communication is best when it is carefully planned and tied into a theme that is being developed elsewhere in the service.

4. *Slides.* Close-up pictures (no more than two or three people in each picture) can easily be shown in church services to illustrate the types of ministries which are happening; they can also be used with a rear-projection device in the front lobby of the church to visualize the ongoing ministries of the church.

5. *Video cassettes.* A VCR can be placed in the lobby of the church once a month to provide recorded highlights of church ministry activities during the preceding month.

6. *Media presentations.* Sometimes equipment can be rented or borrowed from a school district or community college which will allow a person to program a tape with narrative, music, and sound effects which can be synchronized with two slide projectors to provide a dramatic, exciting "show-and-tell" presentation communicating the joys of service.

7. *Movies.* From time to time Christian films featuring the Sunday School or other avenues of ministry in the local church can be shown as part of the church service.

8. *Ministry bulletin board.* One large display area in a highly visible location and changed on a regular basis can become a focal point for honoring special people, posting pictures, displaying awards, and featuring ministry needs.

9. *Pins and name tags.* Some means of identifying those already involved in ministry serves as a reminder to other people in the church that they too may become involved.

10. *Posters.* Either the original or purchased variety can reinforce the message that everyone needs to be involved in service. (Don't leave the same posters up longer than two weeks.)

11. *Opportunity sheets.* These can be attractively typed up and distributed periodically through the adult Sunday School classes.

12. *Bulletin announcements.* Though this is often the first

means that we use to recruit volunteer ministers, it should be used in harmony with the many other methods of publicity.

SAMPLE BULLETIN INSERT

Recruitment Countdown

As of the writing of this bulletin feature, the Christian education ministry has a variety of staff needs. These are perhaps greater than any needs we have experienced in the past year.

Why, I am asked, do we have this urgent need at this time? I think we can isolate at least a half-dozen reasons:

The Armed Services Effect. Just as servicemen expect to be rewarded if they "volunteer," many others in our society have become conditioned to volunteer only if they do not have to sacrifice anything (fun, social times, leisure).

Loneliness. Many people feel lost and without deep relationships in our suburban society. Thus, they fear that if they have to serve in Sunday School or children's church, they will lose contact with the few friends they now have.

Continuing Education. The adult classes of the Christian education program bring support and helpful instruction to many adults who feel that leaving their adult classes to teach children will hinder their own personal development.

Working Women. It used to be that men could expect their wives to handle all of the teaching load because they had time to prepare. With the growing number of working women in the church, men are going to have to stop passing the buck and shoulder their share of the teaching load.

Passion Gap. Many people have ceased to believe that boys and girls need to be led into a personal relationship with Christ. Of course, no one says this, but the absence of this passion is evident by our lack of sufficient teachers.

Big Church Myth. "If they need me, they will call me." Or, "There are so many people at our church, I'm sure they do not need me." These and other big church myths keep many from volunteering.

Can you identify with any of these reasons for not becoming involved? I would like to help you deal with any of these negative feelings you may have with regard to teaching. Please take a registration card. Fill it out and indicate if you would like to talk to me about your role in the educational ministry of our church.

TEN

Interviewing
and Placing Teachers

Some lessons are learned the hard way. Like saying no to a person who is convinced that God is calling him to teach fourth-grade boys when that very class has been without a teacher for nearly a month.

Jeff had been the pastor of Christian education at Walnut Heights Bible Church for a little over a year when a fascinating situation arose. Harry Van Horn had been transferred to Atlanta, leaving an opening in the teaching team that spring. For three weeks after Harry's departure, the class was juggled around between substitute teachers and combined classes. "I've done my best to find a replacement," the department leader told Jeff. "I really feel bad about those kids."

"You aren't alone," Jeff replied. "I've asked seven people to consider taking over that position. They all said no. We really need to lift this up in prayer."

Then Marshall Burlington appeared. A telephone call brought the first contact between Jeff and the middle-aged salesman who had moved into the community just nine months before.

"I feel the Lord has called me to teach junior-age boys," Marshall told Jeff after briefly identifying himself.

"A miracle!" thought Jeff. "I can't believe the way the Lord is taking care of this need."

"How did you find out about the opening?" the pastor of Christian education queried. The recruitment process had been carried out without public announcement to avoid getting the

110

overzealous/underqualified applicants that can sometimes be a thorn in the side of any Sunday School department.

"The Lord just told me to call you," the salesman responded, "so I figured there had to be an opening."

"Who can argue with God?" thought Jeff.

The next Sunday morning, despite some feelings of apprehension on Jeff's part, the young pastor met his enthusiastic new recruit outside the Sunday School office at 9:05, reviewed briefly the requirements for teachers that they had discussed on the phone, gave Marshall the teaching materials, and took him to the fourth-grade class to observe. "But why the apprehension?" Jeff wondered. Marshall Burlington seemed pleasant enough and it appeared obvious that the Lord had provided this new teacher for a very teachable group of boys.

The following week Marshall Burlington began teaching. Within three weeks it was obvious that the department was in trouble. The salesman-teacher was loud, aggressive, and always showed up poorly prepared. Each lesson somehow ended up in hammering the doctrine of sovereign grace into the boys, no matter what the text was or what the lesson aims were scheduled to be. It wasn't that the doctrine was heresy; it was simply not synchronized with the Sunday School program for that age-level or in harmony with what the rest of the teaching staff was doing.

Fortunately for the Walnut Heights Sunday School, the problem was solved without conflict three months later when "Gracie" Burlington (as he had come to be called by his ten-year-old students) was transferred to a new territory by his company. Once again the teaching position was open, but this time Pastor Jeff decided to be more careful in his interview and placement procedures.

In the days that followed, Jeff pulled together, for reasons obvious to all, a set of standard procedures for interviewing and placing workers. Guidelines for the interviews were as follows:

1. Interviewers will insure that only qualified people are selected for ministries requiring specific gifts, talents, skills, attitudes, and training.
2. Each candidate will be evaluated in terms of the degree to which he/she would harmonize with other members of the assigned teaching team.

3. Interviewers should tactfully attempt to identify areas in which training or skill development would be helpful.
4. Care must be taken to insure that the ministry expectations of the new volunteer can and will be met.

Invariably, one or more of these guidelines became the basis for a bonding between volunteer and pastor. Tommie Sanchez was a good example. When Jeff interviewed her for a position working with the junior high youth group, he asked what would be the most rewarding thing that could happen as a result of working with junior high girls. Without hesitating a moment, Tommie responded, "I would see some of them come to know Jesus as their personal Saviour." The response had been so decisive that Jeff had nearly omitted the follow-up question he normally asked to such responses. He asked it anyway.

"If you had the opportunity to lead a seventh-grader to Christ today, would you know how to do it?" Jeff asked. Tommie's response was not so definite this time. "I'm not sure I could," she confessed.

Four or five other volunteers had expressed a similar need so Jeff developed a short evangelism training course for the group. Tommie had already begun her work with the junior high girls when the evangelism training program began and before the four-week course was completed, she had led her first young person to the Lord. The first person she called was Jeff. A new level of bonding between pastor and volunteer had been established.

Later, when the ministry had grown so large as to require age-group coordinators, they too found the guidelines for interviews useful in building strong ties between themselves and the volunteers. The interview had become a key tool to help the pastor to better shepherd his flock.

Interviewing Volunteers

A process of trial and error enabled Jeff to develop a rather effective pattern of interviewing volunteers. The procedure was as follows.

1. *Recruitment interviews will be done face-to-face and in private.* Telephone interviews or discussions in crowded hallways seldom allow for accurate perceptions of the volunteer. Nonverbal clues

may be missed. Follow-up questions may not be asked because of uncertainty over who else might be listening to the conversation. Besides, if the person does not have the time to set aside for a personal interview, there is a good possibility that he or she will not find enough time to fulfill the ministry responsibilities listed in the job description.

During the interview the volunteer should be provided with a job description of the position(s) being considered, shown the curricular materials and allowed to review them, given a list of the names of the coworkers, and given an opportunity to view the room where he or she would serve. Each of these face-to-face actions will allow the volunteer to feel more comfortable with the recruitment process.

2. *Recruitment interviews will be preceded by a written discovery process.* This discovery process will normally have two parts to it. The first is the *Volunteer Discovery Sheet* (see page 118) given to the volunteer before the interview so that the questions can be answered at leisure. The VDS follows the same format as the standard recruitment interview and allows the interviewee to know what questions will be asked (some fear interviews and this makes the process easier for them). It also saves time during the actual interview.

The second part of the discovery process includes a personal inventory test which is designed to help the volunteer focus on her gifts and abilities in light of the needs of the position she is exploring. Jeff and Pastor Wilcox reviewed a number of tests. None were perfect but each contributed insights to the recruitment process. Over lunch one day the two pastors talked with Dick Chester, a human resources manager for a large grocery store chain in the area. When asked about the effectiveness of tests in predicting success in ministry, Dick's comment seemed to put into words what the two pastors had been feeling.

"Tests, when properly debriefed, tend to be of more benefit to the person taking them than to the company (or in our case the church) which is administering them. One reason is that the cost is prohibitive. It's expensive to validate the use of tests as predictors of effectiveness and without validation the tests are merely expensive guesswork. With validation, the price is so high that we could hardly justify their use in the selection of a senior pastor, much less each Sunday School teacher.

"A second reason why the current generation of tests may not be effective in helping to place volunteers in the church is that most are looking for characteristics such as task versus people orientation or creativity versus detail orientation. Others are even more specific focusing on such aspects as styles of management that bring about change and leadership. While all of this is potentially useful in the church, the people in our fellowship hardly have the time to determine which of these orientations are best suited for the various positions in the church.

"Even in industry, human resource people are using fewer tests today primarily because of the possibility of lawsuits. Tests generally do not have a good track record, especially when relied upon as a replacement for a thorough interview process."

The three men agreed that the tests which were used would best be considered self-discovery tools rather than primary means of placement. Jeff evaluated the most promising tests and then started a "Volunteer Discovery Class" in which people who wanted to explore their ministry giftedness might do so under the leadership of Jeff or a person he trained.)

3. *Recruitment interviews will follow a standard format.* The information will be written down and retained in notebook, computer, or vertical file for future reference. It is important, however, that this information be held in strict confidence unless permission to disclose the contents has been given in writing. The interview provides the initial basis for determining a person's readiness to accept leadership responsibility. Seven areas of information are included:

Testimony: "Describe your relationship with God and where you are in your Christian walk today." The request is left open-ended and general so that the volunteer will be forced to provide information from his or her own spiritual development, rather than being influenced by the interviewer to give desired answers.

Training: "What type of classes or seminars (if any) have you taken which have sharpened your ministry skills in your interest area?" "What books, audio or video tapes, or other training tools have been of the most help in preparing you for the ministry to which you aspire?" Most of this will have been written out on the *Volunteer Discovery Sheet* so the interview will merely be looking for clarification of how the training contributed to the volunteer.

Experience: "What experience have you had in volunteer or full-time ministry?" Here the interviewer is looking for patterns of effective ministry. Some volunteers will be looking to move into areas of ministry different from where they have served previously, and so the interviewer should be looking for areas of significant contribution rather than for positions which have been held.

Special Interests: "What do you enjoy doing on vacations or in your spare time?" Hobbies, crafts, sports, and skills will serve to suggest areas of service which might be needed on a short-term basis, but might not fit into the week-to-week ministry of the church. For example, a person who enjoys woodworking might have much to contribute to the preparation of props for the Christmas program.

Expectations: "What would you like to see happen as a result of volunteering to serve the Lord through our church?" Most, if not all volunteers, have a specific reason for committing time to minister at the church. The sensitive pastor can insure that these expectations will be met if he knows about them. Careful placement and appropriate personal contacts throughout the year are key factors in bringing about the fulfillment of ministry expectations.

Fears: "What causes the greatest feelings of apprehension as you contemplate volunteer ministry?" Frequently, Jeff found, fears centered around classroom discipline or being "trapped" in the job because no replacements were available. Understanding the apprehensions of a volunteer, the pastor can usually insure that those fears never materialize or are minimized as a result of training and wise placement.

Preferences: "In what capacity and with what age-group would you like to minister?" The interviewer should look for both primary and alternative choices of ministry opportunities and age-groups.

4. *Recruitment interviews will seek to avoid placing people to ministry positions merely on the basis of pressing need.* If a position is open but a volunteer suited to that ministry or to that ministry team does not step forward, then the position will go unfilled. To inappropriately place an individual is to violate his or her gifts in the body of Christ.

5. *Recruitment interviews will be followed by a period of observation by the volunteer.* For one to three weeks after the interview the volunteer will be asked to attend the ministry activity to which she seeks assignment. During that time the volunteer will have the opportunity to meet the people with whom she will work and allow them to meet her. She will see the responsibilities to be accepted and observe the skills which will be necessary. At the end of the observation period a decision will be made about accepting an assignment to that department.

6. *Recruitment interviews will include feedback from potential coworkers.* "Everybody is smarter than anybody," was a comment Jeff had heard at a Sunday School convention workshop. It applies to the recruitment process. Sometimes a fatal flaw in a volunteer may be observed by a potential coworker while it escapes a person so well trained as the pastor. Their observations are to be considered a vital part of the interviewing/placement process.

7. *Recruitment interviews will culminate in the placement of volunteers into ministry positions or in informing them as to why they are not being placed.* Volunteers should not be left wondering whether they have been accepted to serve in the church. Notification, either positive or negative, should be prompt. If a position is not currently open but will be available shortly, the interviewer should notify the volunteer of as many details as possible and continue to inform him about the progress of the position.

* * *

No process is infallible. Even after going through all of these procedures, there were still times when mistakes were made in assigning new staff, but never again was there a placement so blatantly inappropriate as that of Marshall Burlington.

However, there was an unexpected fringe benefit. Those who had gone through the recruitment interview process built meaningful personal relationships with the leadership team and, as a result, demonstrated a greater loyalty to the ministry. The net result was that volunteers often continued in their ministry positions longer than previous staff had done. This meant that *less recruitment had to be done.*

INTERVIEW PROCEDURES

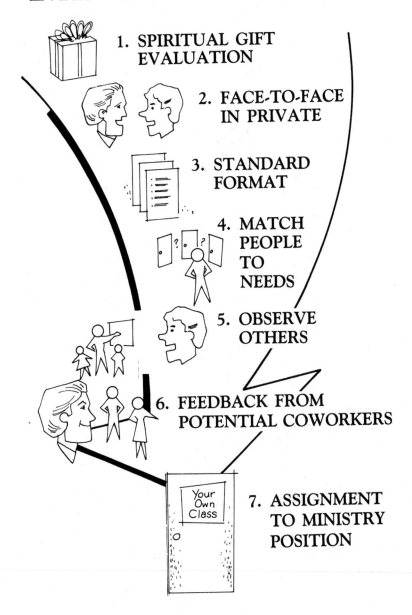

1. SPIRITUAL GIFT EVALUATION

2. FACE-TO-FACE IN PRIVATE

3. STANDARD FORMAT

4. MATCH PEOPLE TO NEEDS

5. OBSERVE OTHERS

6. FEEDBACK FROM POTENTIAL COWORKERS

7. ASSIGNMENT TO MINISTRY POSITION

VOLUNTEER DISCOVERY SHEET

Name: _____

Address: _____

Phone: _____

Interview Date: _____   **Placement Date:** _____

TESTIMONY

Describe your relationship with God and where you are in your Christian walk today.

TRAINING

What type of classes or seminars (if any) have you taken which have sharpened your ministry skills in your interest area?

What books, audio- or videotapes, or other training tools, have been of the most help in preparing you for the ministry to which you aspire?

EXPERIENCE

What experience have you had in volunteer or full-time ministry?

SPECIAL INTERESTS

What do you enjoy doing on vacations or in your spare time?

EXPECTATIONS

What would you like to see happen as a result of volunteering to serve the Lord through our church?

FEARS

What causes the greatest feelings of apprehension as you contemplate volunteer ministry?

PREFERENCES

In what capacity and with what age-group would you like to minister?

CRITIQUE OF PERSONAL ASSESSMENT TOOLS

From: Jeff Thompson
To: Christian Education Committee
Date: November 14, 1989
Re: Personal Assessment Tools for Recruitment and Placement
of Volunteers

In keeping with our discussion of personal assessment tools to help develop volunteers within the ministry of Walnut Heights Bible Church, the following is an informal critique of several of the primary assessment tools available at this time.

Name: "Spiritual Gifts"
Source: Guidance Assistance Programs, P.O. Box 105, Winfield, IL 60190
Description: A four-page forced choice test designed to help individuals learn how to use their spiritual gifts in the church. The tool is designed to be self-scoring and uses a graph to plot outcomes. Ten categories of ministry concerns are identified: teaching, Christian education, counseling, preaching, children, youth, visitation, caring, pastoral, and evangelistic.
Critique: "Spiritual Gifts" is more of a ministry preference test than an indicator of spiritual gifts. Though it does not attempt to link spiritual gifts to the categories of ministry concerns nor provide suggestions of how to interpret the results of the test, the tool could easily be used by a person working with volunteers as a means of gaining further insight into individual ministry preferences — through discussion after the test has been completed and the results plotted on the graph.
Time required: Fifteen minutes.
Validation: None claimed.
Cost: $.30 each; slightly less when bought in lots of 100 or more.

* * *

Name: SIMA (System for Identifying Motivated Abilities)
Source: Mattson, Ralph and Miller, Arthur. *Finding a Job You Can Love.* Nashville: Thomas Nelson Publishers, 1982.
Description: The book adapts a system developed for making

personnel decisions in Fortune 500 caliber companies and makes it available to individuals without the hefty "consultant fee" charged when trained staff members debrief and interpret the results.

SIMA is based on the premise that each person is created uniquely yet in God's image and therefore resists the standard agree/disagree, forced choice or multiple choice formats employed by a majority of assessment tools. Instead the person taking the SIMA identifies recurring activities which she has enjoyed doing throughout her lifetime and believes she has done well. Then through a process of analyzing the information which she has written down, discovers a pattern of motivated abilities which should be present in any job (paid or volunteer) to which a person commits herself.

Critique: The process is rather time-consuming and would best be used in a group process. This could occur over a period of weeks where group accountability encourages the individual to complete assignments or with individuals who are actively looking for a "new job."

Though the book does not discuss the concept of "spiritual gifts," the idea of motivated abilities comes very close to being as useful in helping the Christian discover ministry activities for which she is uniquely suited. To direct volunteers into ministry positions, one would have to link motivated ability patterns with tasks available in the local church situation.

Time required: A minimum of three to five hours.

Validation: Extensive validation claimed for the more extensive SIMA process; none claimed for ministry placement of volunteers in churches.

Cost: The book currently lists at $6.95.

* * *

Name: *Team Ministry: A Guide to Spiritual Gifts and Lay Involvement* by Larry Gilbert

Source: Church Growth Institute, P.O. Box 4404, Lynchburg, VA 24502

Description: The *Team Ministry* workbook contains a 108 item spiritual gifts inventory which uses statements to which the reader is to identify: almost always / occasionally / not very often. Responses are recorded on an answer sheet which clusters responses among nine spiritual gifts: evangelism, prophecy, teaching, exhortation, pastor-teacher, showing mercy, serving, giving, and administration. Bar graphs are then used to visually identify primary gifts.

The rest of the booklet is designed to be used in a classroom setting with an instructor explaining spiritual gifts. The information provided assists the volunteer in understanding the types of activities which the author associates with each gift but does not connect these with specific types of ministries.

Critique: In all likelihood the inventory will be most useful in situations where the volunteers being tested share the style of vocabulary most often associated with traditional evangelistic churches. However, a majority of evangelical churches should find the "Spiritual Gifts Inventory" useful.

The author spends time explaining the individual gifts in a very helpful fashion, but fails to provide suggestions as to what it means if a person scores high in two or more categories or what type of ministries should be considered as a result of such combinations.

Time required: One hour for inventory and two to four hours of class time.

Validation: Despite popular acceptance the test claims no validation.

Cost: $4.00 for workbook (including inventory).

* * *

Name: Houts Inventory of Spiritual Gifts
  by Richard F. Houts
Source: Fuller Evangelistic Association, call 1-800-C-FULLER to place an order; California residents call 1-818-449-0425.
Description: The inventory is a self-assessment instrument to help individuals ascertain their ministry gifts and related opportunities for Christian service. The sign gifts of tongues, healing, and miracles are not included.

The test contains 128 statements intended to help the Christian reflect upon her life and rate the extent to which each statement is appropriate in her experience. A worksheet is provided which enables the person to identify the degree to which each of sixteen spiritual gifts are in evidence in a person's life. A glossary is provided to define the manner in which the gifts are understood for use in the inventory.

The final two pages of the inventory provide lists of suggestions of service opportunities. Eight public and four support gifts are identified and five or more types of ministry opportunities are provided for each gift. The person taking the inventory thus has a means by which to make decisions about areas of service within the church community, though not tightly defined.

Critique: Rather than an inventory which identifies a person's spiritual gifts in any permanent fashion, the inventory appears to be a current reflection on a person's ministry preferences. The results may change over time, so the inventory could be used periodically to assist an individual in clarifying the types of ministry for which he is currently suited.

The statements used are satisfactory but not sophisticated. If a person is looking to outguess the test and intentionally score high or low in certain gift areas, he could do so with relative ease.

Though there are lists of service opportunities provided for each gift, there are no suggestions for combinations or patterns of giftedness. If a person is extremely high in two or three gifts, it would seem that this combination would help focus the type of ministries for which one would be best suited. Yet no suggestions are given.

As I used the inventory, I found it to be a rather accurate reflection of where my areas of giftedness lie.

Time required: A half hour to forty-five minutes.

Validation: Despite popular acceptance the test claims no validation.

Cost: $2.00 for the inventory book.

ELEVEN

Evaluation

At first Jeff rejected the idea.

"It seems so contrary to my ideas about human nature," he told Rita at breakfast. "I'm not even sure people will feel comfortable enough to respond positively if they're evaluated on their teaching performance."

"Maybe you need to give people more credit," Rita suggested. "Evaluation is appreciated by teachers who are doing a good job. It's a form of recognition."

As Jeff drove to the church for a meeting with the middler teaching team, the concept appeared to be a real option. What Rita said made sense. "Perhaps," thought Jeff, "if I'm extremely sensitive about how I approach the process, I can turn evaluation sessions into a recruitment tool—at least a method of retaining an increasing number of quality teachers. That way I might not have to recruit as many new volunteers each year."

Nearly a year before at a meeting of the Christian Education Committee, Jeff had raised the idea of evaluating the teaching teams. "I believe if our primary focus is on discovering the strengths of the various teachers and helping them refine and enhance their skills, teacher evaluation could be a productive addition to the program," he had said. After several months of discussion, the committee adopted the plan that he had submitted, and the evaluation process was introduced to the teaching staff at the fall workers conference.

The initial flack had been predictable. "Do you mean to suggest," fired Ford Collins, fourth-grade boys' Sunday School teacher, "that someone, perhaps with no teaching experience, can come into my classroom for a single session and get an accurate picture of how well I'm teaching week-in and week-out?" Sandra Swanson felt especially angered by the process. "After all," she argued, "I've been teaching children in this church for seventeen years, and if people haven't liked what I've been doing, they would have told me long before now!"

Others expressed similar, though not as defensive, responses at the conference. More concern was expressed to Ernie Larson, chairman of the CE Committee, in the days that followed. But to each person the response was the same: "Pastor Jeff is an easy person to work with. Let's give the process a try, and if it makes your whole team uncomfortable, then we'll reevaluate it — teachers included."

Jeff's role was the key to the idea, and he knew it. He was dealing with volunteers who sincerely wanted to serve the Lord, many of whom felt nervous over having a seminary graduate "peering over their shoulders" in class on Sunday morning. In recognition of their feelings, guidelines were set which, it was hoped, would minimize the teachers' concerns.

1. Teacher teams would be notified two weeks before an evaluation took place to allow teachers to feel adequately prepared for the pastor's visit.

2. The evaluation would take place over three consecutive weeks in order to obtain a balanced view of what happens in the various CE departments.

3. The CE pastor would be in the classroom from fifteen minutes before the scheduled starting time of the session until after the last activity was completed (when the children were turned over to either parents or the church-time leaders).

4. The CE pastor would remain in the department to talk with teachers after each teaching session for as long as they wished to talk. The main discussion, however, would wait until the three weeks were completed.

5. The CE pastor would use an evaluation form with which the teaching team was acquainted to reduce the fear of being critiqued in aspects of the teaching art in which the teachers were not trained.

6. The CE pastor would remain as inconspicuous as possible in the room while doing the evaluation.
7. The CE pastor would meet with the teaching teams as a group within two weeks of the in-class evaluation to share his observations.

Sandra Swanson's kindergarten was the first teaching team Jeff visited. It was not that he had anything against the kindergarten department. He'd just spent so much time on the phone with Sandra explaining things and smoothing ruffled feathers that he thought it would be wise to get the process out of the way quickly. Allowing the evaluation to hang over the veteran teacher's head for months could trigger a buildup of tension and resentment.

The kindergarten evaluation, to Sandra's surprise, was a very positive experience for everyone involved. Though Sandra was not a perfect department leader, she had a number of strengths. Jeff focused on these, suggesting some innovative ways in which these abilities could be channeled to make the teaching experience even more effective. Finally, after nearly an hour and a half of creative affirmation, brainstorming, and instruction, Sandra blurted out the question Jeff hoped someone would ask.

"Nobody's perfect, Pastor Jeff!" the veteran admitted. "What were we doing wrong? Where do we need to improve?"

Jeff was prepared to answer such questions, but he felt reluctant to do so. The meeting had gone so well and so much valuable teacher training had taken place, that he simply didn't want to jeopardize the impact by the negative reaction which even mild criticism could stimulate.

"Come on, Jeff," Sandra chided. "We really want your evaluation on where we could improve."

For the next twenty minutes, Jeff shared helpful observations with the now eager volunteer teachers, offering training resources and practical tips that could strengthen the learning process in the kindergarten department. To his immense relief, it was gracefully received.

Months passed. The third evaluation since the kindergarten teaching team visit had been completed. As Jeff reflected back on the evaluations of the primary and middler departments as well as his time with Sandra Swanson's staff, one fact was obvious: These were dedicated, sincere and, in most cases, gifted people who needed the affirmation, encouragement, and instruction of a person whom they loved and respected. The time and sensitivity he'd invested in the process expanded into a stronger bond of loyalty by teachers toward the church and toward Jeff. There was a new confidence that they were doing a commendable job in their teaching ministry.

In the years that followed, Jeff's idea of using the evaluation process as a tool for recruiting volunteer workers proved to be valid in two respects. Just as he'd hoped, fewer people had to be recruited because department turnover was lower. Second, Jeff noticed that people who felt affirmed, supported, and assisted at the points of their needs would attract other people to volunteer for teaching. The evaluated people became key influences in the recruitment process.

Despite all the positive aspects of this approach to evaluation, the pastor of Christian education found that the process was simply too time-consuming to be practical. After all, it was nearly a luxury to be isolated in one department for an hour and a half, three weeks in a row. Other people needed to see the church's foremost educational resource person during this time. The solution was to train others to do the evaluations.

The next two evaluations gave Jeff the opportunity to teach his age-group coordinators how to assist the teaching teams through the evaluation process. The coordinators were briefed on how to use evaluation as a positive tool, then were given classroom observation assignments.

After each teaching session, Jeff met with the coordinators to discuss the evaluation process. He provided feedback on their comments and observations, the effectiveness of their evaluations, and what should be looked for in the next session. The response of the coordinators was excellent, for they were upgrading their own skills while building better relationships with their teaching teams and upgrading the quality of the teaching/learning process. It was an "everybody wins" proposition.

In the years that followed, the age-group coordinators remained the primary evaluators of the various departments. But Jeff found himself reentering the process for one of two reasons: to train new age-group coordinators as staff changes occurred and to keep in touch with the grass-roots level of what was happening in the educational ministry of Walnut Heights.

TEACHING TEAM EVALUATION FORM

Department _____

Date _____

Evaluator _____

The purpose of this evaluation is to build on the strengths of the teaching team and to expand the horizons of the teachers with regard to the teaching/learning process.

Check evaluated items on the lines (continuums) provided and include comments as frequently as possible.

PERSONAL CHARACTERISTICS OF TEAM MEMBERS
1. Warmth
   Friendly, loving |___|___|___|___| Cold, distant
   Comment:
2. Enthusiasm
   Appropriate |___|___|___|___| Inappropriate
   Comment:
3. Self-revealing
   Open |___|___|___|___| Closed
   Comment:

PREPARATION FOR LEARNING
4. Arrival time of team members
   Early |___|___|___|___| Late
   Comment:
5. Room preparation
   Attractive,
   uncluttered |___|___|___|___| Dull, messy
   Comment:
6. Lesson preparation
   Mastered |___|___|___|___| Dependent
   Comment:

METHODS EMPLOYED

7. Circle the methods used:

Buzz groups	Discussion	Object lessons	Quiz
Case studies	Drama	Overhead	Reports
Cassette tapes	Field trip	projector	Review
Chalkboard	Filmstrips/	Picture studies	Role Play
Charts	slides	Playing Bible	Singing
Conversation	Flannelgraph	learning	Skits
Choral	Interview	Problem	Story telling
readings	Lecture	solving	Testimony
Creative	Making things	Projects	
writing	Maps	Puppets	
Direct Bible	Memorization	Question/	
study	Models	answer	

8. Appropriateness

   Communicated
   well |___|___|___|___|___| Unrelated to lesson
   Comment:

9. Skill in use

   Effective |___|___|___|___|___| Ineffective
   Comment:

TEAMWORK

10. Cooperation among teachers

    Strong |___|___|___|___|___| Weak
    Comment:

11. Discipline

    Appropriate |___|___|___|___|___| Lacking or excessive
    Comment:

12. Organization

    Effective |___|___|___|___|___| Ineffective
    Comment:

CONTENT OF LESSON

13. Biblical basis

    Adequate |___|___|___|___|___| Inadequate
    Comment:

14. Mastery of biblical teachings
    Strong |___|___|___|___| Weak
    Comment:
15. Practical application
    Life related |___|___|___|___| Theoretical
    Comment:

STUDENT PARTICIPATION

16. During early arrival activities
    Strong |___|___|___|___| Weak
    Comment:
17. In large group settings
    Strong |___|___|___|___| Weak
    Comment:
18. In small group settings
    Strong |___|___|___|___| Weak
    Comment:

IMPACT OF LESSON

19. State simply the apparent lesson
    Aim _____

    _____

    _____

20. To what extent were aims accomplished?
    Largely   Largely
    accomplished |___|___|___|___| unaccomplished
    Comment:
21. Evidence of learning
    Strong |___|___|___|___| Weak
    Comment:

SUMMARY

22. What were the strengths of the teaching/learning process observed today?

_____

_____

_____

_____

_____

23. What were the weaknesses of the teaching/learning process observed today?

_____

_____

_____

_____

24. What strength can be used even more effectively? How?

_____

_____

_____

_____

TWELVE

But We Don't
Have a CE Minister

Thanksgiving was always a festive occasion for the Thompson family, but this year's celebration featured a new attraction — Jeremy Wilson Thompson. Rita had given birth, appropriately enough thought Jeff, on All Saint's Day, November 1. Being the baby of his family, Jeff and his wife Rita proudly returned to the family farm in Michigan to show off the child that Jeff's family had thought would never come.

Twenty-three people crowded around the table which had all eight oak leaves inserted for the occasion. Conversation was nonstop except for the few moments when Dad Thompson had taken little Jeremy in his arms and dedicated this new life to the Lord. It was a family tradition that even the youngest of the grandchildren understood and appreciated.

By four in the afternoon, Jeff found himself washing pots and pans while Nick, his oldest brother, dried the last of the serving plates. Nick was a practical man. Even the manner in which he stacked the platters and bowls evidenced the functional way in which his mind operated.

Nick had remained on the farm while the rest of the children had gone off to college and eventually had found careers outside the agricultural field. With Nick's rootedness in the farming community coupled to his commitment to Jesus Christ came another responsibility — leadership within Crawford's Creek Baptist Church, the church in which Nick and Jeff had been raised.

"For the past two years," commented Nick, abruptly changing

the topic of conversation from basketball and babies to his concerns as Sunday School superintendent, "I have been having a difficult time getting people to serve as Sunday School teachers at church. I just wish we had someone like you to serve as an associate pastor and work with the children's programs, but with a church that averages only a little over 180 in the worship service, we simply can't afford another pastor."

Jeff had heard the problem expressed before. A number of smaller churches in his denomination were feeling the same tension. At first he had responded to such questions by launching into an explanation of his recruitment strategies which usually overwhelmed even the most dedicated of Sunday School superintendents. After all, most of them were only able to give five hours a week of volunteer time to the church and already that time was more than spoken for. Another breakfast meeting on top of everything else, even for the noble purpose of finding volunteers, was simply out of the question. This time Jeff would try a different approach and see if he and Nick could come up with an answer for the smaller church.

"What is the Sunday School superintendent expected to do at Crawford's Creek these days?" asked Jeff.

"Well, you name it; I do it. Pretty much the same way Dad did it when we were kids. Do you remember getting to church an hour before Sunday School to straighten up the classrooms, distribute take-home papers, shovel snow, and all those other things? Well, I'm still doing the same things." The conversation was broken for a few moments as Nick put some of the serving plates into the dining room hutch. "It's like putting these platters away. Every Thanksgiving I end up putting them away. I wonder if anyone else, besides Mom, knows where they go."

"How about during the week, does the superintendent have to do a lot of duties on any day but Sunday?" Jeff was looking for some of his brother's time usage that could be redirected into recruitment efforts.

"Sunday School executive committee meetings, ordering of curriculum, buying supplies and equipment, organizing quarterly training meetings, and that kind of stuff," responded Nick.

A flood of memories came back to Jeff of all his father had done as superintendent. People at Walnut Heights Bible Church simply did not accept positions which carried that much responsibility, nor were they that conscientious in jobs requiring less commitment. But maybe his brother's recruitment problem was an extension of his sense of responsibility. Nick may not have learned to give up certain activities in order to accomplish the essential responsibilities of the church's teaching ministry. Enlistment of workers was the most important job associated with the superintendent's duties.

"Let me ask you a question, Nick." It wasn't really a request. "Which of the activities you perform as superintendent could be dropped altogether and still allow the church's teaching ministry to continue?"

Nick paused for a moment to think. "Nothing really, all of the duties are important."

"I realize they are all important," pressed Jeff, "but isn't there something that could be omitted without pulling the plug on Sunday School?"

"Not really," persisted Nick.

"How about straightening up the chairs on Sunday morning, couldn't teaching take place without neat classrooms?"

"Well, of course it could, it's just that it wouldn't be as appropriate for helping boys and girls learn about Christ."

"So we could drop the custodial responsibilities if we really had to," confirmed Jeff. "How about Sunday School executive committee meetings? Could we drop those and still have people teaching the Bible to children at Crawford's Creek?"

"I suppose we could drop them but would we ever have a headache coordinating everything. Besides, who would appropriate the money to pay for Sunday School materials?"

"That raises another question. How essential is ordering Sunday School materials? If worse came to worse couldn't teachers merely teach their Sunday School lessons out of the Bible?"

"Of course they could, but within two weeks I would have a bigger recruitment problem than I have now." Nick had always been the practical member of the family. Theoretical discussions were of little use to him. "So what's your point?"

"My point is simply this: You can get along without clean classrooms, committee decisions, or commercially produced curricular materials, but you can't have Sunday School without teachers. The most important part of your job as Sunday School superintendent is getting and equipping committed teachers.

You may have to drop everything else that Dad used to do in leading the church's CE ministries, but make sure you continually recruit and develop your teaching staff. It's a year-round task."

"Be practical," countered Nick, "I can't just drop those other jobs. The place would be a zoo."

"Then look for someone to take some of those other jobs while you focus on the responsibility of recruitment, and if you can't find anyone then be prepared to enjoy your trip to the zoo until you have built a teaching team which can share the load with you."

Big brothers don't like to have their baby brothers show them up, but there was some logic in the point that Jeff had been making. "If all I did on the farm," said Nick, "was to service the tractors and combines, order seed, and clean the barns and silos but never planted the seeds or reaped the crops, I'd be out of business within the year. What is the difference with the Sunday School?"

Ministry By Wandering Around
"So if you were me, what would you do to get enough workers for the Sunday School?" inquired Nick.

"If I were you," stated Jeff, "I would employ MBWA — Ministry By Wandering Around. It's an idea we have adapted from the business world, but it works extremely well in the church. What I mean by MBWA is to drop the busywork that keeps a leader away from the people and focus a majority of your time on helping your team members become effective in their ministries. Part of the wandering will be conversations with people who aren't currently involved in ministry and finding out what they would like to do in the future."

"But what would I do while I wandered around? It sounds a lot like I would be wasting time."

"It was somewhat wasted for me when I began to do it," confessed Jeff, "because I didn't know what to look for. But in time, I began to ask myself several questions and eventually found ways to ask these same questions of the people I met while wandering around."

"So what were your questions?"

"First I wanted to know what a person had succeeded in

134

doing throughout his or her life. The Lord usually uses those successes as indicators of giftedness. I started by thinking about the types of successes I had observed in that person. Unfortunately, there were many times when I had been so preoccupied with the needs of the CE program that I had not stopped to discover a person's giftedness. Rita was especially helpful here. She had a lot of useful observation about people I thought I knew. Soon I discovered that these people were more motivated to serve when I gave them opportunities in keeping with their past patterns of success.

"Next I tried to discover what each member wanted to contribute to the church during the coming year."

"Do you mean financially?" interrupted Nick.

"No. What I focused on was the use of their talents and gifts in expressing their Christian faith. I started off looking for people who could fill next week's teaching responsibilities but found that, like you, highly unsatisfactory to the people at church. Now my focus is on the next school year which allows me to be more relaxed with people, and in turn they are more relaxed with me. They do not seem to be threatened by something they may be committing themselves to three months from now.

"Finally, I ask myself, 'Where can this person's abilities and vision fit into the existing ministry of the church or should she be encouraged to use her abilities and vision to create a new ministry either within the church or outside of its structures?' "

The last pan was now nested in the drawer beneath the microwave oven. The brothers had completed their kitchen task and there would be other times for Jeff and Nick to complete their conversation about recruiting in the smaller church.

As the two men walked back into the living room, Nick summarized their conversation: "What it all seems to come down to is that recruitment of volunteers, even in the smaller churches, is a people proposition. Our most important responsibility is to become acquainted with the people who attend our church. Then, when we have gotten to know the folks that God has placed in the congregation we will discover the people with abilities appropriate to carry on the church's many ministries."

"That's about the way I see it, too," affirmed Jeff.

THIRTEEN

To Fire a Volunteer

Pastor Thompson should have known better. After all, it had only been a year since he badly bungled the firing of a Sunday School teacher. But no, there he was again up to his neck in angry people. All he wanted to do was remove one immature youth sponsor. Yet from the reactions you would think Jeff was committing some sort of crime.

Looking back, Jeff realized he had handled the situation poorly. Sending that letter to Christopher Swartz asking him to resign as a Sunday School teacher was not the smartest way of firing a guy. "Old Chris," as the students called him, deserved better treatment after teaching in the high school department for five years. Yet Jeff's stomach knotted up every time he had thought of confronting Chris on his lack of teaching skills. So Jeff had taken the chicken's way out. He wrote a letter.

Even the boys in Swartz's class got on Jeff Thompson's case when they heard what happened. Not that they liked "Old Chris" as a teacher; they simply felt bad about the way in which he had gotten the ax.

Then came October. Jeff was determined there would be no letter used when Earl Benson was asked to step down as a club leader. Besides, this one should have been easier. Everyone was aware that Earl was more immature than many of the freshman guys. In some ways his role as "leader" appeared to be a means of gaining the status that he was never able to achieve as a computer whiz at Wheeling High School a few years earlier.

However, there were a couple of factors the associate pastor had overlooked. One was that Earl was the nephew of a very influential former church board member who was never satisfied with the manner in which the weekday program had been handled during Earl's high school years. The other was that a person who is fired without prior warning, tends to fight back to save face before his peers.

So when the grade school boys arrived home from the fall campout at Starved Rock State Park and Jeff could put up with Earl's sophomoric actions no longer, the Christian education minister single-handedly "called" a special church board meeting. The problem was that Jeff was the last person to know about the meeting. All he had done to convene the special session was to sit on the back steps of the church and tell Earl that he should take the rest of the year off as a club leader and get involved in the church's college group.

At least it was better than sending a letter. The results, however, were not much different.

Though again the young minister was able to weather the sudden deluge of misunderstanding, he was beginning to feel as if he would be permanently stuck with any teachers or leaders who were associated with the Christian education ministry of the church. Most of them were fairly effective, so he didn't have anyone on a "hit" list. But what if someone turned out to be an X-rated video freak or theological heretic of some sort, or what if a person who had looked like a winner in the interview process was unable to work with the other people in his department? Jeff wondered if he would be willing to take the chance of getting struck by another bolt of criticism.

Several weeks later Pastor Wilcox and his assistant had a long conversation about Jeff's frustrations over the problems which would be created if he was not permitted to, as he put it, "fire volunteers when it was necessary." The idea was foreign to the senior pastor. In all of his years of ministry he had never found it necessary to take such drastic steps, though he did admit that he had "prayed a few people out of their positions."

"I understand why you would want a volunteer to resign," commented the pastor, "but what would require such drastic action as forcing it to happen?"

Herb Wilcox was a shepherd at heart. He had spent his entire

137

ministry pastoring people at times of need, encouraging dispirited parishioners, holding the hands of hurting church members. The very idea of telling a person that he or she could no longer serve in a ministry position was foreign to his understanding of the pastorate.

"Mediocrity (or something worse) in the educational ministries of the church may be all we will have if we don't have the option of pruning unproductive branches from the church tree." Jeff hoped that the use of biblical images might enable the pastor to understand his point. "And one of the major reasons for mediocrity is the dissension created by people who are poor leaders, weak teachers, or who simply do not work well with others. I would have lost two or three good club leaders, for instance, if I had not asked Earl Benson to resign. Then I would have had to recruit and train new leaders in the middle of the year and that would have hurt the ministry to the boys."

"But do we have to *fire* them?" replied the pastor. "Can't we simply work with them to help them improve? This whole firing idea is so disruptive. The person who you fire gets hurt. Their friends and family get upset, and we spend the next three weeks putting the church back together after the explosion."

For the next hour or so the two men discussed the issues involved, when suddenly Jeff was struck with a blinding flash of the obvious — most of the problems which had been created had to do with communication. He had not been careful in telling volunteer workers what he wanted them to do, how he wanted them to do it, how their progress in ministry would be assessed, or what was expected of them in their personal development. No wonder people were upset. Even if his assessments of people were correct, he had been rather insensitive in how he had acted.

A four point "Firing Prevention Program" emerged in the next few minutes. Jeff was good at creating catchy names or slogans, but it took a solid four hours of work that afternoon to carefully define and write out what the four points included.

Careful Recruitment was the first and by far most important step. The process of interviewing prospective Christian education workers, which had been developed after the Marshall Burlington fiasco, had already helped Jeff avoid surprises later on as people worked in the educational ministry at the church.

All volunteers would have limitations, even if it were no more than a lack of time to invest in the ministry. But Jeff had learned to carefully discover positive spiritual and character qualities before asking a person to minister in the church. If he could be assured that a volunteer was walking with the Lord, a person of integrity, and able to get along with others, most other skills of ministry could be developed in time.

A second step would be to provide *Clear Direction.* Jeff was doing this on one level but needed to strengthen it on a second level. Written job descriptions provided for each ministry position allowed everyone involved to know what was expected of them. The specific ministry objectives needed strengthening. These would be established so that each youth worker could focus on the most important aspects of the job.

A ministry objective which Linda, a junior high sponsor, selected was to have each of her class members over for Sunday noon meal each quarter and have each girl share a prayer request for which Linda could pray daily. With this ministry objective so clearly stated, both Jeff and Linda felt comfortable with her ministry activity for the year.

Consistent Communication would become the third aspect of the "Firing Prevention Program." Jeff had been consistent about having Christian education worker meetings but most of the time he had talked about the wrong things. The bulk of the time had been spent on details of planning. A heavier (though not exclusive) emphasis should have been placed on the teachers and leaders sharing their progress in their own spiritual pilgrimage and in attaining their ministry goals.

By doing this, Jeff would not have to worry about directing a conversation to problem areas. He could affirm a person when he saw signs of progress and encourage or nudge one when progress was slow or nonexistent. It would also provide a forum in which questions could be raised about the best place of ministry for a volunteer and, if necessary, lovingly attempt to redirect one's energies for the glory of God.

Concern for the Individual was the final step in the plan. As he looked back, Jeff was convinced that most of his concern was for himself or for the program. He allowed Earl to continue as a club leader and avoided confronting him because Jeff wanted to be liked. He didn't want to disrupt a relationship even though it was not especially healthy.

What the CE minister had to recognize was that part of ministry was assisting volunteers to become whole persons as they ministered. Sometimes this would mean redirecting a person into a different area of ministry because her abilities simply did not match the requirements of the task. Other times it would mean confronting a volunteer with the fact that he was not living up to the ministry potential which God had given to him. Always it involved praying for the person and thinking in terms of his or her best interests.

By the end of his creative afternoon, part of the problem had been solved. Pastor Wilcox would be much more comfortable because these ideas provided a method for caring for people while still maintaining the integrity of ministry leadership. Still the problem nagged Jeff. If he had to fire a volunteer worker again, how would he do it?

Fortunately, Jeff didn't have to test his new system for nearly two years. By that time the ministry was growing fast. Actually, growth was a major part of the problem.

Ted Wilson was one of the first children's church workers Jeff had recruited when he came to his job. Ted was as sharp a person as a pastor could have wanted to minister beside. As soon as Ted graduated from college he had taken a sales position with a pharmaceutical firm and had been one of their top salesmen. At the same time he maintained an amazing "quiet time" and commitment to his group of preschool children. He was almost too good to be true. Jeff's "Firing Prevention Program" seemed irrelevant with Ted.

As the educational ministry grew, it became obvious that Beginner's Church needed to be split into two sections, one for four-year-olds and the other for kindergarteners. Though there were enough staff most of the time, the room was simply too crowded for the children to worship without having unnecessary discipline problems. So Jeff split the Beginner's Church and when Wanda Buckingham, the Beginner's Church team leader, requested the opportunity to work with the kindergarten children, Jeff turned to Ted for help.

After developing a workable job description and ministry goals, Ted agreed to take on the responsibility. That's when the problems began.

At first it was only little things. He would miss appointments with Mary Ellen Watkins, the early childhood coordinator or show up unprepared to planning sessions for the newly created department. Jeff tended to excuse this due to Ted's growing sales responsibilities. But matters came to a head when Ted apologetically bowed out of the children's ministries workshop at the last moment. It was not as if the workshop had been a surprise to Ted. Both Jeff and Mary Ellen had talked with Ted about his participation in the workshop when the new department was created. Besides, it was written into his job description and was included in the ministry goals to which Ted had agreed. Though his reasons for missing the workshop seemed valid and his walk with the Lord was as strong as ever, Ted's heart simply did not appear to be with the Children's Church for four-year-olds.

Jeff faced an agonizing decision. After bathing the matter in prayer for several days, the CE minister concluded he was going to have to fire Ted — or at least reduce his responsibilities in the Children's Church. Mary Ellen fully agreed but felt uncomfortable breaking the news to Ted.

After the monthly meeting of preschool departmental leaders, Jeff and Mary Ellen asked Ted to evaluate the job he was doing in leading the newly created department. Reluctantly, and yet with no apologies, Ted critiqued himself with his usual crisp, analytical style. Each failure which Jeff would have suggested, Ted described in detail. In fact, Mary Ellen ended up defending Ted from his own criticism, feeling he was being too hard on himself.

As they concluded their conversation, Jeff asked Ted what he thought should be done to resolve the problems.

"Unfortunately," Ted responded, "the problem is me. My heart is just not in it. I'm going to have to step aside and let someone else do the job."

Realizing that even his old commitment to work as a table teacher with four-year-olds was no longer appealing to him, the three leaders set a date a month later for Ted to turn over his leadership role to someone else.

An emptiness echoed within Jeff as he walked to his car that night. He had just "fired" a friend. There would be no special board meetings or angry phone calls. There would only be an open spot in four-year-old Children's Church and an empty niche in Jeff's heart for a friend with whom he would no longer spend as much ministry time.

The story ended happily—and sadly. Two years later Ted asked Jeff to do the premarital counseling and wedding ceremony for him and his lovely bride Lynn. That was a supreme honor, since most of the couples in the church were married by Pastor Wilcox.

Then, less than a year later, the honor was amplified under sadder circumstances. On his death bed, dying of a rare liver ailment, Ted asked if Jeff would perform his funeral. Through his own tears the young pastor agreed.

Three days later Jeff eulogized the volunteer he had fired.

*   *   *

STEPS IN FIRING A VOLUNTEER

When a Christian educator concludes that the efforts of a volunteer worker must be terminated, three factors should be taken into consideration: preparation, timing, and procedure.

Preparation
1. *Prayer.* Before rushing out and firing a volunteer, the careful minister of Christian education will spend time asking God if, when, and how the person should be terminated. Prayer should be focused on both the best interests of the ministry and the person.
2. *Documentation.* Write down the problems that have been observed as they occur. Though the Christian educator should avoid bringing this information into the conversation when dismissing a person, at least as proof of the fairness of the decision, the documentation does help a pastor avoid emotionally based decisions. It helps maintain objectivity.
3. *No surprises.* Firings should not catch the person being terminated off guard. Some type of ministry performance review should be provided for all volunteers, and in this process areas of concern or failure should be brought to the attention of the offending party. Then if the person does not respond to such suggestions he or she should not be shocked by the

firing procedures. A similar procedure is outlined in Matthew 18:15-17.

4. *Keep pastor posted.* In circumstances where problems may result, it is best to explain to the senior pastor why and how the firing will take place. His wisdom and experience may make the process easier.

Timing

1. *Don't rush.* Rapid termination of a volunteer rarely is done well. Emotions may blur good judgment. Facts get confused. Task orientation sometimes hinders sensitivity to people.

2. *Don't renew.* If possible, rather than fire a volunteer, it is better not to invite the person to teach or sponsor for another year. This means that each volunteer should have an automatic "sunset" on his or her commitment. A ministry cut-off date usually occurs at the end of a school year or at the beginning of the next one.

   Absence of renewal, however, does not mean an absence of communication. The volunteer deserves the right of an honest appraisal even if not asked to continue in the current capacity.

3. *Don't delay.* In situations where moral or theological problems are involved, the Christian educator must act with all deliberate speed. As soon as the facts are verified, action should be taken. Remember, however, this type of action is not designed to destroy the volunteer. On the contrary, every effort should be made to be redemptive — both for the person and for the ministry.

Procedure

1. *Private appointment.* Firings should not be done publicly. A specific time should be established when the CE minister (or other supervisor) and the volunteer can evaluate the ministry effectiveness of that person.

2. *Self-evaluation.* Rather than dumping a load of complaints on the volunteer, the wise supervisor will first ask the person for an appraisal of the year's ministry in the light of the job description and ministry objectives. A majority of the time the volunteer will be harder on himself than the supervisor would have been.

3. *Confront if necessary.* If the volunteer appears blind to the weaknesses which seem obvious to others, then the person will need to be told of specific shortcomings. This must be done in a spirit of love and respect.

4. *Affirm positive qualities.* Sometimes the self-evaluation or loving confrontation will obscure the positive contributions that a person has made. Such activities should be complimented specifically and genuinely to avoid this problem.

5. *Allow resignation.* After the problems have been examined, ask the volunteer what should be done. If he or she resigns, accept the resignation with humility of spirit. If the person still does not get the picture, the Christian education leader will have to ask for the resignation.

6. *Redirect talents.* Usually there is another place in the church or a nearby parachurch agency where the fired volunteer could put his or her skills to better use. The mature pastor spends sufficient time getting the fired volunteer settled in a different and more appropriate ministry position.

7. *Follow-up.* Even if the fired volunteer does not become settled in another ministry position, the education minister/supervisor should check back with the former team member to insure continued Christian growth and fellowship.

FOURTEEN

Recruiting When No One Wants the Job

Jeff Thompson was beside himself. For three years his recruiting system had gone very well. Though there had been occasional problems, not one major Christian education position had been without a qualified person on promotion day since he had introduced his process of personal interviews which matched people's gifts with church ministry needs. But that was before Mary Jenkins had retired from Children's Church for three-year-olds.

For three months Jeff had known that on promotion Sunday a bumper crop of wigglers would come pouring into a department staffed only by a rookie helper. No one seemed willing to follow "Mom" Jenkins as the preschool Children's Church leader. She was a legend at Walnut Heights Bible Church. For eighteen years, sometimes with only the silver-haired lady present, children had been touched by her love.

Mary Jenkins' longevity was part of the problem. Potential department leaders balked at the very idea of being held captive by three-year-olds for the next two decades. So the opening remained with but four days left before promotion Sunday. Dozens of people had been considered for the position. Ten capable workers had been approached and had declined the ministry opportunity. Matters had come to the point where Jeff was about ready to accept any warm body who would say "yes" to his inquiries.

Jeff was aware that most pastors face similar problems. Junior high youth sponsors, Evangelism Committee chairmanship, or

145

the Vacation Bible School director's shoes may go unfilled. Most vacancies represent thankless jobs which seem to gather comments only from parishioners who are unhappy with the way the responsibilities are being handled. But the young pastor thought he had overcome those problems with his recruitment system which included continual affirmation of even the most obscure volunteer worker.

"I might have expected this to happen," complained the frustrated CE pastor to Roy Mayfield, the recently appointed Christian Education Committee chairman, "if we had not developed a year-round strategy for matching gifted people with the church's ministry needs through a placement process. Or if we had given the recruitment and development of volunteer ministers little, if any, thought until the moment a personnel shortage stared us in the face, then we would have reaped in vacant positions what we had sown in systematic neglect."

Roy realized what was happening. Jeff was defending himself from blame for the key vacancies in the fall program. As secure as Jeff Thompson had appeared when Roy served as the age-group coordinator for the young people's ministries, this was a new revelation. There was a sense of vulnerability as well as frustration in Jeff's voice. Roy just listened.

"If our church had a declining membership or a static but aging pool of potential workers I would expect to have this problem," continued Jeff, "but not here at Walnut Heights where the increase in Sunday School attendance has been 8.6 percent over the previous year. Roy, I have just about run out of ideas for filling Mary's position. It looks like I may have to do the job myself until a recruitment miracle happens."

"Let me tell you about our experience on the West Coast before I was transferred here," ventured Roy. "We had a very creative woman, Francis Clancy, who was the chairwoman of our Christian Education Committee. When faced with a similar situation she tried a variety of approaches to secure enough teachers for the children's ministry. Pleading was her first approach. Then, when the buttonholing approach proved ineffective, she turned to public announcements in the church bulletin and from the pulpit. Finally, our pastor was enlisted to give one of his patented "volunteer-for-the-gipper" type messages with only modest and exclusively short-term results.

"In the meantime, Francis had gone to part-time helpers in Children's Church. Teachers were asked to volunteer for a month at a time with two months off so they could participate in the worship service before their next tour of duty with the two- and three-year-olds. The problem with the system was best illustrated by the crying of the DeHaan twins on the Sunday of the monthly leadership change. Jamie and Lori DeHaan simply could not tolerate the cycle of "strangers" parading through their lives. They needed the security of familiar faces every week. The only other option for staffing the children's church seemed to be a paid attendant, but with the church already strapped by payments on the new building, the idea was not realistic.

"Just before throwing up her hands in despair, Francis began asking questions which cast light on the dreary recruitment situation before us. While the questions did not solve the long-term recruitment problems, they did give us handles on how to deal with short-term emergencies."

For the next forty-five minutes the two men discussed the four questions and the implications of employing them at Walnut Heights. Stimulated by the breakfast conversation, Jeff returned to his office, canceled his other appointments for the morning, and began calling a number of his friends who were also members of the National Association of Directors of Christian Education (now called the Professional Association of Christian Educators). He asked them if they had ever been bold enough to ask the questions in their churches and what the results had been. To Jeff's relief, he found that all of the questions had been used by one colleague or another and had proved beneficial in the recruitment process.

A summary of Jeff's findings were presented to the Christian Education Committee when they met on the following Tuesday evening. They were explained as follows.

Drop?

What would be the impact of discontinuing the program? From time to time each ministry of a local church should reexamine its current effectiveness and contribution to discipleship ministries of the church. A lack of workers in a program, especially when such a shortage becomes a chronic situation, may be an indicator that a ministry has outlived its usefulness to the local Christian community.

Released-time classes for children from Lowell Elementary had been held at Abel Memorial Church for over forty years. Spurred on by the slogan, "By God's grace we're able," the church viewed the prospect of discontinuing the class as a concession of spiritual defeat. That a majority of the children currently enrolled at Lowell were of Hispanic descent and that none of the members were conversant in Spanish was not considered as a significant factor. Yet the language problem hindered the church from securing permission from parents for their children to be released to attend the Wednesday afternoon classes. Attendance had dipped to five or six children per week.

When surgery put the veteran teacher on the disabled list, the Christian Education Board had to ask, "What would be the impact of discontinuing the program?" The conclusion, honestly stated, was that they would have a bruised self-perception but nothing more. The released-time program, seen as the church's effort to evangelize a changing neighborhood, was totally irrelevant to the Hispanic children as it had been run. To drop the class might even force the church to become more realistic about its relationship to the neighborhood.

But this was not an option for Mary Jenkins' department of three-year-olds. There had to be another solution for the present crisis, though the committee could foresee the time when the "drop" question might be asked about certain other church ministries.

Harm?

A second question which should be asked is "What would be harmed by continuing the existing program without the needed staff?" Unfortunately this question is answered most frequently by adults who have not sat for an hour in an inadequately staffed Sunday School class, club program, or youth group meeting. Seldom do adults consider the feelings of anger, hostility, resentment, loneliness, and even fear which may be experienced by children subjected to poorly supervised Christian education conditions.

Jeff had talked with the CE minister at Bellwood Community Church which had tripled in size within the space of four years. One of the keys to the church's growth was the dynamic Sunday morning adult Bible classes which complemented the worship service. Classes were so meaningful to adults that few wanted to leave and teach children. There was a *severe* shortage of volunteers. To make matters worse the rapid growth of the church necessitated placing twice as many children into classrooms as the fire code, much less good teaching recommendations, would allow. When the church asked the "harm" question, the board came close to shutting down an adult class or two until appropriate staff and space were found for the children.

There is a time, Jeff found, when the short-term harm is an acceptable risk to endure. If a greater harm may be inflicted upon children by rushing adults, who are spiritually or socially immature, into leadership positions, then inadequate staffing is preferable. But the emphasis must be placed on the description, "short-term." If there is long-term risk it may be wiser to discontinue a program than to sponsor a weekly "zoo."

Though some ideas drawn from this question were possibilities at Walnut Heights, the committee preferred to discuss all the questions before they acted. Jeff continued with his report.

Alternatives?

If discontinuing a program is not a wise option and continuing with inadequate staff is sufficiently harmful, a third question should be asked: "Are there other possible activities which would accomplish the same ministry goals for the church family?" Jeff had found the question asked at the Greenwood Assembly of God when the children's church had become impossible to staff. For one thing, no one really understood the purpose of children's church, and furthermore, there were few adequate curricular materials for the volunteers to use. The program had chronically lacked staff until one day when Lenny Fletcher suggested that the grade-school children be taught to worship by creating puppet programs for the preschoolers. With Fletcher's enthusiasm, the sewing ability of old Mrs. Collingsworth, and some children's Bible story and musical tapes, "Churchtime Puppets" became a part of the educational program. Volunteer puppet workers were much easier to secure since most adults had seen the Muppets on TV and had enough "child" in them to be willing to work with this new idea. Innovation captured the imagination of people whose abilities had been overlooked in the previous recruitment process.

But for three-year-olds in "Mom" Jenkins' former department, the idea probably wouldn't work. The children were too young to form a puppet ministry unless the department could be restructured to utilize puppets or something similar to communicate God's truth to them. The idea was left open as the committee heard Jeff's report on the final question.

Dramatize?

When the previous questions have been asked without producing a satisfactory solution to recruiting workers for an unpopular position, a fourth question might be asked: "How can we dramatize the need for workers in this area of the ministry?" Two words of caution must be inserted here. First, such drama should not primarily be used to create feelings of guilt or shame among church members. Such feelings will usually prove counterproductive in the long run. Instead, the drama should be aimed at creating a vision for ministry.

Second, workers obtained in this manner will be much more likely to need immediate on-the-job training to become effective in ministry. The church that is unprepared to train new workers should refrain from the use of dramatic recruitment methods.

The job of obtaining teachers for Sunday morning preschool children in a major West Coast church seemed an impossibility. The church had already invested financially by providing a full-time staff member and two part-time helpers to work exclusively with these children, but still the ratio of learners to teacher was in the neighborhood of thirteen to one. So one Sunday, at the invitation of the pastor, the entire three-year-old department was led, hand in hand, down the center aisle of the church during the morning worship service. Upon reaching the front of the sanctuary, the pastor walked down onto the lower platform and sat down with children all around him. In a pastorly manner he expressed his deep concern that Christian people were not available to teach the love of Christ to such wonderful children as these. It was a lesson that few in the congregation that day soon forgot and for the immediate future the recruitment problem was solved.

A second way to dramatize recruitment needs was demonstrated by a Florida pastor who printed in the bulletin, "Due to a shortage of volunteer teachers in the Primary Department, only the first sixteen first, second, and third grade children who arrive at Sunday School next week will be permitted to attend classes. The Christian Education Board is sorry for any inconvenience caused by the understaffed condition of our church's teaching ministry." The CE pastor was prepared to personally stand at the Primary Department door the following week and turn away the seventeenth child and any that followed. Fortunately, the dramatic shock of the announcement brought forth enough volunteer workers to continue the teaching ministry without interruption.

The discussion which followed Jeff's report was relatively short. It was obvious to all of the committee members that a dramatic step would be the best response to the current situation.

After briefing Pastor Wilcox on the emergency plan which he and the committee had devised, Jeff prepared two announcements—one for the bulletin and one to be posted outside the three-year-old department on Sunday morning. They read the same way:

Due to the lack of personnel, the three-year-old Children's Church department will not be open as of next Sunday morning, October 28. Please return to pick up your child immediately following Sunday School. The department will be closed until qualified staff members are in place. The Christian Education Committee regrets any inconvenience which the closing of the three-year-old Children's Church department might cause.

Jeff's hope was that the "scare" tactic would motivate people to volunteer before the Sunday the three-year-old department was actually closed. Unfortunately, people apparently thought that Jeff was merely trying to be dramatic and no one volunteered.

On Sunday October 28 the three-year-old department was closed during Children's Church. Jeff placed a notice on the door and then took up a position in the hallway before Sunday School to answer the questions which surprised parents might have. He was prepared to take children to the sanctuary to find their parents in the event that they were not picked up after Sunday School. Most of the parents were understanding. A couple were upset. One visitor was obviously not impressed at the manner in which the educational program was being run.

At the end of the morning Jeff was exhausted. He had not expected the emotional drain that came from facing all those parents. Yet he knew he had done the right thing. The discouraging thing was that, even with this dramatic gesture, no one had volunteered to serve in the three-year-old department.

It was not until Wednesday that someone called to inquire if Jeff could use him among the three-year-olds. That call was followed by two other calls the same day and by the following Sunday three placement interviews had taken place, along with a brief planning meeting, and the three-year-old department was back in operation.

FIFTEEN

Trends in Volunteerism

Working with volunteers had become one of the central themes of Jeff Thompson's ministry. Seminary had not prepared him for this challenge. Most of his education in church-based volunteerism evidenced what Allen Tough would call an adult learning project (*The Adult's Learning Projects*, 1979). He had to get information wherever he could—from friends in the ministry or in other parts of the not-for-profit sector, magazines and journals, and seminars and workshops as well as books on the subject.

One of the important discoveries which Jeff made in this process of self-education was how to get information at the time he wanted it. At times there was the sensation of being trapped between his impressions about the current state of volunteerism and what he was hearing "authoritative sources" say about current trends. The working woman, for example, was a favorite target of certain speakers. Yet Jeff's experience told him that women were still the vast majority of his volunteers, even though they tended to be more selective in the tasks for which they made their time available. His impression was verified at the public library when Jeff discovered that those who are employed part-time (of which women were in the majority) are more likely than others to spend some of their time volunteering (Gallup, *American Volunteer*, 1986, p. 15). Women who have never been married allocate significantly more hours per week to volunteer service than married, divorced/separated, or widowed females (Sasser, doctoral dissertation, 1983, p. 144).

Young adult professionals were another group which tended to get criticized by people in the church. Jeff, like many others, had written off the Yuppies as the spoiled remnant of the narcissistic "Me" generation and had conceded their collective worthlessness to local church ministries, at least until they had married and had children. Thus, he was shocked to read a description of "The New Volunteerism" which announced that "high-paid Yuppies are penciling compassion into their calendars" (Newsweek, 8 February 1988, 42–43).

A quick look through the list of Christian education staff seemed to confirm his hunch and contradict the findings of the article. Yuppie-types were not well represented throughout the ministries of the church. But why? Gradually the Christian education pastor realized that he had made an assumption that young professionals would not be stable enough to make a valid contribution to the church's educational ministry and as a result the belief became self-confirming. When his recruitment committee members had reported that certain young adults "were never home," Jeff had taken the comment as an indicator of irresponsibility. It had never occurred to him that the mobile lifestyle of young adults might be an asset rather than a detriment, or that the best time to call single people without families might be after 10 o'clock at night, a time at which most families would resent the noisy intrusion of a ringing phone.

The larger problem was not that he had misunderstood the role of women or single young adults in the educational ministries, though these were problems at the church, but that he had blind spots in his thinking about volunteerism. To deal with the gaps in his thinking, Jeff determined that part of his normal monthly activity was going to include research. He would start at the public library looking for articles on current trends.

In addition he would talk to people who were active in the not-for-profit sector and who actively recruited and utilized volunteer personnel. Hospitals, YMCAs, scouting programs, service clubs, libraries, schools, PTAs, athletic leagues, and many other agencies had a massive amount of experience which could benefit the church's ministry to and with volunteers.

Conferences and seminars focusing on the issues of volunteerism were another source of research data. Even governmental resources were becoming more apparent. President Bush spoke of "a thousand points of light" to describe "that vast galaxy of people and institutions working together to solve problems in their own backyard" (*Newsweek*, 10 July 1989, 36–38).

Jeff found it necessary to set up a filing system to preserve the information which he was collecting. Though he began with one file folder, he soon found that information rapidly degenerated to a disorganized "piling" system. So the folders were organized in the following manner:

Volunteer — General
   Volunteer: Bibliography
Volunteer: Management
   Volunteer: Motivation
   Volunteer: Placement
   Volunteer: Selection
   Volunteer: Training
Volunteer: Publicity
Volunteer: Research and trends
Volunteer: Resources

The following samples of articles placed into each file will illustrate the types of information which Jeff Thompson found useful.

Volunteer — General

> "Dear Pastor Potter:
> " . . . I think I'm burned out — spent, pooped, empty. I've been hearing about it lately, and they say that if you're not careful, it can lead to dropout. I always used to say I didn't mind burning out for the Lord, but lately I've been afraid I might go up in one big poof."
> Ronald E. Wilson, "Letter from an Ex-Volunteer," *Leadership* (Summer 1982): 50.

"What is your definition of volunteering?

"The paid volunteer . . . [is the beneficiary of] the 'third party payment' system that we are developing in the volunteer field. In [these] instances the agency accepts individuals who are 'volunteers' only in the sense that the *agency* doesn't pay for the person, *not* in the sense that the individual is not ultimately paid.

"The coerced volunteer . . . [finds his] motivation to volunteer is initiated and directed by an outside force . . . it is likely that without that outside force the volunteering would not occur.

"The 'selfish' volunteer . . . stresses the 'What's in it for me?' theme.

"The 'unintentional' volunteer . . . one receive[s] credit for doing good without knowing it and without intending [to do] it."

Stephen H. McCurley, "A Volunteer by Any Other Name," *Voluntary Action Leadership* (Winter 1985): 24-26.

Volunteer: Bibliography

Christian Education Journal. Scripture Press Ministries, P.O. Box 650, Glen Ellyn, IL 60137.

Journal of Volunteer Administration. Association for Volunteer Administration, Box 4584, Boulder, CO 80306.

Nonprofit and Voluntary Sector Quarterly. 5 Jossey-Bass Inc., 350 Sansome Street, San Francisco, CA 94104.

Voluntary Action Leadership. Volunteer — the National Center, 1111 N. 19th Street, Suite 500, Arlington, VA 22209.

Volunteer. Lutheran World Ministries, Volunteer Services Office, 360 Park Ave. S., New York, NY 10010.

Volunteer in Education. National Association of Partners in Education, 601 Wythe, Suite 200, Alexandria, VA 22314.

Volunteering. Volunteer — the National Center, 1111 N. 19th Street, Suite 500, Arlington, VA 22209.

Volunteer: Management

"The most important volunteer position is that of volunteer coordinator."

Cheryl A. McHenry, "Library Volunteers," *School Library Journal* (May 1988): 44.

"The Social Welfare Research Centre at the University of New South Wales found in 1982 that nationally, volunteers worked the equivalent hours as for 125,000 full-time jobs. The commensurate annual wage bill for this would be $1.5 billion, or 1.1 percent of the gross domestic product. The most recent major study of volunteerism in Australia . . . found that more than 800,000 Victorians, or 28 percent of the population, spent more than 100 million hours of their time doing organized voluntary work in 1982. This is the equivalent of 60,000 full-time jobs."

Martin Mowbray, "Volunteering for Nothing?" *L.A.M.P.* (December 1983): 19.

"From among the ideas in *In Search for Excellence*, the eight principles of excellence can give volunteer managers some 'food for thought':

1. A bias for action: a preference for doing something (anything) rather than sending a question through cycles and cycles of analyses and committee reports.

2. Staying close to the customer—learning his (her) preferences and catering to them.

3. Autonomy and entrepreneurship—breaking the corporation into small companies and encouraging them to think independently and competitively.

4. Productivity through people—creating in all employees the awareness that their best efforts are essential and that they will share in the rewards of the company's success.

5. Hands-on, value-driven—insisting that executives keep in touch with the firm's essential business.

157

6. Stick to the knitting—remaining with the business the company knows best.

7. Simple form, lean staff—few administrative layers, few people at upper levels.

8. Simultaneous loose-tight properties—fostering a climate where there is dedication to central values of the company combined with tolerance for all employees who accept those values."

    Karla A. Henderson, "In Search of Volunteer Management: Ideas for Excellence," *The Journal of Volunteer Administration* (Fall 1985): 38–39.

Volunteer: Motivation

Why do people volunteer?	
I want to help others	97%
I enjoy the work	93%
The specific work or cause interests me	89%
I feel a responsibility to volunteer	75%
Someone asked me to volunteer	59%
I have free time on my hands	41%
To make new friends	40%
To get job experience	15%
My employer encourages volunteering	14%
Required for membership in an organization	10%
To get freebies such as complimentary tickets	7%

    Source: Gallup Organization, *Psychology Today*, October 1988, 6.

"Seventy-five percent of all the volunteers [surveyed] cited a specific support behavior of a person . . . was influential in their continued involvement in ministry."

    Gary C. Newton, "The Motivation of the Saints and Interpersonal Competencies of Their Leaders," Unpublished paper, 1986.

"Most of the reasons for volunteering can be categorized as: Achievement motives, affiliation motives, power/leadership motives, or duty motives."

Karla Henderson, "The Motivations of Men and Women in Volunteering," *The Journal of Volunteer Administration* (Spring 1983): 21.

Volunteer: Placement

"It is my conviction that volunteer work in the church is more greatly enabled by spiritual gift theology than by any other single factor, training technique, or conceptual base."

Carl F. George, "Recruitment's Missing Link," *Leadership* (Summer 1982): 55.

Volunteer: Training

"Here are the six most frequent recommendations from church leaders who are successfully training or being trained.
- Recognize that training is hard work
- Be sensitive to training resistance
- Understand lay [feelings of] inferiority
- Tailor training programs
- Challenge volunteers
- Recognize the limitations of training."

Terry C. Muck, "Training Volunteers: A Leadership Survey," *Leadership* (Summer 1982): 40-48.

"In designing the training, focus as much as you can on the volunteer . . .
1. Establish personal relationships with the volunteer, based on shared information and goals.

2. Find out how the volunteers hope to benefit from their work and help them achieve their goals.

3. Use the training to promote the organization's mission.

4. Gather input from the volunteers concerning what training they believe they need, and integrate their suggestions into established training programs."

Jeff Orr, cited in "Training Volunteers," *Voluntary Action Leadership* (Spring 1985): 28.

Volunteer: Recruitment

"The selection process should be looked upon as just that — a selection process. It should not be simply a process of getting 'warm bodies' or filling a sheet with names."

Jack L. Giles, "Recruiting Volunteers," *Lutheran Education*, March–April 1982, 227.

Volunteer: Research/Trends

"Who Volunteers and Why:

About 45 percent of adults eighteen years of age or older reported volunteering in 1987.

Time given to volunteer work averaged 4.7 hours a week.

People sixty-five to seventy-four volunteer the most (six hours a week), followed by those 45 to 54 (5.8 hours).

People with household incomes of $20,000 to $30,000 volunteered most often followed by those earning $50,000 to $75,000.

People volunteered to do something useful (56 percent), because they would enjoy the work (34 percent), a family member or friend would benefit (27 percent) or for religious reasons (22 percent)."

Source: The Gallup Organization, *Time*, 10 July 1989, 37.

"A Gallup survey . . . released by Independent Sector, a Washington based philanthropic group . . . shows that many Americans are willing to volunteer but are not being asked. Three-fourths of the respondents believe that they should volunteer to help others, but half did not volunteer in the past year."

Roger Thompson, "An Untapped Resource," *Nation's Business,* March 1989, 50.

"Nine out of ten congregations reported that they used volunteers to perform work in their congregations. There were 253,000 volunteer clergy who gave an average of seventy hours per month. Overall, 10.4 million volunteers, other than clergy, worked an average of ten hours per month in congregational programs. Fifty-two percent of those volunteers were devoted to religious programs and the other 48 percent to other congregational programs, including elementary, secondary and higher education (18 percent), human services and welfare (12 percent), health and hospitals (7 percent), public or societal benefit (5 percent), arts and culture (6 percent), international activities (5 percent), and environmental quality (1 percent). Overall, volunteers represent 85 percent of the total employees at religious congregations."

Source: Gallup Organization/Independent Sector, *Voluntary Action Leadership* (Winter 1988-89): 6.

Volunteer: Resources

Association for Volunteer Adminisitration
Box 4584
Boulder, CO 80306

Volunteer — the National Center
1111 North 19th St., Suite 500
Arlington, VA 22209   Phone: 703-276-0542

SIXTEEN

Recruitment as Shepherding

It must have been a dream. Jeff couldn't remember. It seemed so real, so vivid, so comfortable. As far as his eye could see, shepherds moved like ants among the gently rolling hills. Westerly breezes whispered among the patches of trees which seemed to frame the pastures, creating a gigantic patchwork quilt in shades of green across the luscious hills. Yet, oddly enough, something was missing. There were no sheep. Just shepherds, talking and waiting. But waiting for what?

Trudging into the pastures himself, he wandered the rolling hills. Jeff was amazed at the diversity he found among the people present. Primitive tribesmen from the "outback" of Australia, Scotsmen with their kilts and sheepdogs, family farmers from neatly run farms in Ohio, Palestinian nomads from the Negev, rugged herdsmen from the seemingly endless land-grant acreage in Texas. Their languages and dress were as diverse as the lands from which they'd come and yet, to his further amazement, conversations flowed like the gentle murmur of Appalachian streams.

From group to group Jeff wandered, listening, watching, tempted to question the uniformly hospitable strangers about the purpose of their gathering and the object of their waiting. Yet each time the words were formed on his lips he could not break into the conversation with the people.

Common interests dominated the friendly chatter. Favorite breeds of sheep constantly entered the discussions: Romeldale,

Shropshire, Panama, Corriedale, Romney, and other equally unfamiliar names emerged as breeds were described and lovingly
compared.

Unfamiliar? Yes, and yet not strange and unknown. The more
he listened to the conversations, the more Jeff realized he knew
(or was coming to know, as sometimes happens in dreams)
about the sheep being discussed.

Problems of breeding, feeding, health care, protection, shear-
ing, and a thousand other details crowded conversation after
conversation. Marketing of products occasionally surfaced in
discussions, but only briefly as the shepherds appeared most
interested in their flocks and in the personal needs of individual
sheep.

Once again Jeff was tempted to inquire about the purpose of
the gathering when the myriad conversations suddenly melted
away into silence. Heads turned as if on an inaudible command,
and each eye became riveted on a Shepherd who stood quietly
on a grassy knoll. Yet He appeared to belong to each group,
each language, each type of native dress.

A hush of anticipation settled over the multitude. The waiting was over. Whatever had been anticipated was about to
happen.

There was no fanfare as the Shepherd began to walk down
the knoll toward a group of shepherds. Quickly, He blended into
the crowd, while at the same time (and this is one of the ways in
which Jeff knew that the events were a dream of some sort) the
Shepherd remained perfectly visible to everyone present. No
fanfare was needed, for His very presence commanded the total
respect of every living being.

Now He was in the thick of a crowd on the flatland between
a stand of birch trees and the steep incline which led to the
ridge on the west. He had paused beside a shepherd whose gaze
had fallen, as if in genuine embarrassment, to the feet of the
One to whom everyone else looked in anticipation.

"Joshua," said the Shepherd in a voice that barely exceeded a
whisper and yet was totally audible wherever the sheep-loving
people stood.

"Joshua," He spoke again with a greater strength that commanded the sheepish herdsman to look Him in the eye. "I will
present to you a reward that will never tarnish or fade away.

Here are the people whom you shepherded during your lifetime."

With that, all of the angry people on whom the simple shepherd had poured the oil of healing, all the growing people to
whom he had fed words of encouragement, all of the confused
people to whom he had provided insight and direction, all of the
lonely people to whom he was available, all of the healthy people to whom he was a model, as well as ones who needed the
correction, rebuke, punishment, or instruction which he had
provided—all came and formed an appreciative crowd around
the embarrassed herdsman. One by one the people expressed in
warm measure the deep felt appreciation which each had experienced in a lifetime of following their shepherd.

Ages seemed to have passed (as could only happen in a
dream) and still the people came and spoke. Sometimes tears
glistened in their eyes. Then they drifted back into their own
circle of friends. Finally, just as it appeared that the line of
friends might come to an end, there came a second gathering of
sheep—new people. These, though seemingly not familiar with
the modest shepherd, had been touched by the lives of the
people to whom the shepherd had ministered directly. Each
person told of how he had been cared for in ways learned from
Joshua. This group was far larger than the first crowd because
for every person to express appreciation in the first group there
were 5, 10, 25, or even 100 who stood in line to add their
appreciation to the unassuming tender of this flock.

About the time that this second flow of people had dwindled
to a trickle, another flock of sheep gathered around, then a
fourth and a fifth, as if the ever enlarging crowds of people
appreciative for the faithful service of one conscientious shepherd would never fade away or cease.

All the time that Jeff was observing the events taking place
around this first shepherd, the great Shepherd had remained
active. He had moved from shepherd to shepherd initiating the
same chain of events for herdsmen as far as the eye could see.
Endless lines of appreciative people formed a fluid pattern of
shepherds both expressing and receiving affirmation for obedient
service to the master Shepherd.

Gradually, the picture blurred, much the way binoculars do
when trying to refocus from some distant scene to an object

close at hand. Sounds too became indistinguishable, a gentle murmur of contented voices. Perhaps the dream was over — or could this be what the Prophet Joel might have referred to as a vision?

Either way, the CE pastor still had to finish his preparation for the Christian education staff meeting the following evening. His Bible lay open to 1 Peter 5:1-4. That's what he was! That's what they were! Shepherds — shepherding the flocks of God.

For a few moments Jeff thought back over his ministry at Walnut Heights Bible Church. Maybe that was why recruiting and training of staff for the education program seemed so much less difficult in recent days. He had not simply been recruiting workers. He had been shepherding one of God's flocks.

His thoughts wandered from person to person — old and young, male and female, sophisticated and naive, all with one common bond: Jeff had touched each one in a time of need.

There was Andy, the fifth-grade Sunday School teacher, who had lost his job due to personnel cutbacks in middle management. Jeff was no career counselor, but he was available to listen, question, provide feedback, pray, suggest resource people within the church and community, and finally rejoice when Andy landed a new job.

Larry and Charlene also came to mind. Charlene was a self-assured professional woman in her mid-twenties when she began teaching in the early childhood children's church program at the church. Jeff's first impressions had been verified throughout her first year of teaching. She was capable, sensitive, organized, and loved by her little learners. Then shortly into her second year of children's church leadership, "Miss Composure" appeared to be falling apart.

A phone call by the CE pastor served to bring the "Larry" problem to light. Charlene just couldn't decide whether she loved him enough to take the chance of losing her career in favor of a life of "wifery," as she perceived it.

Shepherding had taken the form of counseling this time — to each individually, then both together. The decision was not an easy one. Though Larry and Charlene were able to work through certain apprehensions each had about self-worth and the institution of marriage, their final conclusion was not to marry.

Other shepherding events flooded Jeff's mind. There was the hospitalized department leader he'd spent time with, whose doctor suspected cancer. A single mother needed a sounding board when her ex-husband failed to send Christmas gifts to the children, leaving her stuck with the question, "Doesn't Daddy love *us*, either?" The club leader who knew that Jeff was interested in him and could share "very special" prayer requests with him, both as friend and pastor. Memories of shepherded people marched through his mind accompanied by the feelings of celebration associated with an Independence Day parade.

Gradually, the dawn had come.

Jeff had come to realize that recruitment and shepherding are inseparably linked together. Without the balm of shepherding, recruiting would be almost unbearable. Without the practical consequences of recruiting, shepherding would become inbred, isolated, abstract. On the other hand, with shepherding, recruiting became an exciting opportunity to extend present ministries; and with recruiting, shepherding became a natural expression of God's love toward others.

Jeff's mandate was becoming increasingly clear. Tomorrow evening's talk to the Christian education staff would take the form of a shepherd talking to his under-shepherds. Thoughts, experiences, and biblical insights would be shared to encourage and lift the entire staff, to inspire and permeate them with loving shepherding principles.

The message that Tuesday night was quite simple. It was built around the sign posted at railroad crossings: **STOP! LOOK! LISTEN!**

> **Stop** to think about the people with whom you are ministering
> . . . their joys . . . their hurts . . . their pressures . . . their successes.
>
> **Stop** to pray for the people with whom you are ministering
> . . . responding to their stated needs . . . their nonverbal clues . . . their observable frustrations.
>
> **Stop** to switch from task orientation to a personal perspective

. . . not so much program as people . . . not so much numbers as needs . . . not so much doing as being.

Look at people's faces to become aware of their sensitivity
. . . at their smiles to perceive their receptivity . . . at their
eyes to share their celebration of life . . . at their shoulders
to understand the loads they carry.

Look at people from their own perspective
. . . what is shaping them? . . . what is concerning them?
. . . what is crowding them? . . . what is pleasing them?

Look for God in people
. . . through His Word . . . through the predictable crises
of life . . . through responses to the mistakes of others.

Listen to what is being said
. . . when it is not convenient . . . when it is uncomfortable . . . when it is obviously biased . . . when someone
less wise is speaking.

Listen to what is felt
. . . when words mislead . . . when smiles obscure . . . when
eyes cry out . . . when confusion reigns.

Listen to what God says
. . . through the Bible . . . through His Spirit . . . through
circumstances . . . through people . . . through rejection . . .
through life.

Though the words, approach, and context of Pastor Jeff's
message were fresh to his audience, the ministry staff of Walnut
Heights Bible Church recognized something very familiar about
it. A few of them smiled to themselves. It was a theme they had
seen emerge, grow, and blossom in their pastor of Christian
education over the years. He was living it.